PENGUIN BOOKS

NUNS IN JEOPARDY

Martin Boyd was born in Switzerland in 1893 of Anglo-Australian parents. He was brought to Australia when six months old where the Boyd family made impressive contributions to the artistic and intellectual life. At the outbreak of the first world war he travelled to England and joined an English regiment and later the Royal Flying Corps. In 1948, at the height of his literary success, he returned to Australia to make a permanent home near Berwick.

Most of his novels maintain an Anglo-Australian theme and are based on his preoccupation with his own family. Martin Boyd moved to Rome in 1957 and lived there till his death in June 1972.

BY MARTIN BOYD

FICTION

Love Gods (1925)
Brangane: A Memoir (1926)
The Montforts (1928, revised edition, 1963)
Scandal of Spring (1934)
The Lemon Farm (1935)
The Picnic (1937)
Night of the Party (1938)
Nuns in Jeopardy (1940)
Lucinda Brayford (1946, revised edition, 1954)
Such Pleasure (1949)

THE LANGTON QUARTET (in reading order)

The Cardboard Crown (1952, revised edition, 1964)
A Difficult Young Man (1955)
Outbreak of Love (1957)
When Blackbirds Sing (1962)

The Tea-Time of Love (1969)

AUTOBIOGRAPHIES

A Single Flame (1939)
Day of My Delight: An Anglo-Australian Memoir (1965)

NON-FICTION

Much Else in Italy: A Subjective Travel Book (1958)

CHILDREN'S NOVEL

The Painted Princess: A Fairy Story (1936)

MARTIN BOYD

Nuns in Jeopardy

With an introduction by Leonie Kramer

PENGUIN BOOKS

Penguin Books Australia Ltd,
487 Maroondah Highway, PO Box 257
Ringwood, Victoria 3134, Australia
Penguin Books Ltd,
Harmondsworth, Middlesex, England
Penguin Books,
40 West 23rd Street, New York, NY 10010, USA
Penguin Books Canada Ltd,
2801 John Street, Markham, Ontario, Canada L3R IB4
Penguin Books (NZ) Ltd,
182-190 Wairau Road, Auckland 10, New Zealand

First published by Penguin Books Australia, 1985
First published by Penguin Books Australia, 1986

Made and printed in Hong Kong by
L P and Associates

CIP

Boyd, Martin, 1893-1972.
Nuns in jeopardy.

First published: London: Dent, 1940.
ISBN 0 14 007228 4.

I. Title.

A823'.2

INTRODUCTION

'All good art is religious.' So Martin Boyd ends his account of how he came to write *Nuns in Jeopardy*. The story is best told in his own words:

In 1938 Daryl and Joan Lindsay were in London. One day, when she was lunching with me in Holland Street Joan said: "It's no good writing today a novel assuming that society is stable. You must either deal with the mess we are in, or else write of something quite fantastic, say, a lot of nuns wrecked on a desert island and call it *Nuns in Jeopardy*." I said: "Very well, I will" and I did.

From this, some connection has been assumed between *Nuns in Jeopardy* and *Picnic at Hanging Rock*, but apart from the fact that both writers found the mode of fantasy a convenient way of examining relationships between people, there is no family likeness between the two novels. For one thing, Boyd concerns himself with ideas as well as people, and his interest in mystery is different in kind from Joan Lindsay's. He reaches after the ineffable, whereas she mystifies the reader in the manner of a writer of detective stories. *Nuns in Jeopardy* dramatizes intellectual arguments; *Picnic at Hanging Rock* the power of the Australian landscape.

Why, one wonders, did Boyd so readily adopt Joan Lindsay's suggestion? Many fictional possibilities must present themselves to a writer as active and observant as he was. Why should this one have captured him at that time? Answers to such a question can only be speculative possibilities, but hindsight can furnish hints which might explain Boyd's prompt response.

The first world war had affected Boyd deeply; on the eve of the second world war it would not be surprising if his thoughts had turned to 'the last things'. In 1928, under the pseudonym Martin Mills, Boyd had published *The Montforts*, an early attempt – and one which he later saw as a waste of good material – to deal with his family history. Then came a number of novels dealing lightly with love, religion and romance – books which are more interesting today than they might have appeared at the time because they hint of concerns to come. Now he became more deeply engaged with the nature of man's spiritual destiny. *Nuns in Jeopardy* looks forward to his Anglo-Australian novels, *Lucinda Brayford* and the Langton series. In the event, its timing proved perculiarly apt. The *Princess of Teck*, the ship taking Boyd's characters from Australia to England, is overwhelmed by a violent storm; and most of the first edition of the novel was destroyed in the Blitz in 1940. It is as though Boyd's fictional metaphor was translated into reality, and as though the tropical-island paradise he created for the purposes of his moral fable anticipated the actual purgatory in which so many innocent people were to suffer.

Boyd was one of the first novelists to recognize that the first world war changed the course of European civilization; *Lucinda Brayford*, which deals with both wars, for all its apparent preoccupation with the traditional continuities of life in England and between the wars, has disintegration as a central subject. The action of *Nuns in Jeopardy* takes place in a world where, in the words of its most enigmatic character Mr Smith, 'there is no financial insecurity, no threat of poverty, no slums, no smoke, no disease, no policemen, no politicians, no war, no taxes, no time even, unless you wish to observe it'. Relieved of these accidentals, the characters are faced with the realities of their own nature, and through them Boyd provides a preview of the ideas and values which are refined and deepened in *Lucinda Brayford*. The paradisal laboratory which he creates for his characters is also a proving ground for the author.

Early in the novel, even as the storm is increasing in intensity, Mrs Bright, the richest and silliest passenger on board the *Princess of Teck* insists on reading aloud a story by Stephen Leacock called *Red Love on a Blue Island*. Sister Agatha, the nun whose experience is central to Boyd's purpose, is one of her reluctant listeners, and registers that 'she had never heard such nonsense as Mrs Bright was reading'. However casual his manner may appear at times, Boyd is never careless. Leacock's story is about a couple who are wrecked on a tropical island. They are prudish and affected in manner, and pretend, since each is married, not to notice that they are flirting with each other. One day they decide to explore the island, only to find that it is the site of a large hotel. On the beach they find their respective partners enjoying an illicit relationship. Boyd does not mention that the subtitle of Leacock's story is 'Broken Barriers', and in failing to do so robs the casual reader of the only element in the story he has adopted. *Red Love on a Blue Island* bears as little resemblance to *Nuns in Jeopardy* as does *The Count of Monte Cristo* to Solzhenitsyn's *The First Circle* (in which, however, Dumas' book is mentioned). In both cases romance is replaced by reality; and Leacock's superficial encounter with the breaking of a moral convention is in sharp contrast to Boyd's investigation of chastity and sensuality, puritanism and pleasure, instinct and will, and of the idea of nature.

Nuns in Jeopardy is not, however, a didactic or abstract novel. As he does in *Lucinda Brayford* and the Langton tetralogy, so here Boyd matches the literal and non-literal elements so that there are no abrupt transitions between them. It is always clear, indeed obvious, that one is reading a fable; but there is extraordinary attention to detail. The storm is brilliantly described, and Boyd keeps changing the angle of vision so that the reader has a total picture. Just before the *Princess of Teck* sinks he inserts one sentence which is vivid in its impact, yet at the same time makes one reflect on the novelist's art: 'From this distance it was like some ghastly mid-Victorian lithograph.' What a strange and compelling comparison that is, not least in its comment on temporal distance.

The natural events, for all their vivid actuality, are part of the fabulous mode of the novel. The storm disrupts all normal relationships and expectations. Its aftermath – days of peril and suffering in a lifeboat – reduces the characters to hallucination and despair. The island, with its man-made garden of Eden – the *locus amoenus* of classical literature – appears to offer them respite and restoration of their bodies and minds, yet challenges their deepest convictions. The nuns are deprived of their inviolate community, and their spiritual discipline begins to fail. A journey of exploration undertaken by two of the male castaways ends in the death of one of them. And finally, the *locus amoenus* is virtually destroyed by a volcanic eruption and tidal wave. The Paradise Garden vanishes under volcanic ash; and just as they begin to rebuild it, their rescuers arrive, ironically searching not for the nuns and their assorted companions, but for the large, rich Mrs Bright, delighted reader of Leacock, who has been drowned in the storm (from which Leacock no doubt would have rescued her).

This pattern of destruction and renewal is convincingly presented as a credible natural sequence of events, but also functions as a metaphor for the discoveries that individual characters make about themselves. Sister Agatha's spiritual discipline is threatened by the sensuous luxury of her island home. Religious austerity seems at odds with the abundance of nature, and she struggles to maintain the forms of her faith, in order to preserve their spirit. Any expectations the reader might have that Sister Agatha will be converted to secular life are disappointed. She learns to respond to the natural beauty and vibrancy of the island without succumbing to it; and in the end is able to say, reflecting on her hitherto imperceptible move from instinctive to manufactured kindness, 'What I have learned on the island, and which I hope I shall remember, is that it is as easy to be corrupted by one's virtues as by one's vices, and that it is more tragic, because then one turns a little of the good in the world into evil.'

All the characters are challenged by the realities of an existence which, though ideal in its physical environment, nevertheless offers none of the protection they have enjoyed in their previous lives. Even when a chapel is built so that the nuns can resume their spiritual regimen, discipline is undermined. Central to Boyd's examination of the changes in his characters is the concept of nature. For Sister Agatha the human embodiment of natural forces is the castaway Harry the Islander, though the narrator describes him as 'a Christ in a pietà'. He is chosen to dedicate the nuns' chapel, because, in the words of Mr Smith, acknowledged leader of the group, 'he is still able to see God in clouds and hear him in the wind. If you want God brought into your chapel, he alone can do it.' Agatha feels that Harry had dedicated the chapel to his own god, but is honest enough to recognize the force of the natural world. Sister Hilda's puritanism, on the other hand, makes her fearful of nature, because 'to her sterilized mind an enjoyable sin seems far more wicked than one which merely brought the sinner deprivation and suffering'. (Boyd in later novels develops the puritanical character more fully, and in particular suggests the power of negative and proscriptive attitudes to engender evil.) Winifred, the novice, is innocently open to the power of natural instincts, and therefore recognizes that Harry is in harmony with the environment as no one else is. Yet she is still constrained by her training and background, and her struggle against the passionate desires of Dick, her would-be lover, makes her feel 'that she understood something more about life, and that the more one understood, the more one's happiness died'. Here Boyd anticipates the theme of inevitable disillusionment which so forcefully informs *Lucinda Brayford* and the Langton tetralogy.

The voluptuousness of the garden and the intoxicating sensuousness of the island are emblematic of Boyd's interest in the varieties of eroticism of which humans are capable. At one extreme is the ill-concealed lust of George and Tom; at the other the fearful prudery of Hilda. The romantic love of Dick and Winifred accepts the formal convention of marriage, while the child Marcella's innocence tempts Ursula's unfulfilled desires. But sexual ambivalence is a powerful theme, and is realized in the relationship between Joe and Dick. Joe's homosexuality is made quite explicit in a curious scene in which Smith shows him his former lives – as a 5th-century B.C. heathen disbeliever, in love with a young prince; as a Boetian peasant who had seventeen children; as Canthus who accompanied Jason in search of the Golden Fleece, and was inspired by love for Atalanta, whom he thought to be a man. Smith brings Joe's imaginary history down to the reign of Henri Quatre. Three times Joe had caused the death of the person he loved, because he demanded 'an unhampered love', 'of the free spirit, and the spirit of course is only free in death'.

Dick is the object of Joe's affection, and his sexual ambivalence is resolved late in his attachment to Winifred, and then only because Joe is killed during their exploration of the island. In fact, Boyd clearly constructed this whole strange episode in order to bring the relationship between Joe and Dick to a climax, and to enable Dick fully to realize his love for Winifred. But he returns to her 'calmed by tranquil sadness', 'his tragic face, young, and yet seeming to know so much'. Once again, suffering shades the romantic aspirations of youth.

At the centre of this network of relationships stands the mysterious Mr Smith. It is he who steers the lifeboat to safety, who reveals Joe to himself and indeed encourages his 'free spirit', who organizes the building of the chapel, persuades Ursula not to light the bonfire which might lead to their rescue, elicits Hilda's anxious negation of life, and a violent reaction from Dick whose sexual ambivalence he reveals. Smith is *agent provocateur*, expositor, philosopher, aesthetician and critic. He has been thought to represent the devil, but that is how he can and does appear to some of the characters, not how he is.

Smith has two principal functions in the novel. One is to force the characters, one by one, to face reality. What he says to Joe applies to the others, 'I've shown you the reality of your own nature'. Joe gets it right when he says that they are all 'artist's models for old Smith'. Smith's other role is to disseminate ideas, and these form the substance of the novel. The governing idea is the force of nature, made explicit in the storm and the eruption, but also in the passions and fears of human beings. Balancing this, however, is the life of the intellect, which combines with the senses to produce works of art, and to develop insights into man's relationship with himself, his fellow beings, and God. Thus when Agatha rejects the notion that Neptune can have any effect upon her, Smith reminds her that 'the early church admitted the existence of the old gods', and goes on to conclude that 'we are the heirs' of both classical and Christian culture.

The island chapel, built on Smith's architectural principle of the 'metacube' – the Golden Rule – is dedicated by Harry the Islander. This episode represents the marriage of instinctual life and classic form, Christianity being the unifying force. It in turn leads to Sister Agatha's perhaps reluctant speculation that 'God is a natural force', not the powerful authority Hilda would prefer to worship.

In the end, when the castaways are rescued, it turns out that the island is known as Hell Island, and thought by sailors to be inhabited by dead souls. But the only victims of its evil reputation are its original owner – who made the garden – and his son, who kill each other in a struggle for possession. The castaways are redeemed, by devotion, love or innocence, and Mr Smith's final speech is a celebration of life and the 'bounding heart'. Yet even at this moment he is credited with 'evil intentness', a knowledge beyond the ordinary.

Boyd was impatient with the criticism that the novel was 'marred by an uneasy air of symbolism'. 'The whole book,' he wrote, 'was a symbol of the transmutation of the human soul, told in physical terms'. Despite its undisguised and purposeful allegory, *Nuns in Jeopardy* is tantalizing and compelling. For one thing, while offering explanations, it leaves unsolved mysteries. It moves easily between sensuousness and rationality while insisting on their interdependence. Seriousness is refreshed by a sense of the absurd, and the commonplace is elevated by insight. Sentences, even phrases, constantly arrest our attention. '. . . memory had not much to do with continuity.' 'The important thing about beauty and happiness is its quality not its permanence.' 'English grammar can't cope with all aspects of time.' Isolated, these might seem sententious, even trite. In context they alert the reader to the fact that this unconventional island romance is a serious essay on the flesh and the spirit, the human and the divine.

Leonie Kramer

1

The *Princess of Teck* was rolling heavily, but Sister
Agatha was dreaming that she was at a garden party
at Bishopscourt. The sunlight was more dazzling than
she had ever known it in the natural world. Its warm
effulgence, which seemed to enfold her in soft golden
wings, had the quality of spiritual benediction as well
as of physical warmth. As often in her dreams, she was
talking to the most important person present, here the
archbishop. They chattered with an intimacy unknown
in her actual experience. Then the governor-general
arrived, and she somehow had become archbishop. She
continued to chat to the governor-general with the
same intimacy. He was wearing a bright yellow uniform,
exquisitely embroidered with small blue flowers and
silver filigree. She was faintly worried by the fact that
his face had not Lord Bletchingdon's round red fatuity,
but was finely-drawn, cynical, and intelligent, with
pointed nose and eyebrows. She took him round the
garden whence the other guests had disappeared.

'This gum tree,' she said, standing by a huge old
eucalyptus near the gate, 'was going to be cut down,
but Fieldflowers Goe who was then bishop, quoted to
the gardener:

> "O woodman spare that tree,
> Touch not a single bough!
> In youth it sheltered me
> And I'll protect it now."

'Fieldflowers Goe!' exclaimed the governor-general.
'What an Elysian name!'

When he said the word 'Elysian' there was a sort of ping in Sister Agatha's brain. There seemed to be delicate bells ringing in her ears. The governor-general's uniform became confused with the garden which was now a brilliant field of spring flowers. She was poised in the golden air a foot or so above this lovely surface. She moved her feet and danced, skimming over it, and opposite her, smiling, dancing, and flying with her was the novice Winifred. She was so happy that the tears streamed down her face.

She awoke with a gasp to black fear.

At first all she knew was that she was drenched to the skin. Then she remembered that she was on board ship, and she stretched out her wet hand to the electric light switch. She was shuddering with fright, more than cold, as the water in these tropical seas was almost tepid.

She felt that every stitch of her bed was sopping wet, and her suitcase was floating in four inches of water on the cabin floor. She heard the sounds of the storm, the wind howling, and the thud of waves against the creaking ship. Apparently the steward had forgotten to shut her port-hole and several gallons of the Pacific Ocean had invaded her cabin. When she saw that this was all that had happened she gave a rueful smile, and with shivering fingers shut the port, before another wave could add to the confusion.

Although she now had no cause for fear, she was suffering from the jolt from her warm, relaxed sleep to this extreme of discomfort. She took off her dripping nightdress, and disregarding the rule of her order, which enjoined the sisters to observe the maximum of modesty, even when alone, she stood naked trying to dry herself with a rough towel which had only half escaped the deluge. She then lifted her suitcase from where it was swilling to and fro on the miniature lake of her cabin

6

floor, and dumped it on the soggy berth. As the ship rolled the water washed in little rills round her feet. She opened her suitcase and was vexed at her foolishness in not lifting it up sooner. The water had seeped in and wet the lower contents, but the clothes on top were still dry. She hung a set of dry underclothes on a peg, and standing on the squelchy bedding she managed to put them on without any excessive damp contacts. She was about to lean over to open the narrow wardrobe to take out a dry habit, when the ship gave a lurch, and she clung to the peg to steady herself. With her cropped hair and her utilitarian underclothes, she looked like a kind of frightened, elderly boy as she crouched on the bunk in graceful ungainliness. Although she was forty her body was still beautiful, its slender virginity preserved like that of a September flower, which remains through the cool, still days in static bloom.

As she hung there, facing the port-hole, suddenly the disk of glass framed a face. There was a man looking in at her—a native. He stared a moment, his white eyeballs and teeth flashed in a grin, and he disappeared.

Her brain whirled and her heart beat violently. She was so faint that she longed to sit down, but there was nowhere dry to sit. She had to step into the lake again to pull the short red curtain over the port-hole. She leant with closed eyes against the wardrobe door, while her shoes floated idly about her feet.

For her the incident had enormous significance. After forty years of absolute modesty, she had been seen practically undressed by a man—by a black man. She was not sure whether this made it worse or better. She had not heard of the Russian lady who used to let her butler come for orders while she was in the bath, as she felt the man so far removed from her that modesty was superfluous, but something of the same idea occured to her. She was already miserable with discomfort and fright, and now she felt that she had sinned and that virtue had gone from her, because a man had seen her in her underclothes.

Suddenly she had what was almost a new spiritual sensation, a sort of resigned acceptance of an occurrence which formerly would have worried her for days. After all, she thought, life was a continual struggle with the devil, and she had simply lost a point. It was the first time she had admitted to herself frankly that one could not win every round. A queer kind of peace descended on her, in spite of her discomfort.

She managed to finish dressing, and when she had put a clean, starched wimple her head and taken a dry pair of black cotton stockings from a drawer, she stepped out into the corridor, but her wet feet made patterns on the carpet and she leant back into the cabin for a towel. As she turned with the towel in her hand, she saw a man coming down the corridor. She was surprised that any of the passengers should be about so early. As he passed he glanced at her bare feet and at the towel, and his face showed a flicker of amusement, but his expression was kindly and without impertinence.

She was puzzled, as she had not noticed him before among the passengers, and yet his face seemed familiar. Then she realized that it was the face of the governor-general in her dream, the same pointed eyebrows, and the same air of cynical intelligence. It was odd that she had not noticed him about the ship, but that subconsciously she had registered his features and they had come to her in a dream. It was also odd, she reflected, that in her dreams she so often held conversations with important people, such as the governor-general and the archbishop, and once she had a long talk with the Duke of Windsor. Sometimes the pope received her, and at her request recognized the validity of Anglican orders.

She did not like to disturb the stewardess at this hour, and steadying herself with her hands against the close bulkheads, she walked along to the other sisters' cabins. The corridor, with its red carpet and steadily glowing electric bulbs which quivered slightly from the throbbing engine, in spite of its lurching was warm and secure, though up above the noise of the gale was terrific. The last time she had walked along a corridor in the small hours of the morning was when she was staying with some enclosed nuns, and she had got up for Matins and Lauds, and had been inwardly thankful that she had not felt that kind of vocation. Being shut off completely from the world had frightened her. In a way she felt more secure in this lurching corridor than she had in that midnight cloister.

There seemed to be swirling waterfalls in every direction. Sometimes the ship stood and quivered when a huge wave struck her bows. And yet she did feel secure, because she had such faith in the captain and sailors, who with their skill and courage directed the ship through this lightless, landless turmoil of waters. It was like being in the church, secure amid the raging evil of the world.

Certainly the wave in her cabin had shaken a little her sense of security, and the sea had become more definitely a symbol of evil. Weren't sailors supposed to be unusually immoral, with wives in every port? Anything as loose and fluid as the sea must bring looseness and fluidity to those associated with it. Her cousin Thelma, who had been such a nice girl, had lost all her reserve on a P. & O. liner, and had married a dreadful man, a fortune-hunting actor. Although Sister Agatha had enjoyed being on the ship and the cosy feeling in the midst of danger, she had found it much more difficult to pray than on land—perhaps because the cosy feeling of being protected in the ship by strong men had supplanted a little that feeling of spiritual security she had on land, protected by angels and ministers of grace.

Of course one had to pray from stability in oneself. How could one be stable, physically or spiritually, on this heaving sea? How could one feel God dwelling anywhere in a thing so amorphous. There was no fixed place in it. She was accustomed to think of God as more strongly present in fixed places—on the altar of course, and even in various pleasant corners of the convent garden. Although she must continue to say her offices and her private prayers, she would deputize the ever-obliging Virgin to give importunity to her petitions until she arrived at the mission station. Was she becoming free-thinking and heretical? She would have to have a good confessional clean-up when she landed.

She hesitated outside the cabin shared by Sister Hilda and the novice Winifred. Perhaps she ought really to go to Sister Ursula, the next senior to herself, who also had a single berth cabin, but she had a sudden longing to see what Winifred looked like asleep. This might be the only opportunity in her life to see her so. She knew it was a temptation, but she did a kind of short circuit in her mind, and opened the cabin door before she had time fairly to meet and resist the temptation.

'Sister!' she called in a gentle, lilting voice, not to make too abrupt an awakening. She opened the door wide to let the light from the corridor into the cabin, to show who she was so that they would not be frightened, but she did not switch on the cabin light. Sister Hilda sat up at once.

'Who is it? What is it?' she demanded in a shocked whisper. It was a wanton breach of the Rule for sisters to speak between Compline and Terce, the after-breakfast office.

'It's me,' said Sister Agatha. 'I've been nearly drowned and I've nowhere to sleep. May I switch on the light?'

She did it without waiting for permission, and saw Winifred asleep in the top bunk, her eyelashes resting on her rosy cheek, her face like a flower, quite close to her own. She felt a sudden stab of sadness in her heart and longed to lean forward and kiss her, but this would have been a sin, and anyhow Sister Hilda was sitting up in the bunk below, like a cross suspicious gnome guarding a treasure. Sister Agatha would have loved to share a cabin with Winifred, but as she was the senior and Superior of their small company, she had to accept the unwelcome importance of a single cabin. Hilda, on the other hand, would have been delighted with a single cabin, and hinted at a sense of ill-usage at having to share with a novice.

Winifred opened her eyes, stared in expressionless wonder at Sister Agatha, gave a delicious sleepy smile, screwed up her eyes against the light, and turned over to face the wall. Agatha had the feeling that in the morning she would have no recollection of waking.

Meanwhile, Hilda was fussing in the bottom berth.

'What is it, sister?' she whispered crossly. 'You're breaking the silence. Did you fall over-board?'

Hilda looked more like a rabbit than a gnome, and Agatha began to feel little convulsions of laughter which bubbled up in her. Now that the worst discomfort was over she had a pleasurable reaction of excitements. She had a sense of triumph at having seen Winifred asleep, and at having seen her awaken like an unfolding rose—so tenuous are the sentimental gratifications of a nun. She felt proud of her adventure, and this elation made her no longer envious of Sister Hilda, but even gave her an amused affection for characteristics which before she had found irritating—her meticulous fussiness about the Rule, her perpetual air of suspicion, as if someone must be deceiving her somewhere, and her prim, snappy way of speaking, her habit of leaping to extremes.

'I want to borrow a rug,' said Agatha.

'You know very well I haven't a rug,' said Hilda. 'Sister Ursula has a rug. Please put out the light.'

She was so funny trying to be cross and prim in a whisper that Sister Agatha's laughter bubbled right over, and giggling weakly and feeling rather light-headed, she left the cabin. The lurching of the ship made her giggle more, and she thought that if any one saw her now they would think she was drunk. The idea of any one thinking that she was drunk seemed funnier still, and she could not stop laughing.

She knocked on Sister Ursula's door, but there was no reply beyond the steady ron-ron of her snoring. One might almost have mistaken it for one of the ship's noises, for part of the engine, whose steady throbbing was an undercurrent to the whining of the gale, the pounding of waves upon the deck and the rush of falling waters. She opened the door and switched on the light but still Sister Ursula snored, her head buried in the clothes, her back, a huge bulwark of indifference, thrust insolently towards the world exterior to her snug dreams.

'Sister Ursula,' said Agatha, without effect. She had a temptation to slap that enormous behind, and then made an effort to pull herself together and become more sedate-minded. It seemed as if the wave had washed away her sense of propriety, or else that in the small hours of the morning she was capable of a levity which did not effect her at other times.

Agatha called again, louder, and Sister Ursula's snoring suddenly ended with a protesting snort. The large behind disappeared, and Ursula's red, thick-muscled face came into view.

'What is it?' she growled. 'Have I overslept?'

'No. A wave came into my cabin. I want to borrow your rug.' Ursula had a red tartan rug, which now lay across her feet, in spite of the steamy warmth of the cabin. She was a Highlander by birth, and somehow had managed to retain this individual possession in spite of poverty and obedience. As it was her only distinctive possession she was intensely proud of it, partly also because it emphasized her superiority of race to the other sisters, who had the misfortune to be Anglo-Australians. When Sister Agatha asked to borrow this treasure, Ursula made two funny little noises in her nose, and looked obstinate. She had the same feeling about lending her rug to someone who was not even a Scot, let alone a member of her clan, that she would have had if she had seen a priest giving the Sacrament to a Nonconformist.

'Mrs Bright has a good 'possum-skin rug,' she said at last, not meeting Agatha's eyes.

'I don't like to wake her up,' said Agatha.

'I'll do it,' said Ursula. She stretched out her hand to the precious rug, and draped it about her before she descended, a miniature Scottish avalanche, to the floor.

'There is no need for you to go. If she must be woken up I may as well do it.'

Actually Sister Agatha had thought of Mrs. Bright's 'possum-skin rug, but it did not seem to her right to disturb a stranger when one of the sisters had a rug. She took it for granted that a nun had less right to a comfortable night than someone who had not renounced the world.

She turned to leave the cabin but Sister Ursula pushed past her, so she remained where she was, thinking that after all as Ursula would not lend her rug she might as well have the unpleasant task of waking Mrs Bright. Ursula was performing this not so much as a service to Agatha, as to her rug, her symbol of race, as a young subaltern might do a service to his flag. She knew that she kept this possession in defiance of the Rule, and there was always the danger that her Superior might suddenly wake up to the fact and make her give it up. The

13

Reverend Mother had ignored the indiscipline, finding Ursula enough of a bear without giving her a sore head, but now Agatha was her Superior and if Agatha found that the possession of the rug was leading her into selfishness she might command her to give it away, so in a desperate display of unselfishness she left her bed and lumbered along to Mrs Bright's cabin, where she roughly shook her by the shoulder.

Agatha remained leaning against the open doorway to steady herself. The events of the last half-hour were vivid in her mind. She began to smile at them again, when in the middle of all these sharp but jumbled pictures, her shoes sailing on the floor, Winifred's smile, Ursula's insolent behind, appeared the native's face and his grin as he stared at her, clinging almost naked to the clothes-hook. Her heart sank a little. The native's smile seemed in a way to negative the effect of Winifred's smile which had made her so happy.

She was standing there pensively when the man who had been the governor-general in her dream came back along the corridor. She moved a little to let him pass, but he stopped and said courteously:

'You have been afflicted by Neptune, *ma sœur*?'

Agatha was a little startled at being addressed by a man, though pleased at being called *ma sœur*, which somehow made her feel more Catholic, She murmured a shy reply.

'Neptune is an uncertain quantity,' the man went on. 'His higher vibrations produce the great mystics, his lower the extreme of human depravity. On the material plane he can provide a happy paddling place for little children, or the dark and treacherous caverns of death— or perhaps mere discomfort such as you have just suffered. But in all his works there is a strange beauty.'

'There isn't much beauty in my cabin at the moment,' said Agatha drily.

14

'Perhaps there was when the wave came in.'

She did not know what he meant. She thought that possibly he was impertinent, but there was nothing offensive in his manner.

'As a Christian,' she said, 'I don't expect to be affected by Neptune.'

'The early church admitted the existence of the old gods,' he said, 'and called them devils—mistakenly I think. Our culture without either the classical or the Christian ingredient would be poor in texture. We are the heirs of both worlds.'

Sister Ursula, a mountain of fur and tartan, was returning along the corridor. The man looked at her, gave a faintly amused smile, bowed to Agatha, and walked away in the opposite direction.

'What an odd conversation to have in a ship, in the middle of a storm, at four in the morning!' thought Agatha. He was an odd man anyhow, probably an Oxford don, a scholarly bore, who spent his time travelling round the world in search of beetles or orchids or anthropological data. She shivered, beginning to feel the after-effects of shock.

Ursula handed her the fur rug in an off-hand manner, and gave a slight grunt when Agatha thanked her. Ursula often performed small services with less ulterior motive than the borrowing of Mrs Bright's rug, but she could never accept thanks gracefully. She did not seem able to endure the slightest emotional link with another human being, even that created by mild gratitude.

Agatha made her way unsteadily up to the lounge. She had to stop twice on the companion-way, clinging to the banister lest she should be flung backwards down the steps. This no longer seemed an amusing adventure. It was really horrid of Sister Ursula to grudge the loan of her rug. It was a sort of denial of the oneness of their community, of the religious love which should

15

bind them nearer to God and nearer to each other, which inflamed the young novices like Winifred, but which the professed sisters were apt to smother under mutual distaste for their idiosyncrasies. Without this love it was painful to continue in religion. One could only endure material barrenness if it was compensated by spiritual richness.

She settled herself on the stuffy red velvet seat at the side of the lounge, and wrapping the rug round her she tried to sleep, but it was impossible, because although by now she had become fairly accustomed to the sea-noises, she could not relax or she would roll off on to the floor. Also the rug was much too hot. The storm did not make the tropical seas any cooler, and she did not need the rug for warmth, but simply because she did not like to lie down in a public place, even though there was no one about, with nothing over her. She lay in the corner behind a fixed, brass-rimmed table, which smelt horribly of stale nicotine, but without its support she could not have stayed on the seat.

She lay there miserably until the hour of Prime, when, tired but relieved at having an excuse to move, she went down to warn the five other sisters that Prime would be said in Sister Hilda's cabin.

She then went to her own, which was still in its drenched, disordered condition. She rang for the stewardess who, when she saw the mess, shrugged her shoulders and said that she would make the steward clean it up. After all it was his fault for leaving the port-hole open. She was very vexed with the steward but made no reference to Sister Agatha's discomfiture. Apparently the steward would not be able to attend to the job for another hour at least.

The sisters crowded into Hilda's cabin, where she and Winifred were now dressed, and had made their beds tidy. It was already rather stuffy as the port-hole had been closed all night, and in this old-fashioned ship the ventilation was not very efficient. Magdalene and Cecilia were bursting with curiosity to know why they were to say Prime here instead of in Agatha's cabin, but they might not speak until after breakfast.

Hilda hung her large crucifix on the hook on the door, where it swayed with the movement of the ship, sometimes hanging away from the door, as if it were offering its feet to the nuns to kiss. They faced it, and Agatha began the office. They were so crowded together that when they crossed themselves they bumped each other, and now and then they clutched wildly at anything within reach to stop themselves falling over.

Hilda felt awful. She was in one of those dilemmas which seemed so frequently to afflict her, when whatever she did would be wrong, and which gave her eyes that suspicious look, as she had come to believe that all life was a trap for her. The door on which the crucifix swayed was a kind of religious sanction, denying her air and freedom and the decency of vomiting in private. Its brown polished surface was as forbidding as the door in that picture by Watts, which shows a disconsolate Eros beating his delicate fist against a surface of adamant bronze. Her suspicious eyes glared at it. She gulped once or twice and then turned and was sick in her wash-basin.

When a situation became really dreadful Agatha always wanted to laugh. She felt the corners of her mouth twitching and she could not go on with her psalms. She did not know whether to interrupt the office and go elsewhere or to ignore Sister Hilda, as a priest ignores someone who faints in church. But it was difficult to ignore someone being sick in a tiny, crowded cabin. At last she said quietly: 'You had better lie down on your bed, sister.' She finished the office but she was very glad to get out of that cabin.

She took the fur rug back to the lounge and tried to rest there again until breakfast time. It was light now, and through the windows she could watch the heavy seas. Sometimes a wave would come right on to this upper deck, and for a moment the windows darkened as if they were solid green glass, and when they cleared the spume dribbled down them like water inside a fishmonger's window. The sea seemed so powerful that Agatha had a brief qualm of doubt of the captain's and crew's ability to bring the ship safely through the storm. And yet one could not imagine it sinking, all those cabins and corridors, the lounge and the large saloon plunging beneath the waves and filling with roaring, rushing water. It would be like a hotel sinking, and somehow far more terrifying than if one were to be capsized in a small boat, even though the danger of drowning was the same.

Marinella Dawes was the first passenger to come up into the lounge. She was a bright, fair-haired, self-assured little girl of eleven or twelve, who liked talking to people. She was nearly always the first on deck, and there was no one to talk to, except busy stewards whom she rather despised, so she was pleased to see Sister Agatha, and danced up to her, as much as one could dance on a heaving floor.

'You are up early,' she said. 'You don't generally get up till breakfast.'

'I don't generally come on deck till breakfast, but I am up long before,' said Agatha. She really ought not to go on breaking the silence she thought, but it would be difficult not to answer the child, and it would be wrong to let her think that nuns led a sluggish life. There was a dispensation about the silence when travelling, but it was only meant for when it was absolutely necessary to speak.

'Then why are you here now?' asked Marinella.

'A wave came into my cabin.'

'A wave? How could a huge wave get through a tiny little port-hole?'

'Well, a wave broke on the deck and quite a lot of water managed to get through the port-hole.'

'Were you in bed?'

'Yes.'

'Did you get wet?'

'Yes.'

'Wet through?'

'Yes. My shoes were floating on the cabin floor.'

Marinella stared brightly for a moment at Sister Agatha, then she burst out laughing. She doubled herself up, dramatizing her laughter, and the high silvery sound filled the lounge.

Agatha smiled, but not with unqualified pleasure.

Mrs Bright, who weighed sixteen stone, came swaying up the companion-way. Agatha was afraid that her weight would be too much for the strength of her hands, which clutched at the banisters. But Mrs Bright held herself gallantly erect, waiting now and then to recover her balance, and arrived in the lounge with an air of breezy triumph. Her light curls were golden and glossy beneath their net, her round, rather puffy face was powdered to an even bloom, her mouth was scarlet and her double row of large pearls rose and fell on her bosom as she recovered her breath after climbing the stairs.

'Good morning, sister,' she called cheerily. 'You've had an experience. How are you now?'

Choosing a moment when the deck was level she managed to reach the seat.

'Well, young lady,' she said to Marinella. 'You seem very amused.' She turned to Agatha. 'I've brought you some brandy.'

Agatha abandoned all hope of keeping the silence.

'That is very kind of you,' she said, 'but, really, I don't need any.'

'It'll warm you up,' said Mrs Bright, ignoring Agatha's refusal. She took a silver flask out of her bag and poured some brandy into the stopper, which served as a small cup.

'But, really—' Agatha protested.

'Come on, now. It'll do you good. It wouldn't harm a baby. It's lovely stuff—'85. My brother gave me six bottles for the trip.'

'Six bottles!' exclaimed Agatha.

'Yes, you can never have too much brandy at sea.'

'I hope you don't mind this stormy weather?' Agatha said, looking doubtfully at the brandy.

'Oh no! I'm an old sea-dog,' said Mrs Bright.

'I love the sea!' cried Marinella, who thought she was not receiving enough attention. 'I love it when it's stormy—I wish I was a sea-gull.'

'Well, mind you don't fall overboard,' said Mrs Bright. 'I did once.'

Agatha looked a little startled. The idea of Mrs Bright's sixteen stones, surmounted by its meticulously arranged curls, sploshing into the sea made it difficult to suppress a nervous giggle. Marinella burst out into another fit of laughter.

'It wasn't so funny as you think, young lady,' said Mrs Bright, a little piqued. 'I was no bigger than you at the time, and the ship was in port—in Sydney harbour it was—but I might have been eaten by a shark. They gave me brandy afterwards. You drink that up!' she said to Agatha.

Agatha thought the brandy would be like rather nasty medicine, and made an attempt to gulp it down. But she had almost never taken alcohol, certainly not for many years, and even the mellow spirit was fire in her throat, and the fumes got in her nose. She coughed and spluttered and wiped her eyes.

'Oh, it's much—much too strong,' she said. Mrs Bright stood up and lurched dangerously to the stairs. In a little while she returned, carrying with surprising success a glass half-full of water. Agatha thought she was like an elephant in an egg-and-spoon race, and then blamed herself for being amused at Mrs Bright when she was so kind.

The brandy was easier to drink with water, and it did warm her and make her feel more cheerful. Mrs Bright had a nip to keep her company, and when Marinella asked to taste it, she gave her a tiny sip. Marinella screwed up her face, half-sneezed, smiled, and asked for more. Mrs Bright gave her another tiny sip, which rather shocked Agatha.

However, she sat there laughing and talking with Mrs Bright and Marinella until the bugle went for breakfast. The silence had been so much broken that it hardly seemed worth while trying to retrieve the rest of it. All this could go into the bag for her next confession.

The breakfast bugle startled Agatha. Its notes sounded eerie against the storm. They were blown away over the endless, angry mountains of water. Her mind was stimulated by the unaccustomed alcohol. Again she had a vivid awareness of the ship as a mere speck of civilization in a vast primeval waste. The challenge of the bugle was frightening in its impudence.

'Aren't you feeling well?' asked Mrs Bright.

'Oh yes, thank you, I'm quite well,' said Agatha. She stood up and clung to the metal-rimmed table for support.

'Can I help you down?' she asked Mrs Bright, knowing quite well that she could not possibly lend any useful support to such a weight of flesh.

'Each man for himself, I think,' said Mrs Bright with a hint of rebuke for the insincerity.

When they came into the saloon they were laughing at their misadventures. The other sisters were already silently but unsteadily eating their breakfasts at a table where the fiddles failed to stop a good deal of sliding and upset. They looked up shocked when they heard Sister Agatha laughing in the public saloon before the end of silence.

Agatha felt a little ashamed of herself, but more irritated with them for being so particular. Surely her discomforts had excused her? It was very unpleasant to feel the disapproval of people who were in her charge. She bowed with sudden primness to Mrs Bright, and crossing herself, sat down between Hilda and Ursula.

After breakfast she found her cabin in order again, with a dry, newly made bed, and dry new curtains and carpet. They always seemed to have plenty of everything on a ship. She let down the shiny metal basin to wash her hands, when suddenly she was overcome by nausea and collapsed on the bed.

The shock and its reaction had used up her reserves of vitality and she felt exhausted. She was just beginning to recover a degree of composure when the sisters trooped into her cabin to say Terce.

She waved a limp hand and murmured: 'Go away!'

'Are you ill, sister?' asked Hilda, peering down at her with suspicious eyes.

'If you make me speak I'll be sick,' said Agatha.

They chattered anxiously round the bed, but Hilda had smelt the brandy and stood apart, her mouth pursed and her eyes turned inwards almost to a squint.

At last Agatha braced herself to sit up. 'Oh, do go!' she shouted. She then flopped back on to the pillow and turned her face to the wall. This open human anger, so contrary to the spirit of holy religion, startled the sisters, and they trooped out of the cabin to say their office elsewhere. Winifred went last. She drew the curtain over the port-hole and closed the door softly behind her.

Agatha lay debating with herself whether to get up and be sick or whether to lie still in the hope that the nausea would pass. Before she had decided the point she fell asleep.

She woke up just before luncheon feeling perfectly well, but she rose and moved about gingerly, not to put her condition to too hard a test.

At luncheon two of the passengers were bandaged. Mrs Stevens had been flung against an iron railing and had hurt her hand. She had dyed auburn hair, a very much painted face, and had acquired a bogus upper-class manner through living in the tropics and ordering native servants. She talked loudly and cheerfully of her injury, and seemed to enjoy the prominence it gave her. Like Marinella she declared that she adored the storm, implying that she was a creature of heroic blood. There was a slight rivalry in social importance between Mrs Stevens and Mrs Bright, the former's based on the number of her black servants, the latter's on the wealth of her brother in Sydney.

Mr Dawes had bumped his nose on something, and wore a cross of sticking plaster. He was a small mouse-coloured man who had married early a girl a few inches taller and a few years older than himself. He had been a clerk in Melbourne until six months ago, when his wife had inherited some money, and Mr Dawes had revealed that his life's ambition was to be a planter. He was not quite sure what he wanted to plant, whether tea or coffee, rubber or coco-nuts, but he had a nostalgia to walk in the tropical dusk through leafy groves, for the dancing girls an sweet birds' cries, the scarlet hibiscus, for the cool verandas, and the bronzed obedient slaves. He was now touring the South Seas in search of a place where these things might be found. His wife was a little uneasy about it, but at intervals she told Agatha that it was 'a great adventure.' Being so much larger than her

23

husband, and happening to provide the money, she was pathetically anxious to be dominated by him. She did all she could to bolster up his importance, and she often quoted him, saying: 'Mr Dawes says——' as if that authority were final.

It was strange that such a sedate couple should have produced anything as bright and assured as Marinella, but they were so obviously proud of her that she had become proud of herself, and did not imagine that any one could fail to find her entertaining and sweetly pretty, as she had often overheard people describe her. Her frocks were spotless, and she never crushed them in rough play. She wore two little gold bracelets, and even had a tiny ring. She almost vied with Mrs Bright and Mrs Stevens to be the social leader of the ship. There was a queer affinity between them, Agatha thought, and she had often noticed women of their type on the few ships on which she had travelled. Their colour was always a little too gay to be natural. She could imagine Marinella in thirty years time a replica of Mrs Stevens, and even now her pretty eyes were a china blue. Perhaps it was the influence of Neptune as that man had said. Agatha looked round the saloon for him, but she could not see him. Perhaps he was injured too, or he might only be seasick.

At the end of luncheon the captain came over to their table and asked them how they liked the weather.

'We don't like it at all, I'm afraid,' said Agatha. 'We're longing for dry land.'

'You needn't be nervous,' the captain explained. 'I've turned a bit off our course to make the going easier.'

'Oh, we're not nervous,' said Agatha.

'There's only one thing to be afraid of at sea, and that's fog. I'd rather be in a typhoon than in a fog.'

'Isn't this a typhoon?' asked Hilda.

The captain laughed.

'This is just a stiff breeze,' he said. He nodded and walked out of the saloon. Agatha had a return of her confidence in him, a warm feeling that was almost affection.

After luncheon Mrs Bright stopped her in the lounge and asked her to come to her cabin. 'I'll make you some really good coffee,' she said. She also collected Mrs Dawes and Mrs Stevens.

Mrs Bright's brother had paid for her to have a three-berth cabin to herself, so that she would have room to move about. It contained other evidences of wealth. The inevitable stuffiness was relieved or accentuated, Agatha was not sure which, by lingering aromas of expensive perfume—there was powder spilt on the floor by the washstand—of Egyptian cigarettes, and of brandy. Some full-blown pink roses brought aboard in bud and kept alive with aspirin were stuck in the water-bottle. There were several large boxes of chocolates tied with satin bows, one of which lay open on the bed, amid a disarray of crinkly paper. On a shelf were half a dozen new novels in brightly coloured wrappers. The 'possum-skin rug and a cerise satin dressing-gown, flung down beside the chocolates, gave a final touch of opulence.

While Mrs Bright made coffee in a silver-plated machine, shaped like a long egg, Mrs Stevens did the honours of the cabin. She could never help acting as hostess wherever she was. She gushed over Agatha, and called her 'Reverend Mother.' Soon the aroma of coffee mingled with the other smells, and though the mixture was even richer it was a slight improvement, as at least the coffee was fresh.

Mrs Dawes sat stiffly upright on the settee-berth under the port-hold. To her a party of any kind was simply an occasion for a display of good housekeeping, though of course it was difficult to display much housekeeping in a ship's cabin.

'This is certainly very good coffee,' she said at intervals, but no one heeded her, as Agatha was occupied in refusing Mrs Bright's offer of more brandy and Mrs Stevens in accepting it.

'Oh, Mrs Dawes, some brandy,' said Mrs Bright, suddenly noticing her.

'No, thank you. I am quite well,' said Mrs Dawes. 'I do not really mind the rough weather. This is excellent coffee.'

'Glad you like it. Have some chocolates. There's rum in the blue and silver ones.'

'What a royal box!' exclaimed Mrs Dawes. 'Are there any with hard centres?'

'Let's shut out that damned ocean,' said Mrs Bright, and drew the curtain over the port-hole, above which the waves rose at intervals, filling the cabin with green gloom.

Mrs Dawes looked more shocked than Agatha, who hardly noticed the profanity as she was so used to the sluts and whores using far worse language outside the mission-house windows in Little Bourke Street. Mrs Dawes looked in every way far more respectable than Agatha. There was a kind of passionate respectability about her. Mrs Bright had fixed a rosy lampshade to the electric bulb, and in its glow Agatha's face looked softened, amused, and almost worldly in its tolerance, but no light could soften the grim lines of Mrs Dawes's cheek-bones, nor dim the gleam of fanatical respectability in her eyes. She looked to Agatha like some stern Covenanter, who would gladly die, or if necessary butcher someone else, for her faith—not that she had any faith in anything beyond her husband and her bank balance.

Mrs Bright having told the others to help themselves to chocolates, brandy, or cigarettes, if they wanted more, tucked herself up on her bed and opened a book called *Red Love on a Blue Island*, by Stephen Leacock.

'This book's a scream,' she said. 'Shall I read you some?'

Mrs Dawes was relieved, as she thought reading aloud a very genteel pastime, but as Mrs Bright read no smile flickered on her face, which remained stern and puzzled. Mrs Bright and Mrs Stevens became hysterical with laughter, and Agatha began to laugh with them. Mrs Dawes was shocked at Agatha's laughing, but she had heard that Catholics and High Church people had no morals. She had never heard such nonsense as Mrs Bright was reading, and thought the three women must be tipsy. When the story was finished she stood up and said: 'Thank you for the coffee, but I must go now to Marinella.'

Agatha left with her, as she felt that when Mrs Dawes's forbidding presence was removed the remaining balance of raffishness would be too great for her to remain with propriety. She felt that she had already been far too careless about self-discipline to-day. She had a horrid feeling that her character or her faith was disintegrating. It went somehow with the sensation she had at those recurring moments when she doubted the safety of the ship.

After tea all the passengers were gathered in the lounge. Mrs Stevens with her bandaged hand, and Mr Dawes with his plastered nose were still the only casualties. The lounge opened on to a veranda, which faced aft over the well-deck. This seemed to be the highest and driest part of the ship, though every now and then a wave broke over the boat-deck and the veranda was like the inside of a waterfall.

In spite of the captain having turned off the course to avoid the full onslaught of the weather, the ship was still rolling heavily.

Agatha was seated with Winifred in the corner by the brass-rimmed table, where she had spent the hours before breakfast. Mrs Bright was near them in her cane chaise-longue. The ship descended in a roll to starboard, but instead of coming back it went on—and on—and on. Mrs Bright's chair began to slide. Agatha put out her left hand to grab it, and with her right she clung to the fixed table. The angle of the ship was so great that she had almost the whole of Mrs Bright's sixteen stone to sustain with her left hand. People were screaming, but she hardly heard them as she was concentrating on holding Mrs Bright. The ship went farther over still, and she thought it must be going to turn upside down. She was coldly curious to see what would happen. At last the pull on her hand was so great that she either had to let Mrs Bright go, or to go with her. There seemed no sense in two people falling together so she let her go, and felt a little ashamed of herself. Mrs Bright's chair shot downhill across the lounge, and crashed sickeningly into the opposite wall. Mrs Bright fell and then as the ship came up again she rolled back enormously across the floor. The other passengers were all clinging to something fixed, and could not go to her aid, while the unfixed articles, chairs and books, fell and slid about with Mrs Bright, whose skirt had rolled up, showing her huge fat knees and the elastic bottoms of her pink drawers. She still clutched the copy of *Red Love on a Blue Island*.

As soon as it was possible to stand without support Agatha, Mr Dawes, and half a dozen others rushed to help Mrs Bright to her feet. It was slightly more shocking to them, more of an affront from nature to human standards, that the richest woman on the ship should be rolled across the floor with her knickers showing. It accentuated the impersonal fury of the storm. Protected by her layers of fat Mrs Bright had broken no bones, but she was white and shaken, and she could not speak. Mr Dawes helped her down to her cabin.

When the excitement had died down and the passengers had settled themselves again, smiling uneasily because they had been so scared, Agatha turned to Winifred and said quietly:

'Were you afraid?'

'I think I was more curious to see what would happen.'

'So was I. I thought she would roll right over. Did you say any prayers?'

Winifred blushed. 'No, I forgot. At least there wasn't much time, was there?'

Agatha was looking anxiously at the floor. When the ship rolled to port she still seemed to have a slight starboard list. Perhaps it was the wind blowing from the port side, but she had not had this list before.

The man who had been Lord Bletchingdon in her dream, and who had spoken to her about Neptune in the corridor, now appeared in the lounge. It was the first time that Agatha had noticed him among the passengers. He stood easily on the sloping floor and announced in a cheerful voice:

'The cargo has shifted.'

He caught Sister Agatha's eye, smiled, bowed courteously, and passed out of the other door of the lounge, on to the deck. There was a sudden howl of wind, and Mrs Stevens, who was seated near, was wet with spray before the door slammed behind him.

Dick Corkery, the fourth officer, who had come in as the man made the announcement, looked extremely annoyed, and said: 'There is no danger. We're filling the port ballast tank.'

He was standing close to Sister Agatha, who said: 'Excuse me, what is that man's name?' She nodded towards the door on to the deck.

'Smith,' said Dick.

'Oh!' Agatha laughed. She had expected him to have some double-barrelled, English-gentlemanly name.

Dick smiled back at her, glanced at Winifred, remained a moment with his lips parted, and then disappeared, amid another howling of wind and spray, on to the deck.

'That's a nice boy,' said Agatha, but Winifred did not reply.

The ship gave a further roll to starboard, even worse than the one which had dislodged Mrs Bright. There was a distant thud, somewhere away in the innards of the ship, and she lay and quivered. She did not come up again nearly to her normal level. One propeller must have been almost continuously out of the water as there was a terrific vibration.

No one fell in the lounge, as they had all stationed themselves by something to hold on to, but all the loose articles, books, chairs, and rugs, were heaped against the lower wall like rubbish in a second-hand shop.

Mrs Stevens screamed: 'We shall all be drowned!' Her terror made her painted face and her dyed hair look inhumanly grotesque.

Agatha said quietly: 'They are filling the port ballast tanks.' She did not know what this meant, but it had a reassuring sound. She felt that if she repeated it enough it would act as magic to save them.

Hilda kept on exclaiming: 'We shall die without the Sacrament!' She took out her breviary and fussily turned over the thin India paper, which always stuck together at the pages she wanted.

Mrs Dawes, holding Marinella by the hand, came up into the lounge. They climbed more up the banisters than walked on the stairs. Marinella was screaming horribly. Mrs Dawes cried:

'Where is Mr Dawes?' She looked like Niobe, or some stern archaic figure of tragedy.

Marinella went on screaming until she saw that Mrs Stevens was screaming too. The screaming woman and the screaming child stared at each other and suddenly they both stopped.

Agatha began to say: 'He's helping Mrs Bright——' when the steamer's siren hooted pitifully out into the gale.

The second officer pushed his way into the lounge upwards from the starboard deck. He was tall and strongly built, with a square jaw, a straight nose, and straight black eye-brows. He was like a handsome sailor in a magazine illustration. He squared his shoulders and looked impersonally across the room.

'Boat stations!' he snapped out. 'And keep calm.'

He expected to be dead in half an hour at the most. He was certain of this immediate death, but he was determined to act nobly. In fact to act nobly was the only pleasure left him, though he did not realize how much satisfaction it gave him to stand there, affecting indifference to death, and snapping out 'Boat stations!' He was at last what he had always longed to be since he had learnt *Vitai Lampada* at school—a heroic Englishman. He had his reward. He was given what is allowed to very few—to realize his dream of himself.

*

Dick pulled himself along the deck. For the moment he had forgotten the storm and the shifted cargo. His expression was tranquil and serious. He had never thought of a nun as being beautiful before.

As he came for'ard beyond the shelter of the bulkhead a seaman blown by the wind collided heavily against him, and grabbed him round the neck to stop himself rushing overboard.

'Hell!' said Dick, and disentangled the man from his neck and pulled him up until he could reach the stanchion.

'Oh, it's you!' he said crossly. The sailor was a young man of about his own age, whom he had noticed about

31

the deck, and to whom, for some reason which he could not understand, he had avoided giving orders when he might have done so. It was something to do with the way the man had looked at him. He looked at him in an amused, comradely way, which ought to have been offensive from an A.B. to an officer, but which somehow was not. In the army this expression might have been classified as 'dumb insolence.'

'Thanks, very much,' said the sailor, and he burst out laughing. His voice was not uneducated, though a little Australian.

Dick was furious with him for laughing and said: 'You might let me pass now,' but he spoke huskily as he found it difficult to stand on his dignity, especially as at that moment the ship rolled heavily to starboard, and neither of them could move. They heard the thud of the shifting cargo, and then the melancholy hoot of the siren, which made the ship seem like an animal lying on its side in pain.

Dick forgot his dignity, and stared with frightened eyes at the young seaman.

'Listen!' said the seaman. 'We'll both be dead in ten minutes, and you won't be an officer any more. I'll tell you something. You seem to me a damned nice chap, and I like you a lot.'

'What's your name?' asked Dick.

'Joe.'

'Good. Mine's Dick.'

They parted, and Dick climbed up to the boat deck.

*

Mr Dawes, dripping with sweat, managed to bring Mrs Bright to her cabin. The stewardess had been in after the coffee party and had tidied up, emptying the ash trays and drawing back the curtain again, so that looking out one could see the ruthless, curling waves above one, until they swooped down and the cabin was a dim green, like the inside of an aquarium. Mrs Bright sank heavily on to the settee below the port-hole. Mr Dawes watched her anxiously, uncertain what further attention he could decorously offer.

'My brandy flask,' said Mrs Bright tonelessly, 'on the washstand.'

'Shall I pour it out for you,' he asked with eager politeness.

'Yes—a good nip in the tooth glass.'

'Water?'

'My God, no!' Mrs Bright gave the first sign of returning energy since she had fallen over. She gulped down the neat spirit, and paused as if to let the life creep along her veins.

'I hate water,' she said. 'Ugh!' She offered him the brandy flask. 'Have some.'

For reply Mr Dawes shot across the cabin, and knocked the flask on to the floor, where it emptied itself on the carpet. Mr Dawes sprawled across Mrs Bright, while behind the clatter of falling objects he heard a thud somewhere in the bowels of the ship, and she stopped and shuddered. Mr Dawes was so horrified to find himself lying on top of Mrs Bright that it was a moment or two before he realized their danger. The cabin was now filled with unrelieved submarine gloom, as the port no longer rose above the solid mass of water. It was like some fantastic nightmare to find himself in this queer green light, struggling off this scented mountain of a woman.

Above them, away up in the wild gale, the siren began to hoot.

A steward, clambering along the corridor, showed a scared, green-white face at the door.

'Boat stations!' he yelled hoarsely, 'the cargo's shifted.'

Mr Dawes gave a kind of whimpering moan, not of fear, but of indecision. He was longing to dash off to Mrs Dawes and Marinella, but he could not leave Mrs

Bright unaided. He stayed and tugged at her to pull her to her feet. He was as much a hero as the second officer, but he was unaware of his heroism which was not acted at all, but only sprang from an instinctive conscientiousness, and gave him no satisfaction.

'Let me alone,' cried Mrs Bright angrily, trying to free her fat arm from his grasp.

'Hurry! You'll drown!' he shouted.

'If I'm going to drown, I'll drown here in the dry and comfort,' she shouted back at him.

He did not speak, but continued to drag at her desperately. The brandy and this new shock had given her an access of strength. She rose from her bunk, and somehow flung Mr Dawes uphill out of the cabin and bolted the door against him.

He rattled the handle, banged on the door, and shouted with vindictive hysteria:

'May God help you!'

'Same to you, I'm sure,' Mrs Bright muttered angrily, as she fumbled in her cabin trunk to get another bottle of brandy. She knocked its top off against the wash-basin and lay down on her bed with the bottle and a tooth glass, first drawing the curtains and switching on the rosy light. With a trembling hand she poured out a tumbler full of brandy and began to gulp it down. She must lose consciousness before the unthinkable, the horrible thing happened. She would not think of it, would not name it in her mind. She was trembling with anger against Dawes that he should have demanded of her to face the unfaceable.

But after a tumbler of brandy she no longer felt afraid. She lurched from her bed, and again fumbled in her cabin trunk, from which she pulled out a jewel case. She drew from it diamond stars, emerald bracelets, rings, and ear-rings. She fondled each one, remembering the birthday when it was given her, before she fixed it on her bosom, her finger, or her wrist. Soon she glittered amazingly, and as she fixed the last bracelet on her wrist the fumes of brandy finally overcame her, and she passed into unconsciousness.

*

'Where is my husband?' cried Mrs Dawes, as the second officer withdrew from the scene of his brief apotheosis. She looked more antique and noble, more carved in tragic stone than ever, as she stood unable to move for fear she should be going in a direction away from him, and every minute apart from him was an eternal loss, when there might be so few left in which she could see his face.

The passengers climbed past her up to the door, which gave on to the port deck. The waves were now thudding against that by which Mr Smith and Dick had gone out, and water splashed through the cracks.

Agatha stopped by Mrs Dawes and said: 'He's helping Mrs Bright. He'll be here soon. You must bring Marinella on to the boat-deck.'

Hilda darted down the companion-way.

'Sister!' cried Agatha. She thought she had gone to fetch Mr Dawes, risking her life to comfort the desperate wife. She was surprised that Hilda, with all her fussy observance of the letter, should be capable of such a generous gesture of the spirit. She was ashamed of herself for being surprised, and felt suddenly happy that their life as nuns was justified, the life in which the self is nothing, and the love that is God everything.

A Brisbane solicitor who had come on a holiday cruise was crawling up the floor past her. He tugged at her habit, and said: 'Get a move on.' Beneath all her emotions, her happiness, her steadily mounting fear, it occurred to her that he was unsuitably familiar. He was like a dog urging someone to go for a walk.

The wind was blowing in at the open door, which flapped and banged noisily, and blew back the people struggling upwards against it, so that they all, like the solicitor, had to crawl through on their hands and knees. Everywhere in the ship unfastened doors were banging like loud castanets.

With the first shifting of cargo the captain had turned the ship head on to the wind, but now she was gradually easing away from it, and the danger would be when she was broadside on to the vast waves.

Up on the boat-deck they were faced with the stark reality of their peril. Agatha's instinct, unlike a rat's, was to return into the sinking ship, to enjoy, like Mrs Bright, the brief security of a dry cabin and electric light, rather than trust herself to the small open boat which the sailors with difficulty were now swinging out on the davits.

The faces of the passengers confronted with death were so dreadful that Agatha felt a rise of cold fear in her stomach, and she looked away at the sailors before fear possessed her entirely. The sailors only appeared extremely angry as they tugged and cursed at the davit ropes. Winifred was standing beside Agatha. Her face was pale and serious. She took Agatha's hand, and pressed it, and Agatha's fear sank down again.

Individual life had become unimportant. There was a primitive urge to save life as a whole, but there had to be wastage. Mrs Stevens was the first wastage. Brandy and fear had made her uncertain in her movements, and she slipped on the wet boards and slithered down the deck into the sea, shooting overboard where a boat had been swung out, and there was no railing. They had a glimpse of her painted face, framed in her auburn hair which floated round it like seaweed, staring horror-struck from the green wall of a wave which curled and broke over her, when she was tumbled up and lost in spume.

The laws of proportion had altered. This was dreadful, but it was only an incident. The filthy language pouring automatically from the angry-faced sailors as they grappled with the davits would normally have been appalling, but now it hardly had the importance of an incident. The only consideration of any full-size importance was how many people could get into the boats, and how many boats would survive.

The nuns' veils blew out like black flags. Winifred's blew right off her head and caught on the rigging where it flapped wildly as if mourning the doomed ship. Dick, the fourth officer, was in charge of the boat to which the nuns were allotted, and he shouted at them to get in. With an athletic recklessness which they had been unaware they possessed, they clambered, black, agile, and fluttering, into the swaying shell. Mrs Dawes and Marinella were with them. Mrs Dawes handed Marinella to Ursula, and then, clinging to the davit-post, turned and cried desperately: 'My husband.' Dick took her by the arm and tried to force her into the boat, but with tigerish strength she thrust him aside, so that he nearly fell into the sea.

Marinella screamed 'Mummy!' Mrs Dawes gave a sob and clambered into the boat.

The young sailor called Joe was climbing along the deck to his boat-station. Dick stopped him and said: 'Get in here.'

He replied: 'That's not my boat.'

'I tell you to get in,' said Dick authoritatively.

The sailor grinned. 'You won't be an officer much longer, so I needn't do what you tell me.'

It suddenly seemed to Dick more important than anything in the world that this sailor should be in his boat. He was filled with a passion to be obeyed. A small voice at the back of his brain told him he was out of his senses, but he did not heed it. He seized Joe by the throat, flung him backwards into the boat, and jumped in after him.

'Let her go!' he yelled to the sailors.

At this moment Sister Hilda and Mr Dawes appeared. Hilda had her black American cloth bag, and she and Mr Dawes between them were carrying a yellow, French-polished box. They slid precariously down the deck, and Hilda got into the boat. Mr Dawes was about to follow her, when she pushed him back and said: 'No, no! The altar!'

He picked up the yellow case which he had dumped against the railing, and handed it to her. As he did so a huge wave rose up to the level of the boat-deck, Mr Dawes was up to his knees in rushing water, and the life-boat was actually floating before it had been lowered. The sailors freed it from the hooks, and it was borne away on the wave which had floated it. The ship rose above them, a great black and rusty wall, with waterfalls pouring from the decks. The sailors, their faces once more fixed in that expression of violent anger, tugged furiously at the oars to pull the life-boat clear of the ship, before she came down again to crush them, but it was hardly necessary, as the wind and waves seized the light little craft and bore her away from that particular danger.

Dick was amazed that they had managed to launch the life-boat and get clear. It was that wave lifting them off at exactly the right moment.

'A bloody miracle! A bloody miracle!' he kept repeating in his mind, though it would need another miracle to keep the life-boat afloat in this sea. But he felt exhilarated, and having survived so far, determined to struggle with every ounce of his being to keep alive till the storm slackened.

The most difficult job was to get the life-boat round with her head into the wind, without capsizing in the process. They had blown down wind and he had continued on that course until they were clear of the *Princess of Teck*, but at any minute they might be swamped by the following waves, though they were so huge that the little boat was like a car travelling in mountainous country. He chose a smooth valley between two waves, and at the exact moment shouting 'Now,' he shoved over the tiller and the men brought her quickly round into the wind.

She shipped a good deal of water from the flying spray, and the drenched nuns worked frantically with bailers. Only Mrs Dawes refused to move, and stared with fixed eyes at the *Princess of Teck*, when an intervening mountain of water did not hide her from their sight.

She saw the second boat lowered, but could not see whether her husband was in it. She saw it smashed against the side before it was released from the davit ropes. She heard the cries of the drowning people faintly mingled with the howling of the wind. She gave a shriek, and the nuns stopped their bailing and looked across at the ship.

They saw the third boat lowered, and it looked as if it might get away, when the ship lurched more than usual. Something happened to one of the davit ropes of the fourth life-boat, and it fell at the bows and tipped its occupants into the sea. The people still in the ship were flung after them. From this distance it was like some ghastly mid-Victorian lithograph. The ship rolled steadily on, crushing the third life-boat, like a clumsy animal over-laying its young, like an enormous pig, when its huge black bottom gleamed uppermost, and then slowly sank, until where it had been there was nothing but swirling, angry lace.

2

The *Princess of Teck*, if she had the vices of a sow which destroys its young, had also its virtue, fat, or in this case, oil. Soon, in the middle of the swirling lace where she had sunk, amid the racing air-bubbles as from some mammoth siphon, came up other bubbles, which spread in an ever-widening lake of calm. Within it the waves could no longer express their angry rhythm. They were like a half-remembered phrase of music, of which the notes struggle vainly to rise above a film in the mind.

Before long this spreading calm reached the life-boat, which rowed to meet it. Dick told the sailors to row on, to the spot where the *Princess of Teck* had sunk. The second miracle had happened, and yet he feared a more horrible experience than any they had yet been through. It was possible that there would be survivors swimming about, more than the boat could hold, and he would have to choose which to allow in, perhaps have to beat off frenzied creatures clinging to their only hope of life. He might even have to give his own place up to some woman, and yet if he did who would navigate the life-boat and find their course. As he scanned the water where the ship had gone down his blue eyes were set and hard, and at the same time afraid.

Now they were directly over the place where the *Princess of Teck* had sunk. The angry water bound by the immeasurably fine film of oil, could only achieve a sullen swell on which they rode in perfect safety. Around them on all sides came popping up objects which had been sucked down by the ship, chairs, life-belts, bits of wood, but among them were no people. Dick looked over the side, down into the dark clear water. He stared in fascinated horror, then drew back and called sharply: 'Don't look!'

Sister Hilda gave him a suspicious glance. She thought he was trying to deprive her of one of the available sensations, and she looked over the side. She screamed, and fell in a dead faint on the floor-boards. Below them must have been a hundred or more sharks, fighting over the bodies of their late shipmates as they rose towards the surface. One could see their white bellies as they turned to seize their prey. Here and there blood stained the water in a soft red cloud.

There was nothing the people in the life-boat could do. They remained inarticulate, looking inward, trying to ignore everything beyond the gun-wale of their boat. The sailors kept her as near as possible to the centre of the expanse of oil. They had no difficulty, as this was now a mile or so in width.

The constraint, which arose from a horror so intense that it was almost too great an intimacy to share it, was broken by a voice *outside* the boat requesting urbanely:

'I should be very much obliged if you could help me aboard.'

It was a grotesque voice to hear in that scene of stark terror and desolation. Not only its accent, but its un-ruffled intonation suggested a phase of life as remote from their present condition as Olympus from Tartaras. It suggested the line of festal lights in Christ Church hall, and good wine, or tea on the lawn of a country house. It belonged to Mr Smith, who, wet but showing no sign of distress, was hauled into the life-boat by Dick and Joe. He smiled benignly at the occupants of the boat, as if he were arriving at a party. He bowed to Sister Agatha, and said: 'I need hardly apologize for being so wet as we are all in the same condition. It is extremely fortunate that we are not in a colder latitude. However, the wind appears to be dropping.'

They noted with surprise that this was true. It was no longer necessary to clutch their veils to prevent them blowing away, and it seemed as if the angry sea, having swallowed the *Princess of Teck*, was for the time being satisfied. The clouds broke. There was a patch of blue and a burst of light from the western sky. The light became more brilliant and flung astonishing colours into the retreating clouds. The sunset was more vivid and glorious than any they had yet seen in the tropics. To Agatha, and the same idea occurred to more than one of the nuns, it was as if they had passed through the experience of death, and had come within sight of the Gates of Heaven. In their joyful surprise they forgot the horror being enacted below them, as blissful saints round the throne of God are indifferent to the souls tormented by the foul fiends. Their wondering faces, framed in wet black veils, turned towards the magnificent sky, and were tinged with its hopeful colour.

Hilda stared at the sunset for a while, then she nudged Agatha, and nodding towards Mr Smith said: 'What a good thing we've got a gentleman with us.'

Agatha for the first time had sufficient leisure and composure to take stock of their fellow castaways. Besides Dick and Joe there were three sailors, of whom one was a copper-coloured islander, the same who had grinned through her port-hole in the small hours of that morning. Of the two European sailors, one was a short thick-set man, who looked angry even when he was not afraid. He had a mat of reddish brown hair on his chest, and she learnt later that his name was Tom. The other looked more amiable, though this might have only been due to his projecting teeth and his fair, raised eye-brows. He was called George. The passengers, apart from the nuns, were only Mrs Dawes and Marinella, and now Mr Smith.

Marinella had screamed herself into a state of whimpering hysteria during their worst moments of peril, and finally had sunk into an exhausted sleep in her mother's arms. Agatha gave her a pitying glance, and then was arrested by the expression on Mrs Dawes's face. She was staring at Hilda with a malevolence which was hardly sane.

The only provisions in the boat were biscuits and two water barrels, but the wooden stopper had been knocked out of one and the water had joined the bilge in the bottom of the life-boat. There was also the yellow wooden box, the saving of which had cost Mr Dawes his life. This was a portable altar for use on the ship, should there be a priest among the passengers, or in any place where the nuns might find themselves without a chapel. It had been presented to them before departure by some pious ladies in Melbourne. It contained an ugly little brass crucifix and candlesticks, and a silver chalice and paten.

It was surprising how quickly after the fall of the wind, the sea, helped of course in their vicinity by the oil which had risen from the *Princess of Teck*, settled down to a long heavy swell, on which the life-boat rose and fell peacefully.

By the time the sun set with tropical suddenness Dick and the sailors had rigged the mast and hoisted the sail, which however hung loosely in the still air, while the boom creaked in slow rhythm with the swell.

Even if there had been a breeze Dick would have been undecided on his course. He had no sextant nor instrument for finding his position, of which he was uncertain, as for the last sixteen hours or so the *Princess of Teck* had left her normal route to avoid the full force of the gale. But after sunset the stars in the tropical sky were brilliant, and he calculated that if he steered northwest he might get back on to the regular steamship route, and be picked up by a liner. He had little hope of reaching land, as there was none, he imagined, nearer than a thousand miles. It would need yet a third miracle to save them, but as he had already experienced two, he was not entirely pessimistic. He was, in fact, too exhausted to think much beyond the unlooked-for ease and safety of the present moment.

One by one the castaways fell asleep. The nuns were in the bows, huddled against each other. The sun had been long set when Dick woke up the islander, whom they called Harry, and told him to keep watch for two hours, and after that to wake one of the other sailors to relieve him. Then he sank on to the floor, and, resting his head on his arm, he fell into a heavy sleep.

Throughout the night, now and then someone would stir on the hard seat, and possibly shift the arm or head of a companion, resting too heavily against his side or shoulder, and the companion would let his head be moved as if it were an object without life. Once or twice Agatha half awoke, and dimly knew where she was, and quickly closed her mind again with sleep, unwilling to remember before she need the horror that was passed, or to face the danger and discomfort yet to come. But for the greater part of the night there was no sound in the life-boat but the creaking of the boom, an inter-mittent gentle lap of water, and the steady breathing of sailors and nuns. Ursula, sleeping upright, did not snore.

Marinella woke with the sunrise, and tugged at her mother, saying: 'Mummy, mummy, wake up. I want a drink.'

Slowly the group of huddled women broke apart. Some sleepily protested at being disturbed. Others sat up with expressionless faces, which gradually were filled with sadness and foreboding as they became fully conscious of their situation. They stretched themselves and spread out their damp veils to the hot sun. They were like black butterflies emerging from the chrysalis and drying their wings.

44

Mrs Dawes turned to Mr Smith as the oldest man present, and the one with most air of authority, and said sullenly: 'My little girl wants a glass of water.'

Mr Smith repeated to Dick: 'The little girl wants a glass of water.' Dick had just awakened and was staring rather crossly at Harry, the islander, who was still asleep, leaning across the tiller, and had probably been there all night—not that he would have been any use awake. They had drifted away from the film of oil, but the sea was perfectly smooth, though still moving in a barely perceptible swell.

'I suppose we'd better give out some water,' said Dick. 'We'll have to ration it. We may not be picked up for a week.'

Every one as soon as he was fully awake found that he was thirsty, but there was nothing to drink out of—no cup nor enamel mug, let alone the glass demanded by Marinella. Mr Smith leant over to Agatha and said:

'Isn't there a cup in that?' He nodded at the portable altar.

'Well, yes—there is a chalice,' said Agatha doubtfully.

'That's out of the question,' Hilda protested indignantly. 'I have never heard of such a thing as the sacred vessels being used as a common drinking cup. There must be something else.'

'There's nothing else, miss,' said Dick apologetically.

'Could we not put our lips to the bung-hole?' asked Hilda, 'though that might be scarcely hygienic.'

'We can't afford to risk any waste.'

'D'you mean to say the boat is not adequately stocked with water? Whose fault is that, may I ask?'

'The storm's,' said Joe, sitting up. 'The bung got knocked out in the storm.'

Mrs Dawes suddenly burst out with a horrible cackle of laughter. Marinella screamed: 'Don't, mummy!' and for a moment every one was frozen into embarrassed silence.

Mr Smith said: 'I think we shall have to use the chalice,' and Agatha quietly agreed.

Hilda said to Agatha: 'If it is your command we must obey, but I register my protest.'

Dick handed out a hard ship's biscuit to every one in the life-boat, while Joe took the chalice which Agatha had carefully unfolded from its green baize—Hilda refusing to lend herslf to such sacrilege—and allowed one cupful to each person. That was all their breakfast.

Mrs Dawes, however, refused to drink from the chalice, nor would she allow Marinella to do so.

'I can drink from my hands,' she said.

'You will waste water if you do that,' said Dick.

'I want my drink and I can drink from my hands,' she shouted back at him. The insane gleam was more violent in her eyes.

Mr Smith by a glance advised Dick to give way to her, and she knelt by the cask, while Joe carefully let her ration of water dribble into her cupped hands. Marinella fussed to be allowed to use the chalice, but something in her mother's manner stopped her, and she knelt down, afraid, and drank in the same way, and then asked for more, but Joe dared not give her any. Hilda also refused to drink out of the cup, saying: 'If she can have her way I can have mine.'

Apart from this awkwardness there was something truly sacramental about this first simple meal taken in the early dawn by those who had survived together horror and the close presence of death. The sun glinted on the silver chalice as it was passed along the boat, and to the hungry people even the rough ship's biscuit had a comfortable taste.

Hilda said to Agatha that the men should rig up some screen to make a toilet place for the women. Mr Smith overheard the gist of their conversation and passed it on to Dick, who managed with a useless jib to screen off a small triangle in the bows, though the head of the occupant remained in view.

Throughout the morning, although their hunger and thirst were only half-satisfied, the castaways were not unhappy. The bright sun, the blue and tranquil sea, and the small boat, gave a false suggestion of a pleasure trip, and the contrast with the horrors of the previous day could not fail to produce a reaction of relief and hope. Marinella, at first subdued by her mother's strangeness, became more lively when she heard that they hoped to be picked up by a steamer, and she made a sort of competition of who should see the first trace of smoke, though after a time this became irritating with her over-optimism and her frequent cries of: 'Look, is that smoke,' as she pointed to some faint mirage on the horizon.

At noon they had another biscuit each, and a ration of water. Mrs Dawes and Hilda again refused to drink from the chalice. After this meal there came a return of weariness and despondency. It seemed possible that it might be two or three days before they were rescued. The light beating up from the water was painful to the eyes, and the heat was intense. The only use of the sail was to provide a degree of shade.

The nuns read their offices together, but in silence. In the evening, at the hour of Vespers, as the gorgeous lights again were gathering in the western sky, Cecilia recalled that it was Passion Sunday. Agatha pointed out to Dick and Mr Smith that it was Sunday, and asked if the men would mind if they said Vespers aloud. They made no objection, and the sailors expressed a murmured approval, feeling that some thanks was due to God for their preservation so far, and prayer for their safety in the immediate future. They were rather relieved than otherwise to have professionals to perform these duties on their behalf.

The nuns recited the psalms in a monotone, but when they came to the hymn they lifted up their voices and sang:

> The Royal Banners forward go
> The Cross shines forth in mystic glow.

If an observer could have been poised in the air, a hundred yards or so away from the boat, with its dark hull and idle sail between himself and the splendid sky, he might have imagined that a flock of souls, half-pagan, half-Christian, was journeying to a paradise in the Islands of the Blest. There was something infinitely lonely about the tiny boat on the vast expanse of sea, something immemorial in its hull against the sunset, and as the archaic plain-song melody floated up and meandered thinly across the water, it seemed to express all the pathetic faith of the human soul, journeying uncertainly towards the light through a wide and dangerous world.

In the boat the sailors listened respectfully, and Mr Smith with the air of a connoisseur, to the singing of the hymn, but Mrs Dawes stared at the nuns with a derisive grin. At the hymn she burst out into a cackling laugh. It was a hateful sound, not only mocking, but extraordinarily metallic and cold. When they had finished she spoke into the air above her head, addressing no one:

'They think they're very holy, saying all these prayers. They're Roman Catholic idolaters, that's what I call them.'

'We are Anglo-Catholics, Mrs Dawes,' Hilda corrected her.

The effect on Mrs Dawes of being addressed by Hilda was extraordinary. The derisive grin gave way to an expression of violent hatred. She hissed and bared her teeth like a dog, and Marinella again cried in fear: 'Mummy! Mummy! don't do that!'

When the sun set and it was cooler, and they could see the stars, Dick said that they should row all night to try and make the normal steamship route. He said to Joe:

'I'm still an officer, you see.'

'Maybe I only miscalculated the time,' said Joe.

When Dick was arranging the shift for rowing George muttered to Tom: 'That sod makes thirteen in the boat.' He meant Mr Smith.

Tom swore under his breath and said: 'He'll be a bloody Jonah. Why did we take the sod aboard?'

'Still, the wind dropped when we picked him up.'

'And how the hell are we going to get anywhere without any wind?'

They argued in angry undertones.

Mr Smith told Dick that he had sailed a great deal in the South Seas, that he knew the heavens as well as the streets of Paris, where apparently he had lived for some years, and he offered to help him with the navigation. When he differed from Dick he affirmed that he was right with an air of such calm authority that Dick gave way to him, often with slight uneasiness.

With the help of the nuns who made themselves responsible for one oar, they managed to keep rowing all through the night, though when dawn came they had nothing to show for it, as they found themselves still a spot in the centre of an empty, glittering desert.

After the chalice of water and the biscuit, which did for breakfast, Marinella began the game of looking out for a ship, but she tired of it much sooner than on the first day, and she was too thirsty to talk much. This applied to every one of them, and they sat drowsy and silent through the long day, until Vespers when the nuns again sang their hymn, and their voices faded, sweetly quavering out over the immense ocean.

When Hilda, still refusing to use the chalice, bent down her cupped hands to receive her allowance of water, Mrs Dawes stared at her each time with an

49

increase of hatred. Agatha saw that this produced some agonizing tension in the woman's deranged mind, and she asked Hilda to use the chalice, but Hilda, always suspicious of being the victim of an injustice, said: 'Indeed, I have as much right as she has to drink as I please.'

Agatha felt too exhausted to argue or to command Hilda on her obedience. It always needed a good deal of nervous energy to oppose Hilda's conviction of the sanctity of the letter of the law. Her mouth was now perpetually dry, and she did not care to speak more than necessary. Even when she read her offices silently, in a curious way the mere thought of forming the words seemed to tire her throat.

On the morning of the third day at breakfast, when Hilda took the water in her hands, Mrs Dawes watched her, her hands clutching and twisting in her lap, while her eyes looked quite mad. Agatha determined that she would insist on Hilda's using the chalice after this. However, she delayed the unpleasant task, and late in the morning she fell into a doze, from which she awoke to find the midday ration being issued.

The sailor Tom was crouching at the keg, filling the chalice, and passing it along to the castaways. He said to Hilda: 'You'd better take it in the cup, miss. You waste it in your hands.'

'Indeed, I shan't,' said Hilda. 'You can give me less.' Her throat was so dry that it hurt her to say these few words.

Tom grunted and gave her the water into her hands. He felt unable to cope with the religious prejudice of a nun.

When it came to Mrs Dawes's turn he was more insistent. He thought it sheer pig-headedness on her part to refuse to use the chalice. She was no popish idolater.

'You'll have to drink out of this,' he said, and handed her the chalice of water. She stared at him, but did not reply.

'Mummy, I *want* to drink from the cup,' said Marinella. Tom turned and handed it to her, but Mrs Dawes leant forward and knocked it into the bottom of the boat, where the priceless water was spilt.

Every one was horrified to see the water wasted. Sisters Magdalene and Cecilia gave dry sobs, and the men stared sullenly, except Mr Smith, who watched with the indifferent interest one might give to the antics of dogs.

'Once in Western Australia,' he said, 'a traveller arrived at an up-country hotel in a drought. He told a man to wash his horse's legs, and the man said: "In water or champagne, sir. They're both the same price."'

No one attended to this anecdote. Tom was glaring at Mrs Dawes.

'Damn you,' he said. He bent to pick up the chalice. As he did so the handle of his long knife stuck out from his belt towards Mrs Dawes. She stared at it a moment, then snatching it from its sheath, she leapt across the boat, and shouting: 'You killed him!' she made a lunge at Hilda.

Ursula knocked her arm aside. Hilda exclaimed: 'Oh! Oh!' with much the same degree of indignation she would have shown if someone had trodden on her toe, or denied the Virgin Birth. Mrs Dawes stood staring wildly about her, and then suddenly plunged the knife into her own heart. She gave a cry, fell backwards against the gunwale, and toppled overboard. At first every one was too paralysed to move, but as she fell Tom shouted, and leapt to save his knife. He wrenched it from her body and stumbled, holding the red blade in his hand, and fell across the gunwale, staring down at Mrs Dawes, who with a last convulsive movement had splashed and sunk into the sea, and now came bubbling up again to him, until, only a few feet from his eyes, she was taken by a shark. Tom rolled back on to the floor of the boat and groaned: 'O God!'

Marinella, her blue eyes crazy with panic, clapped her hands over her mouth and seemed to be gasping for breath. Then she began to utter piercing screams. Ursula seized her, held her face against her bosom, and rocked her to and fro.

Tom recovered his composure. He leant down and washed his knife and replaced it in its sheath.

Dick and Joe fixed the oars in the rowlocks and Dick said: 'For God's sake, row.'

They might change the position on the earth's surface, but they could not escape the scene of the tragedy, as it was with them as long as they remained in the boat.

Nor could they escape the sharks. Two or three of these monsters followed them, and now and then their triangular fins showed above the surface.

Harry, the islander, stood up in the stern, and put his long knife between his teeth. He slipped off his slight clothing, and dived overboard, himself like a swift knife cutting the water, down among the sharks. He darted among them, below them, swifter than the fish. He came up beneath them, and ripped up their white bellies. The other sharks fought over the dead and the water was a turmoil. Through it darted Harry, beautiful to watch, golden brown, perfect and sure in his movement, so that if at any moment he had been arrested and turned to bronze he would have been a lovely statue, a bronze enclosed in glass. When he was near the surface the water in his shadow was the translucent blue of an opal. Sister Agatha had never seen a naked man before, and she felt an infinite sadness at his beauty, and felt too that the mystery of creation was partly revealed to her. Her feeling was not sensual, but one of worship. There seemed to her a tragic innocence in that beautiful body, in which in some degree God must dwell imprisoned in animal flesh. When Harry climbed back into the boat, dripping with spray, her parched throat contracted with the sense of love she had for the created world, and with awe that even in this native was somehow seen the Incarnation of God, the ecstatic, terrible union of the spirit and the flesh.

The effort had used up Harry's reserves of energy, and he sank in utter weariness on the floor of the boat. Every muscle was relaxed, his eyes closed, and the water trickled from the hairs on his head and body, and made little pools on the boards. His chest heaved as he recovered his breath, and it seemed to Agatha that his spirit was struggling to be released from its beautiful prison.

The castaways now longed for the night to come, although they feared that if they should see a ship by night they would be unable to attract its notice. The men had three boxes of matches between them. Every one tore a piece of what inflammable garment he might possess—the men gave the tails or sleeves of their cotton shirts—and shredded them up to make a miniature beacon, which they would light if they saw a ship by night.

The nuns still tried to keep their Rule as well as possible under these conditions, and they did not speak from Vespers till after the morning issue of biscuit and water. This was easy as on the third night they gave up rowing, thinking it better to save their energy for a spurt if they should sight a vessel, and on the fourth night they were all too parched to utter a syllable more than necessary. But as they dozed so much in the heat of the day it was difficult to sleep at night. They were like cats, or creatures to whom night and day are indifferent as times for rest. Also the seats were too hard to sleep on for more than an hour or so at a time.

On the third night Agatha hardly slept at all. As soon as she became drowsy some vivid picture of the day's events would flash into her mind and waken her. She saw Mrs Dawes as she leapt at Hilda, or fell backwards to the sharks. She saw Harry standing naked in the stern, the knife between his teeth, or curving among the dangerous fish, or lying relaxed like a drowned man, or a Christ in a *pietà*.

Accompanying these half-waking visions was the murmur of the men's voices from the stern. On this night for the first time they talked much together. Perhaps the danger which they shared, and the secret awareness that they might have a common, dreadful end, made them want to know more of each other, made each one seek to find as far as possible a reflection of himself in his companions, and so feel less alone. Agatha had never before listened to men talking together. At times their talk seemed dull to her, and its murmur lulled her into the doze from which a stark vision of the past day's horror or beauty would shock her back to wakefulness. At times she felt that their talk was just like that of boys, which she had occasionally overheard. There was the same interest in and argument over technical facts. Mr Smith did not speak much, but what he said seemed designed to draw the others out. In the small hours of the morning they lost their self-consciousness, and their talk became more intimate. They spoke of their doubts about religion and of what made them feel fear. Like boys they said: 'That's what I think,' or 'I never felt like that.' Dick and Joe agreed together, as did Tom and George in a more surly way. Mr Smith and Harry were each alone in his views.

Towards morning she heard them telling how they came to be on the *Princess of Teck*. They nearly all cursed their luck, and explained how but for an accident they might have been elsewhere. Excepting Dick, each one had been on his first journey on the doomed ship, and even Dick had been transferred to her only two months earlier, owing to the then fourth officer of the *Princess of Teck* being taken seriously ill.

54

Harry, the islander, explained in his soft, musical, broken English how he came to be with the crew of an Australian ship, where coloured men are not allowed by law. A missionary had shown him a post card of Sydney harbour with its enormous bridge. He had conceived an immediate and urgent longing to see that bridge. It filled his dreams, and he felt that whoever walked across it must arrive in a kind of heaven. Such a bridge could only be built, he reasoned, to let men cross to a place more glorious than any known on earth. They would not undertake that stupendous labour to cross from one ordinary place to another. So he had stowed away on the *Princess of Teck* on her last homeward journey, had been discovered, and was being shipped back as one of the crew when she foundered.

'But when I get home,' he concluded, 'I will say to——' here he recited like a litany a long string of native names, those of his companions and girl friends on the remote island where he lived—'I will say I have seen the big bridge to Heaven and they will know I am a very great man.'

After a while Tom said:

'Ten years ago, when I was twenty-two, my grannie died and left me a paper and tobacco shop she kept in Fitzroy. I was away at sea, and my dad who has the same name as me got hold of it. He fooled the lawyer. He sold the shop and cleared out. Not only that, there was a girl who was sweet on me, or so I thought, but I expect she was only sweet on my grannie's money—'cos she went with him. When I came back to Melbourne after three months, I went to see my grannie as usual, 'cos I knew she was going to leave me the shop, and it was only sense to keep in with her, but when I got there it was all painted up with a new name on it, and the bloke told me what my dad had done on me. Now my dad always was talking about them South Sea islands, and wanting to go there—so I thought I know where to hunt for the bastard and his whore. For ten years I've been on ships in these parts, and every time I can I change to a new route, and every port I go ashore I ask in every pub if they've seen an old man with ginger hair and a face like a sick ferret, who has a Spanish-type tart with him. Well, last month I was in a pub in Sydney and was talking to a bloke there, and he said he knew the South Seas like the lines on his hand, and I asked him if he seen my dad. And he said exactly ten years ago he seen a man what answered to his description at Tonga, and he had a Spanish-type tart with him. So I finds out what ships are going to Tonga and the *Princess of Teck* was the first I could get taken on, and here I bloody well am.' The sense of injustice and of impotence shook his weak body, and he cried hoarsely: 'If I catch the old brute I'll wring his bloody neck. I'll tear his thieving hands off, and I'll do in that sneaking whore. God, he's robbed me and now he's brought me to me death. If it wasn't for him I wouldn't be here. I wouldn't be in this blasted tub.'

His angry voice died across the water and was swallowed in the immense silence of the night. A desultory ripple lapped against the boat. The stars glimmered serenely in the high heavens. Possibly he felt that the rage which possessed his whole being was of no more consequence than the buzzing of a gnat, as he gave a frightened whimper and buried his face in his hands.

'How did you come to be on the *Princess of Teck*?' Mr Smith asked Joe.

'I was walking along the dock and I saw her lying alongside,' said Joe, 'and I thought, that's the ship for me. I felt I simply had to be signed on her. It was a sort of intuition I had. If I hadn't managed it I would have thought I'd missed the chance of a lifetime. Well, it seems I was wrong, but everything goes back to front with me.'

'And you?' Mr Smith asked George.

'Me? I'm a sailor,' said George, 'and I've got to earn me living. So I've got to be on some ship, haven't I? But me luck was out I suppose, and there you are.'

Agatha wondered how they could bear to speak so much, but apparently their dread of loneliness, their desperate longing to know and be known while they still had life, was greater than the pain it caused them to speak. But after this night they hardly spoke again, for as long as they were adrift on the scorching sea.

On the fourth day they reduced the water ration to half, and in all their eyes was that look of dread which they had shown when they came out on to the boat-deck, when the *Princess of Teck* wallowed helplessly with her heavy list, and the sailors struggled with the davit ropes. But now in addition to fear they were marked by the first pangs of appalling suffering.

Agatha did not know exactly at what stage it was that her sense of reality became confused with dreams, in which she sometimes escaped, sometimes enhanced her torments. The night when the men told each other of their thoughts and lives had the quality of a dream, their voices breaking in with a fresh picture on the different visions which flashed across her mind. She saw the newspaper shop in Fitzroy, and the Spanish-type tart, mixed up with Mrs Dawes's falling body, and Harry lying on the floor-boards, like a Christ in a *pietà*.

In two more days there was no water at all, and not a sail nor a wisp of smoke had been seen. When Agatha opened her eyes, seeking escape from some horrid illusion, she would see beside her a face with black and swollen lips, like the face of someone in hell, so that waking or sleeping her mind was hemmed in by the confused phantasms of a nightmare. As her weakness and suffering increased she had a curious dream in which she had left her body, and was suspended in the air a

57

few feet above the boat. It was unlike any other dream she had ever known, as in it every detail was clear and there was no inconsequence. She could see the boat and its occupants even more distinctly than when she was lying amongst them, her sight impaired by her physical distress. But as in a dream nothing is surprising, it seemed to her quite natural to be looking down on her own body, and she was indifferent to her old and yellow appearance. Winifred was lying beside her, but her face was hidden, and she could only see her white wimple, crumpled and stained with sea-water. Dick was stretched along the floor-boards, his right arm flung out towards Winifred, the palm upward as if he were offering her something. Marinella was lying on her back along the seat with Ursula kneeling beside her, her head resting against the child's body. Her rugged Scottish face was turned upwards, the eyes closed. It bore a queer expression of accepted suffering, as if she were saying a *Nunc Dimittis* over Marinella. The sailors in the stern were like a group of macabre statuary, which might have commemorated some martyrdom, but Agatha, looking down in her dream, felt no pity for them, nor even disgust at their blackened lips and their unkempt growths of hair. They were to her only like plants that needed water, and the hair was no longer unpleasant, but also like the growth of plants, something that declared the strength of nature. Mr Smith alone, she noted, was unaffected by the general dolour. He sat upright and though he appeared a little tired, his eyes were open, and he watched his fellow castaways with detached appraisement. She thought: 'He is a human being like myself, but the others are just natural growths, like trees or seaweed.' Her own body with its obvious marks of suffering was also an object of indifference to her. She neither wanted to return to it, nor was she anxious to escape from it for good. However, she fixed her attention on it, and soon she felt a curious dragging sensation. When she was a young girl she had gone up in an aeroplane, and the pilot had dived, and the pressure of wind had been so strong against her face that she had felt as if the flesh were being pulled off her bones. She now had this feeling through her whole body, and with the return of physical sensation the agony slowly crept back into her throat and lips, and the hard pain into her thighs. She opened her eyes and found herself the miserable creature on which a moment since she had looked dispassionately. She saw Winifred close at hand, her coiffed head bowed down as she had seen it from above, and beyond her Dick was lying, his hand out-stretched. But Mr Smith was not as she had seen him in her dream. He was not sitting upright and clear-eyed, but was lying at a painful angle, his lips as black, his skin as yellow as his companions.

She dragged herself to the gunwale and looked down into the cool depths of the sea. She felt it drawing her, and she stretched her head down to reach it. She longed to fall into it, down into the cool liquid shadows, to have enough water, water all round her, easing her skin and her burning lips. Between her and the inviting depths came a vision of Marinella the night before—or was it two nights ago, or a week—struggling desperately with Ursula, who was preventing her from jumping into the sea to lap up the salt water. The vision blurred into the jumble of other pictures in her mind, and she lost consciousness.

Again she had the dream that she was floating in the air above the boat, looking down at its occupants, including her own body. When last time she had contemplated her body for long she had entered it again, and became her whole self. Now she found that by fixing her attention on any one of the castaways she could enter into him, not to become him, but to have complete

59

knowledge of him. This absolute intimacy of knowledge provoked no emotional reaction, neither admiration nor disgust nor love, hardly even understanding. It was like her knowledge that two and two make four.

She found herself with Ursula, knowing every remote and overlaid impression that time had stamped on her brain. New pictures were added to those already teeming in her own mind. Soon she was not only seeing these pictures, but being a person in them, Ursula as a child, as a young woman, a novice. She was in the playground of a school somewhere in the Australian country. She was an ugly little girl, thickly built with a knobbly face and freckles. She was standing in one of those spaces so frequent in Australia, on the hard bare earth beneath the sparse shade of a gum-tree, where grass will not grow, but broken twigs lie about, and there are processions of tiny black ants carrying grains of a sweetish white substance which falls from the trees, and which children call manna. Around her was a ring of hostile mocking faces, most vivid among them that of a girl she loved, a fair-haired blue-eyed child something like Marinella, to whom she had made presents of flowers and sweets, but who now, possessed by an evil genius of destruction, was summing up her character and looks with a child's heartless accuracy, while the others jeered in chorus.

She was Ursula as an adolescent being kissed on a veranda. Beside her was a half-open front door with a panel of ugly stained glass. The man kissing her did so carelessly, half as a kindness, as at that moment she had a touch of flowering beauty which must light now and then on the plainest girl in her 'teens, and he thought it unlikely that she would be kissed often, if ever again. She never was. The kiss had enormous significance for her. She thought it was a certain pledge of marriage, but two days later she found the man was in love with her young stepmother.

She knew now what she had always been curious to know, why Ursula had become a nun. It was to escape defeat, to have a grander love than her school-fellows could achieve, or her stepmother with her secret liaison. It was also to have something to possess and be loyal to, that would give her more opportunity for pride of association than being a Highlander, her habit making her more unique even than her tartan. She had to belong to a superior herd. From her earliest years she had felt excluded from easy contacts. Her ugliness, her shyness, and her misunderstanding of people's motives had prevented them. Finding herself different she had to insist that her difference was a superiority. There was no race so fine as the Highland Scots, no garment so glorious as a tartan kilt. But she found to maintain this pride needed constant argument, and it received a severe blow when an acid schoolmistress in a moment of irritation pointed out to her that the unexampled cultural achievement of the Scots was one poet, one novelist, and two portrait painters, none of the first order. She felt that as a nun her position would be more unassailable and more romantic.

Ursula had adored the novice mistress. The emotional tension without which life was meaningless to her was provided by this relationship. She enjoyed even the commands which were unreasonable. The blow to her pride was followed by a pleasurable easing of the pain, and an increased devotion to the woman who had inflicted it. Her loyalty became focused on her instructor, and almost deliberately she would create some situation, stir up some discord, in which it could be expressed. Once the Reverend Mother had said to her:

'Where people are collected together as we are, it is natural that some will find themselves attracted in friendship. It would be bad if it were not so. But that love must only be part of a wider love. It mustn't be

61

possessive. It mustn't contain the sort of loyalty that leads to jealousy.'

Ursula listened sullenly to this utter denial for her natural impulse. If you were excluded from the general sympathy of your kind, how could you find security except in the possession of another single person's exclusive sympathy? When you were used to fighting day after day to declare the honour of the few things you possessed, how could you relax the struggle, the scoring of points, which were the only things that gave you a kick in life? She tried to obey the letter of the Rule, but she found that by little disobediences, little tales, little acts of ill-nature, she could provoke some of the tension to which she had been accustomed, and she became the grit in the wheels of the community, the cross they had to bear.

Agatha's dream, in which she had become intellectually aware of these facts about Ursula, now acquired sensation. She dreamed that she was actually in Ursula's body—that she was Ursula. She thought that perhaps Ursula was dead, that her spirit had gone away, and her own spirit had taken possession of the empty body. She began to feel dreadful hates and resentments. She thought of all the nuns in an entirely different way. She thought of the Reverend Mother, whom she had always loved as wise and kind, as a shallow, prejudiced woman. She felt physical pains in her body in new places—the weight of thick legs. She was rapidly becoming Ursula, and she fought desperately, while she was still partly herself, to separate from her, to escape from the dreadful identity. All she could do was to make an effort of will against some dark force. She had no conscious weapons to use. She could only make this pressure of her being against something that was also herself. So the earliest form of life which reproduced itself by dividing into two, might have struggled before it split.

The pains in her body increased. Then her lips hurt, and her throat. Her eyes opened, and she found she was completely herself, lying as before amid horror and torment in the sun-parched lifeboat. Almost immediately she lost consciousness.

Again she was looking down at the boat, and she found her sight resting on Harry, the islander, and soon the knowledge of his life came to her. With him she was a small boy, and suddenly she was aware of a delight greater than she had ever known. She was on the shore of some luxuriant island, and was taking such an intense pleasure in the feel of the air, the smell of the sea, the colour of flowers, and the swift sure movements of the body—his or hers, she did not know which—that it was like entering a new dimension. As herself, Sister Agatha, she had always thought that she had a great appreciation of nature, and would often exclaim: 'How lovely is the colour on the hills this evening!' or 'What a delicate shade is this rose!' She knew now that she had never had the faintest appreciation of nature, that she had treated it like a pretty chintz, and that there was no appreciation of nature until one knew oneself identified with it, in an emotion both religious and sensual, like an electric current in the blood. His sudden awareness of the scarlet of a hibiscus or of the intricate growth of a piece of coral or seaweed, startled him into a delight which either made him pause with wonder, or shout with joy.

The native boy grew older, and was still herself. His mind rioted with erotic imagery. The naked girls in his brain were part of the beauty of the flowers he had plucked as a child, and when he sought them in palm groves and on starlit beaches, he fused completely into the nature which he unconsciously worshipped. Again Agatha struggled to free herself, before her soul was blackened with sin, which she was puzzled to find she did not feel to be sin at all. She felt herself drawn to infinite pleasures, down, down among soft shadows of utter assuagement, as she had felt herself drawn to the cool depths of the ocean, when she was tormented by thirst. Only a hard core of reason, still surviving, the centre of resistance built up through years of discipline, held her back. This hard core was like a polished stone in her mind. It was like a stone on which a thousand gossamer webs were caught. It pulled backwards and upwards, drawing all the soft filaments of her desire away from their goal, until she was free, and once more floating, looking down at the pitiful boat-load of castaways.

At once she looked away from them, as she dreaded to be enclosed again in a body that was not her own. If the soul, the flickering pulse of life of Ursula or Harry had finally departed, she might have been left the tenant of one of their bodies for the remainder of its life. She might even by her intrusion have pushed out the other soul, like a kind of vampire. It occurred to her that now was her opportunity to find out something about Mr Smith. She felt her attention drawn down to the boat. She did not want to look, to experience again one of those suffocating confusions of personality, but she could not control her sight. Now all that she did was involuntary, as if a thought became a reality as soon as it was born, before the trained mind could accept or dismiss it.

But Mr Smith was not in the boat, and while she was wondering what could have happened to him, she found him beside her in the air, floating like herself, though her body still lay yellow and emaciated below her, and he either had discarded his altogether, or had brought it with him. He said:

'Up here you are free.'

'No,' said Agatha, 'I'm not free, because I can't move from here except to return to suffering.'

'Have you tried to move from here?'

'I haven't *tried* to do anything.'

'You don't need to try. You only need to think of where you want to be. Surely you must have wanted to be in many places in your time.'

'Of course I have.'

'Name some of them.'

'I have wanted to hear the Pope sing Mass in St Peter's, and I've wanted to be at Evensong in King's chapel in Cambridge, and I've wanted to go to Assisi and Canterbury and Venice, and to see an English spring in Devonshire.'

Mr Smith smiled. 'Well, why don't you do it?' he said. 'Try King's chapel first.'

With no sense of movement nor of the passage of time she found herself seated in a stall on the south side of King's chapel. A don, wearing a surplice over a grey suit, walked through her feet and sat in the next stall. He was Mr Smith. A few undergraduates and middle-aged gentlewomen in summer hats were all the congregation. The sun streamed in the windows behind her, and above, the glorious fan tracery showed dimly behind the coloured shafts of light. The choir in their scarlet cassocks entered, and bowed and took their places. Although she had never been to England she knew that outside were wide lawns and lovely bridges, and the Cam, 'a tunnel of green gloom.' The choir sang more beautifully than any she had ever heard, as not only were their voices remarkable, but their enunciation was that of educated people. They sang the canticles to a *faux bourdon*. Now one of her greatest nostalgias should be satisfied. Here she was in the very heart of that traditional Anglicanism which she had always loved and longed for, where it had its finest expression in beauty of sound and of building, and in the evidences of good breeding. But she only saw that it was good. It produced no feeling in her. She could make no contact with it. She looked towards the altar, and was curious about the design of the candlesticks. Immediately she was there, looking at them, but no one took any notice of her standing at the altar. She felt the same curiosity about the bosses on the vaulted ceiling and she was up there, looking down on the white rows of surplices, whence rose the heavenly strains to which she was able only to give a cold intellectual appraisement. And no one noticed her suspended in the vaulting any more than they had when she was standing by the altar.

Outside, she thought, were the grey courts and the green lawns, the embowered river and ancient peace. She found herself in a punt. Opposite her on the red plush cushions reclined Mr Smith, wearing white flannels and reading the poems of Theocritus. An undergraduate with strength and skill, but apparent laziness, was propelling them up stream. He lowered his pole while they glided under Clare bridge. Agatha knew that she had at last realized a girlish dream. She had always imagined that there could be no greater delight—outside religious joys, of course—than to be punted up the Isis or the Cam on a summer afternoon by a nice-looking undergraduate. At least she thought she had realized a dream, but it gave her no emotion, and when she put her hand down to trail in the water she could feel nothing, and she had a dim idea that it was terribly important for her to be able to touch water and to drink it, and that while she was here she should swallow as much of the Cam as possible. She lifted up a handful of water and put it to her lips, but she could taste and feel nothing.

Mr Smith looked up and said: 'Perhaps St Peter's would be more interesting.'

She was in the huge crowded church. She flitted about from one vantage point to another, seeing but not feeling—quite unmoved by beauty of architecture or sound. She stood by the Pope at the high altar. She noted that with her other senses she had lost all sense of reverence. Mr Smith was a priest in a green dalmatic. 'Look!' he said, and drew her attention to a slight disturbance down in the nave where a woman had fainted.

She looked at the woman, and at once she was lying half-conscious on the floor. She was the wife of a Portuguese wine merchant on a pilgrimage. She struggled with its lawful owner to possess the body. Sensation had returned to her, and though much of it was nausea and fatigue, it seemed to her infinitely satisfying and desirable. She had the real sensation of being in St Peter's. She smelt the incense and the garlic breaths and the women's perfume. She felt new satisfactions in the body she tenanted—the comfort of fat and of appeased desires.

The chanting suddenly blared in her ears, instead of being heard thinly as through glass. She fought the Portuguese woman for her body, resisting with all her will to remain, the other woman's will to drive her out. She felt her hold weakening. The music grew thin again. The smells had gone—and she was in the air a few feet above the Portuguese woman who was now sitting up, while her husband dabbed her forehead with a wet handkerchief.

She found herself at the top of a high tower. Below her was a square, and an Eastern-looking church with a many-domed roof. On the other side was a canal, another domed church, and the sea, stretching placid and blue into the distance. Mr Smith, in a neat suit of grey check, with a camera slung over his shoulder, was leaning against the balustrade.

'What am I to do?' she asked him.

'You are free to do as you please. You may go where you like, see whom you wish. What more do you want?'

'It gives me no pleasure. Before when I saw a beautiful thing, or was in some lovely place, it stirred an emotion in me. Now I only know places are beautiful but don't feel it. Where is this—Venice?'

'Yes.'

'It's one of the places I have longed to see all my life, but I might as well be in the convent laundry.'

'You've not yet learned to make full use of your new freedom,' said Mr Smith.

'What freedom?'

'Freedom from the flesh—from your own body, which you nuns are always seeking.'

'Then where is my body?'

'It's lying unconscious in a boat full of castaways in the Pacific Ocean. It's almost dead from thirst. In its few waking moments it's in agony.'

'If I've left my body I must be dead.'

'You're not dead.'

'When shall I die?'

'Never..unless you return to your body. You'll be outside the order of growth and decay and rebirth—physical and spiritual. You'll be a sort of free-lance.'

'But I must go back to it,' said Agatha uncertainly.

'You will be very foolish to do so. You'll have a much better time as you are. You are able to view from the best seats scenes of the most astonishing brilliance and pleasure, and if intellectual satisfaction is not enough you have only to slip into the body of someone in deep sleep, or, better still, of lovers as they lose themselves in sensual bliss.'

'You have brought me on to this high tower,' said Agatha, 'to show me all the kingdoms of the world in a moment of time.'

'You have only to let your body die and they are yours,' said Mr Smith. 'You would be mad to return to it. You will at once suffer the extreme of torment.'

Of course,' she replied. 'Suffering is a condition of physical life. We make too much of it. A liftime of suffering is only a second in eternity.'

'You think that now, while you have no body, but immediately you have returned to your body a second of physical suffering will seem longer than eternity itself.'

'I shall remember to think as I think now.'

'No you won't. No one ever does. When a boy has made a fool of himself in love and comes out of it, he thinks: "Next time I shall remember not to behave like that. It does not help me to success in love and it destroys my dignity." But next time he behaves in exactly the same way, and makes himself a bigger fool than ever. It is very easy to be rational when one has no desires. However, if you wish to be in a body, there are better things than a half-dead nun lost at sea. Look!'

They were on a sloping hill-side, which ended in a steep cliff. Below the cliff was a little cove, and beyond it the purple sea. There were boulders of white rock dotted over the hill, and the late afternoon sun faintly gilded them and gave each one its companion of blue shadow. On a patch of grass near a straggling olive tree a young goat-herd was lying on his back, playing on a reed. A peasant girl was seated near him, looking a little bored.

She edged closer to him and began to stick grass seeds in his hair. He brushed her hand away and went on playing. She became cross, and took two handfuls of his curls and tugged at them. He gave a cry and rolled over and tussled with her. They lay breathless, and the struggle merged into love play.

Agatha watched them, and then she felt a delicious warmth, a blind animal bliss. She was the peasant girl, and as soon as she had found this body she seemed to lose it again, in a union with all nature, as she had tried in her religious life to lose her soul in a union with all the spiritual force of good. She came out of this dark ecstasy to find all sensation gone, and the peasant girl below her sitting up and tidying her hair, while the boy lay, his head in her lap, in an attitude which oddly suggested both worship and sleep.

Agatha said to Mr Smith:

'You want to have my spirit free from my body so that you may destroy it.'

'You can never be destroyed. You are eternal.'

'But you said I was not dead. Where is God now?' she asked suddenly. 'If I am out of my body in the spirit world, why is God not here to help me? Where are the holy angels? I am in the spirit world but not in God's kingdom. If my body dies before I reach it I am a lost soul.'

She felt pain and fear.

'I must go back to my body,' she cried. 'I must go back!' Her voice croaked and her throat hurt her dreadfully. She awoke from her dream and found herself on the floor of the boat, gasping and making sounds of distress. She raised herself on her elbow, feeling that there was something urgent that she must do. She was facing Mr Smith who was seated at the tiller. A breeze had sprung up, the sail was full, and the life-boat bounced cheerfully across the waves, but Mr Smith, who had appeared so spruce and urbane in her already half-forgotten dream, was as ravaged by thirst as the other castaways, who lay like broken dolls about the boat, and his eyes were as hell-haunted. He was staring ahead of him with so fixed an intensity that, weak and suffering as she was, Agatha could not help turning to see what he was looking at, and as she moved her head she was conscious of some change in the air, of some refreshing aroma above the stinks of the boat.

About a mile away, flung like a hard, brilliant jewel against the cobalt background of the sea and sky, was an island. Its green foliage glittered above a base of dazzling coral, and from the green belt, every crag showing sharply cut in the clear air, rose the faintly smoking cone of a mountain. The beauty of the island was so vivid under the tropical sun, that Agatha would have believed that again she was dreaming, if she had not been certain of reality by the torment of her body. She tried to say 'Land!' but she only made a sound like 'ahn.' and then sank into unconsciousness, from which she was disturbed by a jolt which shook her bones as if they had been flung loosely together in a bag. All the cushions of fat had been wasted away.

3

Mr Smith had steered the boat through a gap in a coral reef, and now ran before the wind across the still waters of a lagoon. The floor of this lagoon was a strange submarine garden, from which sprouted thousands of plants of different sea-weeds, some in small delicate fronds, others in shady groves peopled by brilliant fish. They darted in flashes of colour through the deep shadows, or hesitated, absolutely still save for a faint wavering of their silken green and scarlet fins. The shadow of the life-boat was like the presence of some frightening god, moving swiftly across their garden, and they darted away from it, hiding under ledges of coral or among the thick roots of weed.

Mr Smith had used his last reserve of strength to steer the boat into this place. He could not push over the tiller to turn her into the wind, but let her run straight for the shore, so that she hit the beach with the jolt which awakened Agatha, and having shot half her length up the sands, lay there on her starboard side, her sail flapping in angry helplessness, and her passengers tumbled over each other more than ever like a lot of broken dolls. Mr Smith jerked forward and fell among them.

A few yards to the right of where the boat had grounded, a stream came out from the forest, divided the beach and entered the lagoon. Not only Agatha, but the other castaways were jolted back to consciousness, except Mr Smith, who, on the contrary, had fallen unconscious as his effort was rewarded. They stared about them, hope shining oddly behind the despair on their disfigured faces. They crawled painfully to the starboard side of the boat, so that she lay over at greater angle, and almost tipped them on to the sand, where they could hardly have climbed by their own effort. They staggered up the beach towards a belt of palm trees, but few of them had the strength to reach it, and they fell here and there, so that the beach looked as if an attack had been stopped by a machine-gun.

Harry, the islander, made for the stream, and walking up it to where the water was no longer brackish he fell on his face. No sensual bliss, no ecstasy he had ever dreamed, equalled the rapture of this moment. The water against his skin was more delicious than the body of the loveliest virgin. None of the pleasures he had known in sultry island groves could compare with this delight. Some scent of earth and leaves in the brown water gave him infinite peace, and he knew that he was not after all a native of the ocean, a fish, but a warm-blooded creature, born of the earth and fresh streams, and here was his natural rest and refreshment. He knew that he must not drink too much, and he let the water creep in at the corners of his mouth to slake the agony of his throat.

When he felt sufficient strength had returned to him he went back to the boat and fetched the chalice. He filled it with water, and made several journeys, carrying it first to Mr Smith as he was the eldest, then to Dick as he was the officer, then to Joe as he was normally the most strong and gay and good-looking, then to the other sailors in precedence of their age. It did not occur to him that the women should not come last.

Dick, who had fallen on the sands half-way between the boat and the stream, after he had drunk was able to complete the distance, and like Harry he lay in the fresh water and recovered his strength, and also like Harry he then thought of his companions. He went back to the beach. The castaways lay about on the sands.

The nuns' black veils fluttered in the breeze, giving them a false appearance of life, as when a rag flaps on a scare-crow. Harry, exhausted by his effort, had fallen again. By his hand the silver chalice blazed whitely in the sun. Joe was closest to the stream, and Dick went to him and lifted him up, and helped him to make the rest of the distance.

When Joe was refreshed (it might have been in five minutes or in half an hour—they were still dazed from their sufferings and their first hours on the island were like time in a dream), he and Dick returned to the boat, where Mr Smith remained in a coma on the floor-boards, and took out one of the kegs, which they carried up to the stream and filled with fresh water. Dick retrieved the chalice, and together they went about the beach, giving a little water to each person. They went first to the women, who so far had had none, as Harry had been overcome with exhaustion after he had attended to the sailors.

Dick went first to Winifred. She was conscious, but her eyes were closed against the painful brilliance of the sunlight. She was suffering in her mind as well as in her body. She knew that cool green shade and water were at hand, but she had not the strength to move. This too was like a horrible dream in which one is threatened with danger, and is powerless to move away from it. She was afraid that she might die when she had come within a few yards of the means of life.

She felt her head lifted and water deliciously trickling to her parched throat. She opened her eyes and saw Dick bending over her. The sensation of water in her mouth was so ineffable, that when she saw the silver chalice held to her lips by a young man with a golden beard, she thought at first that she must really have died and that Christ was administering the sacrament to her in Heaven. Then she saw that it was Dick,

74

and her swollen lips tried to smile, and she looked gratefully into his eyes. They were neither of them beautiful at that moment, but their compassion and gratitude joined them together in a bond that was as close as love.

Gradually the whole company made the shelter of the stream and like Harry and Dick they flung themselves gratefully into the cool water. The nuns lay there, their veils and habits waving in the stream like the fins of black fish. Agatha, speaking painfully, warned them not to drink much at first, and Ursula had to hold Marinella back from the water. They were both too weak to struggle, but Marinella's weakness was the greater. When they came out of the water they lay along the banks of the stream, under the overhanging bread-fruit trees. They ate some of the fruit, their first food for days, and then fell asleep.

Dick and Joe were the first to awaken. It was afternoon, but they did not know whether it was the afternoon of the same day they had landed, or the next. They had the sense of having slept for a very long time.

Instinctively they began to wander up the stream away from the sea. The water was shallow and rarely came higher than their ankles. They heard a splashing behind, and found that Mr Smith was following them. He showed extraordinarily few signs of the privations he had suffered. He was even able to smile as he came up with them. He seemed to ask permission to join their explorations, and at the same time to assume that he would be welcome. He walked ahead as if leading them.

After a hundred yards or so he left the bed of the stream, and without showing any hesitation, or surprise at its discovery, he turned up a pathway cut into the forest. Had they been alone Dick and Joe would have been more cautious of entering a place which suggested so many possibilities of danger, but as Mr Smith walked confidently ahead they did not like to desert him, and also by this time, for some unknown reason, they felt more comfortable when they were with him.

The pathway was evidently not an accident of nature, nor due to animals. On either side branches that had been cut back showed the marks of an axe, while creepers looked as if they had been clipped. The foliage met overhead, so that the path was through a tunnel filled with green twilight. Mr Smith was still some way ahead, but Joe and Dick walked warily. Their wet canvas shoes made a flopping, sucking noise as they walked, and they took them off.

They had been walking for some minutes when the path bent sharply to the right, and they heard an exclamation from Mr Smith, who had disappeared round the corner. When they came to the bend they saw him silhouetted against a circle of dazzling light where the tunnel ended.

They found themselves at the edge of a dell of about two or three acres, laid out as a more or less orderly garden. Every kind of exotic flower and fruit seemed to be here. There were the spiky leaves of pineapples, and bananas hung in huge yellow-green clusters. Orange trees bore both white, waxy flowers, and enormous golden berries, interspersed as well with the hard green balls of unripe fruit. There were mangoes and paw-paws and grape and passion-fruit vines. Among the fruit trees were flowers, multi-coloured zinnias the size of plates. There were the honey-yellow flowers of the kapok, the flaming hibiscus, and the sweet creamy frangipani, whose scent mingled intoxicatingly with that of the orange and lemon blossom. The tropical sunlight streamed down on this profusion, glinting on the dark, lacquered leaves of the trees, and giving the flowers the hard edges of jewels. The scene was overpowering in its richness, its perfume, its fecundity.

Even more surprising than the voluptuous garden was the wicket gate which opened on to it from the pathway, and on which was painted in neat, white letters: 'Balmoral.'

On the far side of the garden was a bungalow, which they had not noticed at first, at it was so thickly covered with vines. Mr Smith pushed open the gate, and they went down a path bordered with large shells. The garden was divided by a stream, bridged by palm trunks. It was evidently a tributary of the one up which they had just waded. The soil was a dark volcanic loam which, helped by irrigation and the blazing sun, accounted for the astonishing growth.

The bungalow was built on poles, about five feet above the ground, with steps leading to a vine-shaded veranda. Dick and Joe were longing to pick the splendid purple grapes which hung from the vine, and to break open the green cardboard of the passion fruit and suck its juicy contents. Mr Smith knocked on the door of the bungalow. When he had knocked three times and had received no reply he lifted a wooden latch and went in, and the two young men followed him.

The bungalow was only one long room, but a door at the farther end opened on to a covered way which led to a smaller room with a cooking stove, fitted as a kitchen. In the first room was a double bed with brass knobs, a desk, a table, two or three wooden chairs, and a tool chest. The place appeared to have been shut up for some days, and it had that curious smell which is sometimes found where a man lives alone. It might have been any settler's, but, except for the brass bed and two complete sets of gold false teeth, arranged as ornaments on top of the desk. Above them hung an amateur painting of a woman and child, done in black and white on a wooden panel. The artist had been at pains to perpetuate the woman's fine dark eyes and full-lipped mouth, and he had succeeded in giving them a kind of bold life, which made the drawing more grotesque than if it had been uniformly mediocre.

Mr Smith looked about him, and then with an air of apology opened the desk. It contained a number of exercise books, several pens, and some large earthenware bottles of Stephen's ink. Only one of the exercise books was written in. The others were piled neatly but discoloured, like stock that has been kept for a long time in a shop.

The used exercise book was filled in as a diary. It was headed: 'The Diary of Thomas Macpherson.' The dates of the month were given, but not the year. It began with an entry on 12th October:

'People talk about earthly paradises, but they haven't the sense to go to them. I says to myself long ago I've only got one life, and if I can spend it in an earthly paradise I'm a fool not to, because it's the only paradise I'll ever know. So when I got the chance I came here bringing Belle, my wife, and all we need for comfort. I've got—' Here followed a long list of goods, utensils, plants, seeds, and commodities, including one hundred tins of Heinz's baked beans. The writer then went on to describe how he had landed on this island two days earlier, having paid the captain of a schooner a large sum to bring him here with his gear. He congratulated himself on being far removed from neighbours and, for some reason, from the police. He looked forward to years of idyllic basking and love-making in his tropical paradise. Presumably the lady in the picture was his wife Belle.

The diary went on for some months to record various' incidents, mostly to do with the building of the bungalow and planting of the garden, but the entries grew more and more desultory. Apparently some friction arose between himself and Belle, as he grew more interested in the garden than in love-making, and she taunted him that she would have had more fun if she had stayed at home with the boys than in his 'bloody paradise.' The last abrupt entry again was on 12th October:

'To-day Belle had a kid and died. The kid died too.'

Judging by the colour of the ink this seemed to have been written about ten years. It was hard to say when the bungalow had last been occupied—not more than a week ago, as an orange left on a shelf had just begun to go bad, and its juice had trickled out through a mildewed spot. There were spider's webs between the ceiling joists, but they may have been due to the owner's indifference rather than his absence.

While Mr Smith was reading the diary Joe had opened a cupboard which contained among other things some large rolls of red and white linen and of canvas, an ancient portable gramophone, and some piles of records. He looked through the records, which were all worn and scratched. Half of them were Scottish airs, the rest popular songs of the early 1920's. He wound up the gramophone and put on a record called *Missouri*. The thin, scratchy music startled them, like a voice from another world, but not from a desirable world, only from one that seemed as pathetic and tawdry as it was remote.

Joe switched off the gramophone before the record was finished. He thought he disliked it only because the gramophone was tinny and the record worn, but he was surprised in a way that he did not enjoy any reminder of the civilization from which they were so far removed.

Mr Smith handed Dick the diary, and Joe stood reading it over his shoulder.

'Where is he then?' asked Dick, when they had glanced through it.

'He may have had an accident,' said Mr Smith, 'or he may be away on a fishing expedition. He writes of his boat, but there is no boat except ours in the lagoon.'

'He may be drowned,' said Dick. 'He may have been caught in the gale that sank the *Princess of Teck*.'

Mr Smith nodded. This slight conversation had been an effort for them. Not only the soreness of their lips and throats made them reluctant to speak. They seemed to feel a kind of need to reintegrate their own individualities before they gave away anything of themselves in casual conversation.

They came out again on to the veranda, where they could no longer resist the temptation to take the fruit, and they pulled the fine bunches of grapes from the vine and ate them greedily. After they had explored the rest of the garden they returned to bring the good news of the discovery to their fellow-castaways. Joe took off his shirt and knotted the ends to make a swag, which he filled with magnificent bunches of grapes, with oranges and passion-fruit. He and Dick carried this between them as they waded down the stream. He felt that he had done this before, in another life, or as if he were a character in some antique legend. He felt hope and life rising in him, and he said to Dick: 'I feel like some bloke in the Bible.'

*

The castaways without any qualms took possession of 'Balmoral.' It did not occur even to Agatha, who was most scrupulous in these matters, that they should hesitate to occupy another person's property, to eat his fruit, and use his goods. She felt that their condition gave them the right to whatever shelter and sustenance were available, and she only took what she would have automatically given to others in a similar plight.

The nuns, who occupied the bungalow itself, began by treating it as a house in which they were guests, but as the weeks went by and Macpherson did not return, they unconsciously came to regard it as their own property. They made more drastic rearrangements of the interior, which at first had seemed a haven of luxury, but which they now found increasingly inconvenient. They stowed the brass bedstead under the bungalow, and cut up the mattress into three. They stuffed canvas sacks to make four more pallets. Dick and Joe built themselves a palm-thatched hut in a corner of the garden, while Tom and George built another on the opposite slope. Neither Mr Smith not Harry, the islander, bothered about shelter. They slept undertrees or on the beach. Mr Smith said: 'I find it delightful to be entirely free from the restrictions and conventions of civilization. One is not always in a climate where such freedom is possible. One may as well make the most of it.'

He would sit about watching the others work, sometimes offering criticism or a useful suggestion, but for the most part indulging in semi-philosophical erudite, idle chatter.

'When I was a little boy,' he said, as he sat on a palm log, sucking a passion-fruit and watching Dick and Joe build their hut, 'I was told a story of a child who played truant from school. He imagined that he would have a day of delightful idleness among the creatures of the natural world, which were free from the obligations of labour. But he found that the bee was much too busy gathering honey for the winter to waste time with him, while the bird had to build its nest and so on. I felt sorry for the child, and now I find myself in the same plight. Here we have nothing to do but eat and lie in the sun, but you must build houses and work to satisfy your puritan conscience that you have some purpose in life.'

'What'll you do when it rains?' asked Dick.

'The rain will be warm. I shall take off my clothes.'

It would have been more correct for Joe to share a hut with the other sailors, and for Dick, as an officer, to have one to himself. It showed how far they considered themselves removed from their former condition of life that they ignored this distinction, though Joe had asked Dick in chaff if he still counted himself an officer, and Dick had replied: 'I'll tell you when we're rescued.'

At first Mr Smith was popular. They were all grateful to him for steering the life-boat to the island, and it was he who had discovered the bungalow and the garden. Even Tom and George now regarded him as a mascot rather than a Jonah.

But after a while his popularity became tempered by a slight irritation with his prosiness, and Dick, who at first when he had seen him approaching for a chat would say cheerfully: 'Here comes that old buffer Smith,' would now mutter: 'Here comes that blasted Smith.' He irritated them not only by his prosiness, but by knowing apparently how to do everything better than themselves, while suggesting that it was hardly worth doing, so that he always left them a little deflated and uneasy. He showed the men how to make cigarettes out of dried pandanus leaves, and he pointed out to the nuns a shrub which provided a good substitute for tea. Although much that he said in his urbane discourses seemed to be against effort and order, he had some sense of responsibility, as he made Dick and Joe help him to remove four casks of rum which Macpherson had stored under the bungalow, before the sailors discovered them.

He was most popular with the nuns, to whom it was a treat rarely enjoyed at the convent to have a cultivated man of the world to tea. Marinella spent as much time with him as Ursula would allow her, and their laughter and conversation was a frequent pleasant babble about the garden.

It was surprising how quickly every one settled down to accept the island life as normal. There was plenty of food—yams did for potatoes, there was fresh fish daily from the lagoon, and the men trapped wild pigs in the forest. From Macpherson's diary it appeared that this island was a long way off the normal steamship routes, so that they were unlikely to be rescued unless a ship was sent to search for survivors from the *Princess of Teck*, which, however, they thought certain to happen. It was also possible that a stray schooner might call here. Perhaps one had put in a few days before they landed, and had taken off Macpherson, who might well by then have been sick of his solitary existence. The men searched and shouted in the forest in the neighbourhood of 'Balmoral,' but they found no trace of him. Mr Smith was of the opinion that he had been drowned while out in his boat in the storm, and as Mr Smith was generally right, and as it was rather convenient to accept this explanation of his disappearance they did so, and came to regard 'Balmoral' as entirely their own property.

'I am sure he is dead. I am sure this is our house now,' said Sister Hilda gleefully.

The nuns had begun to keep their Rule again. During the week it had taken them to settle down in the bungalow they had become rather slack about it. Agatha would have imposed only the minimum of discipline if she had thought that they were likely to be rescued quite soon, but after a conversation with Dick and Mr Smith, who both said that it was equally possible that they might be rescued in either two weeks or two years, she thought it advisable to prepare for the worst.

One Monday morning—they had made a rough guess at the date of their arrival, and calculated the days from that so they could say their liturgical offices correctly—she called the sisters together after breakfast and said:

'We mustn't forget that we are dedicated to the religious life, and that it's hardly consistent with our vocation to spend an indefinite period idling in the sun. It is true that we are active sisters, and that here there is little of God's active work for us to do, and He has provided us so generously—almost miraculously—with the means of life. Circumstances seem to point to our becoming, for the time being, contemplative nuns. There is no excuse for our abandoning our work for God. I am sure none of us would welcome such an excuse. The only work offered us at present is that of the contemplative—the duty of prayer and praise. We must, of course, do our share of manual work in the garden. I shall arrange with the men for us to have a part of the garden to ourselves as a sort of cloister. We might even fence it off. That would be some work for us. Also a duty of the contemplative nun is watching—watching by the dead or before the Blessed Sacrament. There is a form of watching to be done here—by the beacon on the shore which has to be lighted if a ship comes in sight. I suggest that we should undertake that work, by day and by night. It will provide an opportunity for contemplation. There is also Marinella's education, though that is hardly work for six women. As Sister Hilda taught in the school at home, she had better take it in hand.'

Agatha felt her voice growing thin and uncertain. It seemed to float away, meaningless on the air, finding no response in her listeners. The nuns were seated round the rough wooden table on the veranda. The floor was diapered with spots of hot light, coming through gaps in the green translucent vines. On the table was the enormous bowl of fruit from which they had made their breakfast, red and green, purple and gold, heaped up in careless profusion. The scent of lemon blossom and frangipani was sweet in the morning air. Tiny beads of sweat were already appearing on some of the women's foreheads.

As Agatha finished speaking the vines by the steps parted and Harry the islander appeared. He was naked except for the briefest loin-cloth, and was carrying a twig on which he had threaded half a dozen brilliantly coloured fish, still palpitating from the sea. He grinned, and held up his gift for admiration.

The force and beauty of the natural world seemed to come at Agatha like a wave. She could not speak nor smile to thank Harry for the fish. She signed for him to put them on a bench, and sat back, turning away her eyes. Harry looked about for approbation, but the nuns all appeared rather sulky. He grinned at Marinella, who smiled back at him, and then, hurt that his gift was not more welcome, left the veranda.

Agatha for the first time felt that the island, or at any rate this garden, held a spirit that was hostile to religion, as if the force of evil, the enemy of God, dwelt here. These fruits and flowers, so huge and brilliant, so wanton, so voluptuous, so suggestive in their shapes and colours, hardly seemed to be the creation of God but rather of some genius of lust. They had no relation to the apples in the orchards at home, to the primroses and daffodils which she had been accustomed to arrange before the statue of the Virgin. The entrance of Harry had seemed to her like the insolent appearance of the genius of the place, at the very moment when she was trying to affirm the claims of God. She was angry with herself that she had ever thought him beautiful and innocent, long ago in that other life, when he had dived from the lifeboat among the sharks. She glanced at the fish he had left on the bench. One of them gave a convulsive flap. Their colour, their beauty, the beauty of the fish and the fruit, the spots of golden light in the green translucence were overpowering. They were more than her senses could stand. As suddenly a chance remark made by someone whom one loves or hates will release a flood of emotion, so the fish flapping at the very moment she glanced at it, seemed to switch on an electric current between herself and the garden, releasing in her forces of life and desire which hitherto she had not known to exist, and which were likely to strangle in their sinewy grasp all her aspiration towards virtue and peace.

'This sort of thing must not happen!' She cried in a voice so harsh and so unlike her usual tones that the other nuns started and stared at her in surprise.

She rose and went into the bungalow, and stood trembling by the desk, under the leering black and white portrait of the woman and child, which Hilda insisted was a madonna. She was irrationally angry with every one, with the other sisters, and with Harry for daring to walk on to their veranda in that state. She had not been so angry for years. It was all very well, she told herself, to tolerate things which were normally intolerable when they were in great danger or suffering. But there was no longer that excuse. And when they had first landed and come slowly back to strength and health she could not insist on much discipline. On the third day after their landing they had sung a *Te Deum* and the psalm *In convertendo*:

When the Lord turned again the captivity of Sion: then were we like unto them that dream.

Then was our mouth filled with laughter: and our tongue with joy.

It had described so well their condition. Wonder and relief at being on land once more, at the clear water and the cool shade, at the profusion of fruit and flowers, had kept them in a simmer of delight which was ready at any moment to break out in laughter. That was like the innocent appreciation of a child, but a child would very soon become lazy and greedy and possessive if it was not checked, and so could the nuns, thought Agatha. What they needed was a sharp tug at the reins. It was shocking to think that, instead of making a greater effort to please God in gratitude for their miraculous rescue, they were prepared to sit back idly and enjoy his gifts. She worked herself up into a state of bitter self-righteousness. Even Winifred had shown no anxiety to return to a strict observance of the Rule.

She heard the other women murmuring together on the veranda, and she thought they must be criticizing her. She had a strong impulse to go to the door and shout at them to stop. She restrained the impulse, a tremor shook her, and her anger died, leaving her exhausted. She passed her hand across her forehead.

'I'm mad,' she told herself. It must be the effect of the heat. She had heard that soldiers in the French Foreign Legion were attacked by a form of madness called the *cafard*. She must be suffering from something of the kind.

She went about for the rest of the day pale and subdued. She did not say any more about discipline or the Rule. She was worried that some spirit outside herself had controlled her even for a moment. She had felt a hard pleasure in calling the nuns to order, and in that very moment of spiritual pride Harry had appeared and toppled over her pride so that she had become angry and wanted to shout.

Marinella brought in a bunch of the largest and brightest flowers, zinnias and hibiscus, and put them in a tin mug on the desk. She wanted to tell her to take them away, but she kept silence as she was uncertain of her motive. She no longer felt that the garden was a heavenly refuge to fill their mouths with laughter. The innocent relief of the first days was over. She walked warily as if she was in the early stages of an encounter with the devil.

The next morning she again spoke about the Rule, but more mildly, and she awoke some response in the nuns. Sister Hilda made a little speech.

'I don't see how we can turn from active sisters to contemplative sisters overnight,' she said, 'and if we did become contemplative what should we do if we were rescued? We're not chamois. But we should certainly keep our Rule strictly. There's no question of that. And for active work I propose we build a chapel. If we're rescued it may be of use to whoever lives here if the wretched man is not dead.' She crossed herself. 'And if we're not rescued, it will enable us to lead a decent Christian life.'

Agatha was pleased with this idea, and the other sisters acquiesced. Cecilia said: 'Wouldn't it be very heavy work?'

'It's heavy work to bear a cross,' said Hilda tartly.

Agatha said that perhaps the men would help them with the roughest part of the work, and in return they might undertake the whole of the watch on the shore.

Dick and Joe agreed to clear a further space in the forest for the building of the chapel, and to cut the timber and erect the frame work. They said there was no need to trouble the other sailors, though they could help if they liked.

Dick went along to Tom and George and asked them if they would like to lend a hand. Their refusal was emphatic.

Mr Smith asked Agatha if he might design the chapel.

'Before the War I was an architect,' he said, 'and I have always been interested in ecclesiastical building. I suggest you should take the meta-cube as the foundation of your proportions. If you cut a cube diagonally the rectangle made by the inner surfaces is a meta-cube. It is the perfect rectangle. The doorways of Greek temples and the windows of Georgian houses often have this proportion. The doorways of the Baptistry in Florence, which Michael Angelo said were worthy to be the Gates of Paradise, also form a meta-cube.'

He drew out a design in one of the exercise books, and the nuns were all delighted with it, except Hilda, who wanted it to be more Gothic.

'For the height of the wall and the ridge-pole,' he said, 'I have used the Golden Section—that is the division of a line so that the smaller is to the greater as the greater is to the whole. I have noticed this relationship in El Greco's composition.'

'It's very nice, I'm sure,' said Hilda, 'but you wouldn't know it was a chapel. There's not one pointed window, and we ought to have an asp. As I suggested building the chapel I think I might be allowed a say in the design. Metal cubes may be all right for heathen temples.'

'You can put a cross over the door,' said Mr Smith, 'and surely it is the prayers that are said there rather than the shape of the windows that will give the place sanctity. Also I think there is a certain sanctity in proportion.'

'That's nonsense,' said Hilda, 'and anyhow, I don't see why we can't have sanctity *and* pointed windows. It won't cost any more.'

However, Mr Smith had his way, for which Hilda bore him slight resentment, and always referred to him as 'That man' or 'That Mr Smith.'

Joe and Dick, after they had completed their own hut, spent most of their time by the sea. Like every one else they did a little gardening, but they preferred to fish as their contribution towards the food of the community. Macpherson had a large stock of fishing-lines which they did not hesitate to use. They rowed out in the life-boat on the lagoon, and fished for the green and scarlet fish with their long silky fins, that flitted between the beautiful weeds of the submarine garden. Joe said:

'I reckon these fish are a sort of Pekinese.'

Often they bathed from the boat, but only in the lagoon for fear of sharks. Even in this sheltered place they swam with a kind of exhilarated nervousness, as they were never quite sure that some dangerous fish or the tentacle of an octopus would not shoot out at their legs from the ambush of seaweed.

When they went out into the open sea they took Harry, and he would dive from the boat among the sharks, and rip up their bellies with his knife.

Of Dick and Joe it could be said that their mouths were filled with laughter, and also that they were like unto them that dream. The hot golden days by the sea for them held nothing but happiness. Once or twice they spoke about the possibilities of rescue, but normally they gave little thought to it, and they were absorbed in their simple activities, swimming and fishing and sailing the boat. They planned, if they were not rescued fairly soon, to sail round the island. There might possibly be some kind of settlement on the other side of the mountain. They also talked of an exploration up the river, and of another one to climb up to the crater of the mountain. But though they made these plans they were in no hurry to carry them out. Their friendship had grown under the drowsy spell of this life by the lagoon. Every simple activity, the walk down the stream in the still morning, the catching of small fish for bait in the shallow pools of the rocks which jutted out and joined the east end of the reef, the first dive from the boat into the sapphire lagoon with the stock joke about an octopus, the peculiar pleasure of bringing in the boat at the end of the morning, the pleasure of the end of an unspoilt pleasure—each of these shared things was a bond which drew them closer together, and they were reluctant to break a routine which held them under a spell, making the island seem truly the paradise which Macpherson had expected. One day Dick said:

'It was bad luck for Macpherson that his wife died so soon. It couldn't have been so much fun for him alone.'

'I don't suppose she came swimming with him,' said

Joe. They were sitting on the life-boat, oiling themselves after a bathe.

'Why not?' Dick's voice sounded a little sharp.

'Well, she couldn't if she was going to have a kid, could she?'

Dick thoughtfully examined his toes and did not reply.

On the same evening Agatha asked them if they would help to build the chapel.

They both agreed willingly, but after she had gone Dick looked thoughtful, and when Joe asked him what was the matter he said:

'It will be a bit of a bore.'

'I think it will be rather interesting.'

'All right, don't let's quarrel about it,' said Dick.

Joe burst out laughing. 'Is that a quarrel?' he asked.

Dick turned and looked seriously at him.

'I wish nothing need ever disturb us,' he said. 'I wish we could go on like this for ever, just doing the same things every day.'

'Yes, but everything has to end sometime. If it didn't it'ld grow stale.'

'Has this grown stale for you then?' asked Dick with a touch of bitterness.

'What?' Joe looked surprised.

Dick could not speak. He indicated the boat and the lagoon.

'Don't be a fool,' said Joe.

The next morning they began clearing a space in the forest for the chapel. They chose a site as near as possible to the bungalow. Agatha gave as her reason for building on a virgin piece of land, that the owner might object, should he return, to their destroying part of his garden to build a chapel, but her more serious reason was that she felt that the garden in its exuberant pride of life expressed in some way a spirit hostile to the Christian virtues. This reason had hardly come into her conscious mind, and if it had she would have hesitated to state it, as it would appear as senseless ingratitude for their good fortune.

When the new piece of ground was clear the nuns came out to do the comparatively light work of fencing, while Dick and Joe prepared the heavier timber for building. During the building of the chapel Harry the islander caught the fish for the community, and he trapped a wild pig and cooked it, wrapping it in leaves and clay, and then burying it in the earth for three days in a nest of hot stones.

Occasionally the men would leave their heavier work to help the women with the fencing. One day Winifred was fixing a post which would not stand straight. Dick came over to her, gave a few more powerful jabs round the base with a spade, and set the post firmly in the earth. His accurate masculine strength gave her a strange sense of peace and security. She thanked him shyly, but did not meet his eyes for long, as she felt his strength in his eyes, and as if somehow it would draw too much of her inner self to the surface. For the rest of the morning she was amused and happy, and she sang quietly under her breath as she fixed the palings, which Joe had split, against the heavy framework of the fence. She thought how lucky the girl would be who had Dick for a brother. She had no brothers nor sisters.

After that Dick kept an eye on Winifred, and often he would say: 'That is too heavy for you,' and would take a piece of timber from her and carry it himself.

He became impatient in the mornings to get to the site of the chapel, and although they rose early to work before the heat of the day, he now hardly waited for the sunrise, and he would shake Joe out of his sleep when the morning light was gilding the palm fronds high above the garden, but when the crimson and purple and yellow of the fruit and flowers in the garden itself glowed dimly in their deep pool of shade. Agatha noticed his attention to Winifred, but did not say anything for fear of making them self-conscious and crystallizing a relationship which would probably fade out when the building was done, and when she might arrange without seeming to that they seldom met. Hilda noticed it, too, and attacked Agatha on the subject.

'That young man, Dick, is making lamb's eyes at Winifred,' she said.

'Yes, I know.'

'What are you going to do about it, sister, if I may ask?'

'Nothing.'

'Nothing! You are going to let a man make love to a sister!' Hilda's eyes goggled, and all the lines round her mouth converged in painful ugliness to a point below her nose.

'He's not making love yet, and she's not a sister yet. She's only a novice.'

'I didn't know that girls became novices to receive followers.'

'She's not a kitchen-maid either,' said Agatha.

'If you allow this sort of thing, where is it going to stop? Shall *we* be safe?'

'Don't be ridiculous, sister,' said Agatha crossly. 'Nothing here is simple,' she added. 'At home one can rule by the simple exercise of authority. Here there seems to be some natural force in power and one can only rule by carefully directing it into the right channels. If you try to oppose it you will bring disaster. I learnt that the other morning, when I tried to impose my will on you.'

'I should have thought God was in power. Not a natural force.'

'Perhaps God is a natural force,' said Agatha.

'Really, sister, I can't pretend to be an expert on

theology, but that sounds to me perilously close to blasphemy.'

'We are perilously close to a good many things besides blasphemy,' said Agatha.

In the hottest hours of the day, when no work was done on the chapel, Joe and Dick would sleep and then go for a swim in the lagoon, before beginning the afternoon shift. One afternoon when they came out of the creek they saw Winifred seated by the beacon taking her turn to watch. Beyond the beacon a square of the red linen was nailed on to a pole as an added signal, but already this had begun to fade in the scorching sun.

Joe went down the beach to the life-boat, Dick trying to appear casual, but with his heart beating excitedly, strolled across to Winifred. It was the first opportunity he had had of speaking more than a few words to her.

Her hair had grown, and a brown curl had slipped out of her coif, and blew about her neck in the breeze from the sea. She smiled nervously at him as he came up. She was not sure that she should speak to him, as, although it was not the time of silence, Agatha had suggested that this watching by the beacon should be performed as a kind of religious exercise. Dick said:

'D'you find it lonely here?'

'Sometimes,' said Winifred, 'but I'm supposed to meditate.'

'There's plenty to think about, isn't there? I suppose you think of home and everything.'

'I do sometimes.' She found it difficult to tell him that her meditation was supposed to be religious.

He sat on the sands beside her.

'What's it like being a nun?' he asked her. 'I've never known a nun to speak to before. Never thought I should speak to one. They always seem to be kind of shut off from other people, under those hoods and everything. You haven't got a hood. That's a funny little cap you wear.'

'My hood blew away in the storm,' said Winifred. 'But I'm not a nun yet. I'm only a novice. I won't be professed for two more years.'

'What's professed?'

'That's when we make our vows.'

'You make vows! What about?'

'We vow to live in poverty and obedience—and never to marry.'

She was looking away from Dick, but she felt him start. He was silent for a moment, then he said:

'You oughtn't to do that. It's not right.'

'We think it right,' she said quietly.

'What made you think of becoming a nun?' he asked. He could see Joe down at the water's edge, sitting on the gunwale of the life-boat and kicking his heels, but an opportunity of talking alone to Winifred was too rare to give up. He had not talked alone to a girl for six months or more.

'I felt that the world was evil.'

'We have to live in it though. D'you reckon this place is evil?'

'It's very beautiful, and I'm not sure about its being evil. It would sound like ingratitude to say that it was. I suppose there's some evil everywhere, but then you see we believe that God is everywhere, too, if you want Him.'

'But you said the world was all evil just now. At least so evil that you had to become a nun to get out of it. You're what a Communist chum of mine used to call an escapist.'

'Well, naturally, I like to escape from what's horrible,' said Winifred, rather indignantly.

Dick smiled. 'There's some sense in that,' he said, 'if you can escape.'

'You can't escape entirely, I suppose, though by trying to escape as you call it I've got far enough away from the world here.' She burst out into extraordinarily youthful laughter. Her laughter had the innocent quality of a child's, and surprised him a little. 'But you see,' she went on seriously, 'if you are with people whose lives are given up to good, you're more likely to do good and less likely to do evil yourself. At least I think I am, because if I can I reflect the people I'm with, and want to like them and be like them.'

'You must have known lots of nice people you could like,' said Dick.

'I didn't.'

He was rather pleased with that.

'Why not?'

'My father was very rich.'

This did not please him at all. He gave a dissatisfied grunt.

'Then you could know anybody,' he said.

'I was much more limited in my choice of friends than the poor. After all, look at the millions of poor there are. They have a wide choice. And my father was not the sort of rich man who has many friends. Once he went bankrupt, and he paid almost nothing to his creditors. Then he became very rich again, and he gave a peal of bells to a church, but he didn't pay any more to the people he'd ruined, and they said the bells used to ring: "I paid a farthing in the pound." A girl at school told me this. It was a horrible school to which my father sent me, because he thought I would make the right sort of friends there. The girls whose parents were very rich were rude to those whose parents were not so rich. It sounds incredible, but in one of its worst phases—it only lasted a week or two—the girls whose parents had three motor cars would not speak to those whose parents had only one. Then just after I left school, when my father was spending thousands of pounds trying to make me socially important, I met Sister Agatha. Up till then

I had only met people whose whole aim in life was to grab and get somewhere—but her whole aim was to give and to make conditions better for other people wherever she happened to be. She didn't even seem to be self-consciously trying to do good. She just behaved as if that was the normal attitude towards life. At once, and almost for the first time in my life, I felt that I was breathing pure air. I went to tea with the sisters, and I found surroundings that I could reflect without feeling that I was straining my own nature.'

'But you can't reflect them,' said Dick. 'Sister Hilda and Sister Ursula. They're no more like you than chalk's like cheese.'

'Sisters have their faults as much as people in the world, but the motive of their life is different. That's why I can live with them. It's true that the religious life is not an absolute haven of peace. One's faults become more noticeable, if anything. But no one is perfect.'

'You are,' said Dick. This speech was a slight effort, and his voice was husky.

She started.

'You mustn't say that to me,' she said.

'Why not?'

'It's not true for one thing, and also I'm a novice and mayn't accept flattery.'

'Most girls like to have that sort of thing said to them,' said Dick.

'I suppose they do. In a way it's rather nice. Sister Agatha says nice things to me sometimes, but only when she means them.'

'I meant it.'

'But you don't know me, so how could you mean it? I don't think that it is really pleasant to have things said to one that can't be meant, or that are only illusion, because when the person who said them got to know you really well he would find out you weren't like that at all, and would be disappointed.'

'Would you like to know me better?' asked Dick. He grinned boldly into her eyes.

'It wouldn't be possible,' said Winifred. 'Please, you really shouldn't sit here talking to me. Look, your friend is waiting for you.'

'All right,' said Dick. He stood up and brushed the sand from his legs. 'But we must have another talk soon. You've got six times as much sense as most girls. They can't talk for nuts. I mean that anyhow. Well, cheero.'

He turned and strolled down the beach to Joe, who was still kicking his heels by the life-boat.

When Dick said, 'Cheero,' Winifred's heart gave a jump, and she felt as if it had turned completely over. She had been sharply aware of him ever since he had spoken to Sister Agatha in the lounge of the *Princess of Teck*, but now she had no more illusions about wishing that he were her brother. She knew that she loved him, but her love had been awakened not by his compliments and tender gestures, which she felt were half a sin, but by this absolutely frank, comradely, commonplace expression. It destroyed in one moment the barriers between herself and the ordinary, friendly world. Also the idea of saying 'Cheero' to a nun seemed to her so funny, like the *naïveté* of a child, that she gave a faint gurgle of laughter and her laughter and love were mixed together, as she watched Dick walk down the beach to the boat. And then when she realized that she was in love she sat still and dazed, not knowing what she could do about it, and the thought of all the complications clouded her happiness, as a drop of ink will spread and darken a glass of clear water.

'Come on,' said Joe impatiently.

'Jealous?' asked Dick.

Joe turned quickly. 'What d'you mean?' he demanded.

'Because I've got the only girl in the place.'

'No. I'm not jealous,' he said thoughtfully. 'Not of that. Anyhow, she's a nun.'

'I reckon nuns have more sense than other girls.'

'You can't marry them.'

'You can marry novices.'

'You can't marry any one here. There are no parsons and no registrar's offices.'

'So if we were never rescued the race would have to die out, I suppose, for want of a registry office?'

'I don't suppose it would die out if you were anywhere in the neighbourhood,' said Joe rudely. Dick said: 'Shut up,' and they sank into an amicable silence, until they reached the middle of the lagoon, where they dived and shouted and tried to drown each other, after the fashion of adolescents.

When they came in from their bathe Dick waved to Winifred, still on watch by the beacon, but by this time she was in a state of fear and doubt, and she returned his wave so timidly that he did not see it, and he waded gloomily up the creek.

'You can't treat nuns like ordinary girls,' said Joe.

'When there's no one else, nuns are ordinary girls,' Dick replied. 'They're all nuns except that kid Marinella.'

'I book her,' said Joe, 'in about three years' time if we're not rescued. You can have your nuns now. That's a fair deal.'

'You can't bargain like that. It's low.'

'It's only natural.'

Dick grunted.

Winifred did not appear at the afternoon spell of building, as she was still on watch. The next morning Dick was insistent in his attentions to her, but she tried to escape them, and when she could not she looked at him appealingly and said: 'Please!'

'When are you on watch again?' he asked quietly, but she shook her head and moved away, and would not reply.

Cecilia and Magdalene saw what they thought was a whispered conversation going on between Dick and Winifred. They were young and recently professed sisters, only about a year older than Winifred. They preferred the romantic and emotional side of religion, and at home had loved to read about 'The Little Flower' and St John of the Cross. They were excited by Winifred's apparent regard for Dick, but they were not ill-natured, and though they whispered together about it as a scandalous phenomenon, they did not think of mentioning it to Agatha, who still hesitated to interfere.

Another infatuation was worrying her more—that of Ursula for Marinella. Ursula had taken charge of the child in the boat, after Mrs Dawes had stabbed herself, and in their first days on the island had shown that she regarded her as her special charge and protégée. She was furious at the suggestion that Hilda should undertake Marinella's instruction, so that Agatha had agreed to leave it to Ursula, thinking it would not be for long. Ursula's ideas of education did not go beyond arithmetic, spelling, and the dates of the kings and queens of England. Marinella's lessons, for about two hours in the morning, lasted for a fortnight, by which time they had dwindled to half an hour a day. Marinella found that by affecting a headache, or by direct, irrational tantrums, she could do what she liked with Ursula, who only called her in return 'my darling' and 'my little angel.' She quoted Marinella's mistakes as if they were the most brilliant witticisms, and her few serious remarks as if they held all the wisdom of the ages. If any one spoke sharply to the child she turned on them spitefully. Marinella who on the *Princess of Teck* had been a lively, only reasonably impudent child, and who had come back to life subdued by the horrors she had witnessed, now went about wearing the smirk of the successful blackmailer. All the nuns were reluctant to cross Ursula, who made herself Marinella's abject slave, so that Marinella felt herself in a position to control the community. Agatha, anxious to avoid any flare-up, only insisted on the minimum of discipline. Her conscience troubled her, and she tried to soothe it by remembering that Marinella was only accidentally and not officially in their charge. 'Though that is no reason,' she told herself, 'why the child's soul should be damned.'

Mr Smith called Marinella 'The Veuve Scarron,' which made her cross, though she preferred Mr Smith's society to that of any of the other castaways.

'Why do you call me that?' she asked.

'Call you what?'

'Verb Scarron.'

'You must ask Sister Ursula.'

'You ought to call me some nice name.' At the moment she was genuinely childlike and pathetic, but she did not seem to touch Mr Smith's heart.

'Sister Ursula calls you nice names, doesn't she?' he teased her. 'My darling and my little angel.'

'She's an old fool!' shouted Marinella, and burst into tears.

Ursula cut up her tartan to make Marinella a kilt, but Marinella refused to wear it. Every one was sorry for Ursula, but when Hilda clumsily expressed her sympathy Ursula snapped at her. She seemed to take a horrible pleasure in the child's insolence, even when it was directed against herelf.

Agatha began to dream again, and the setting of her dreams was always the garden whose thrusting, twining fertility oppressed her, where the fat buds formed in a night and were startling blooms by midday. The faces of the other sisters and of the men—of Mr Smith and

Harry most often—loomed in her dreams. In the morning their faces no longer seemed familiar. The faces of the nuns were no longer the faces of rather commonplace women intent on good works, whose worst faults were an occasional tired fretfulness and the trifling omission of a duty. Glistening with the heat, tinged with the green translucence of the vines, they seemed to show the stirring of new potentialities. As the flowers and fruit in the garden had achieved their greatest possible size and most vivid colour with an easy splendour of growth that could never occur in the suburban gardens at home, so it seemed that every nerve and gland of these women, every atrophied tract of their brains, was stirring to life to achieve the same fulfilment, the same utter completeness of expression as the huge glossy fruits and the flamboyant hibiscus in the garden. The depression, the obstinacy, the bursts of hilarity, the unusual greed that the nuns showed was not so much the result of privation, as of new life stirring in them and almost like a physical growth disturbing their normal economy.

One night Agatha dreamed that she was back on the *Princess of Teck* on the day of the storm. In her dream she knew that the ship would sink and that the sufferings in the life-boat were ahead of her, but she did not know that at length they would arrive on the island.

When she awoke the howling of the wind continued, and she found that the bungalow was shaking in a gale.

The sisters still slept in a row down the length of the room, excepting Ursula, who had insisted on sleeping at a right angle to the others. Marinella lay beside her, her small and beautiful feet thrust out from beneath the tartan skirt which Ursula had laid across them. Ursula was snoring, but the sound was only a slight accompaniment to the roaring of the wind. Sleep, instead of refining Ursula's coarseness of appearance, accentuated it, so that to Agatha she appeared like someone who had been denied a spirit and was too much of the earth, at the same time repulsive and pathetic.

Agatha dressed and went on to the veranda. In the garden the voluptuous plants were shaking and waving their branches, like women in a harem excited by the sounds of battle outside. The sky was an extraordinary sight. Torn leaves flew thickly across the clear space, gulls blown backwards squawked in fear, and a flight of parrots screamed as they were whirled out of control against the wall of the forest. The feathery tops of the palm-trees were blown straight out, like flags or a girl's hair, in one direction away from the sea, and huge fronds fell in the garden. The whining howl of the gale, the cracking of branches in the forest and the thunder of the sea mingled in a furious concert. The hollow garden, though agitated, was protected by its jungle walls from the force of the gale, otherwise it would have been blown flat and destroyed in a few minutes.

She saw something brown and glistening move under a lemon tree. At first she thought it was a wild animal, and she was a little nervous. Then she saw it was Harry crouching for shelter from the wind. It shocked her to think she had mistaken him for an animal, and the fact that she had been able to do so increased the mistrust she had felt towards him when he had brought the fish on to the veranda.

She went back into the bungalow, where the sisters had risen, and were tidying up their pallets, putting them in a pile against the wall so that the floor would be clear to walk on. They were a little frightened by the gale, and exchanged anxious glances, but they could not speak as the silence lasted till after breakfast. Normally Marinella was sent out to play in the garden till then, but to-day she could not go out, and she fidgeted about the room, asking questions and tossing her head irritably when she had no reply. Her manner suggested that the nuns were complete fools not to talk when they had tongues. Hilda said 'Sssh!' to her, and Ursula glared at Hilda. They faced each other across the bungalow when they said Prime, standing in the same positions as if they were in the choir at home. When Hilda who was taking the office said: 'The Lord be with you,' and Ursula replied: 'And with thy spirit,' her expression did not agree with her words. However, for the most part their voices were drowned by the gale, and they could only guess when to make their antiphonal responses.

As soon as the second grace had been said after breakfast there was a burst of chatter. They were all anxious about the safety of the bungalow, but Ursula turned on Hilda, and said that there was no obligation on Marinella to observe the nuns' rule.

'And there's no obligation on her to stop us from observing it,' said Hilda, whose sentences became more involved as her indignation increased.

'She shall do as she pleases,' said Ursula.

The gale lasted for twenty-four hours. Marinella made herself the obnoxious focus of the women in the hut. She spent all her energies in drawing attention to herself. At first she was extremely helpful, and hung round Hilda tidying and polishing what smooth surfaces of woodwork the place contained. She seemed anxious for praise, which she received grudging and qualified from Hilda, who had never given a word of generous approval in her life, and fulsome from Ursula, which she ignored as automatic and valueless.

In the afternoon Marinella became tired of good works. She played at dressing up with some women's clothes which she found in a drawer, and which must have belonged to Belle, Macpherson's wife, who had brought a supply of dresses which she had thought suitable to an earthly paradise. There were four evening dresses of heavy silk, gold, rose-pink, petunia, and vermilion, and one of black velvet. They had hardly been worn, and were wrapped up in tissue paper and smelt of camphor.

Agathà made a mild protest, and said that the dresses belonged to Macpherson, but as she believed that he was dead she did not insist. Also she was grateful for any distraction that would occupy Marinella for an hour or so. As she paraded up and down the bungalow, trailing yards of expensive silk, Ursula said:

'You're like a little queen.'

Hilda said: 'You look to me more like the Scarlet Woman.'

This started a violent quarrel between Hilda and Ursula, with which the air quivered till Vespers.

As they ranged themselves on opposite side of the room to say their office, Agatha felt that the division was almost between those who wished for good, and those who wished for evil. It was perhaps hard to say that Hilda and Cecilia wished for evil, but Hilda's good, to be achieved by the biting erosion of everything extraneous to conventional righteousness, was not her own, while Cecilia's hot house devotional ardour she felt would only flourish in dim corners where the full Christian sunlight had not penetrated. Then she thought of the dark phases of her own mind, of the strange, unnameable sensations produced by the sight of Harry the islander, and it seemed preposterous of her to align herself on the side of infallible virtue. Again she had the feeling, about herself as much as the others, that their atrophied glands were developing. Even more she felt as if they had been put in this place to simmer, so that their individual spiritual elements might become separated and defined.

With this feeling in her heart it seemed to Agatha that the perpetual recitation of offices was almost blasphemous. A group of people full of resentment, suspicion, and dislike of each other, in whom new doubts and lusts were growing, could not bring God into the midst of them. And yet it was unthinkable that they should give up saying their offices.

Mr Smith spent the day of the gale in the hut occupied by Tom and George. They passed the time gambling with a pair of dice he had carved, and by the end of the day between them they owed him forty pounds. As the date for payment was indefinite this did not worry them much. They found Mr Smith's conversation more disturbing. The gist of it was to the effect that rescue was highly improbable, and that the best thing they could do was to settle down and found a new community, after the example of the Pitcairn Islanders.

The next day the gale dropped, but it poured with rain, and the women were still confined to the bungalow.

In the early afternoon the door was pushed open and Tom and George came in. Their torn shirts and trousers, the best, in fact the only clothes they had, were streaming with water from their short walk across the garden, and made two pools where they stood by the door. George's attitude was both sheepish and swaggering, while Tom looked simply angry.

'What do you want?' demanded Ursula.

George tried to appear jovial. 'A bit of company,' he said.

'You won't find it here,' said Hilda.

'We'll see about that,' said Tom. His manner barely concealed an animal threat. He seemed to be encased in a deliberately assumed armour of ruthlessness, against which an appeal to chivalry or to ordinary human decency would be useless. George was more anxious to give the adventure an appearance of jollity.

'What about a game or something?' he said. 'This is the sort of day for a game, I reckon.'

'We don't know any games,' said Hilda, 'and Satan finds mischief for idle hands to do.'

'We could teach you a few,' said George. 'We could teach you quite a lot.' He gave a loud guffaw.

'I'm afraid,' said Agatha courteously, 'that games are not part of our life. You see our lives are supposed to be given up entirely to the service of others and of God. What pleasure we have—and we have a great deal of happiness I think—comes incidentally, when we see our efforts rewarded, in a mended life for instance. And we enjoy the beauty of the natural world. But our Rule does not allow us to seek pleasure, even in harmless games.'

Tom took a step forward. He looked puzzled and more angry. The veins swelled a little on his forehead, and he looked as if he might break out in violence. George said:

'That's all right when you're in civilization like, but what's the use of it here? There's no sick and poor here. There's plenty of everything, and now's your chance to have a good time. If we all got together like, it'ld be real nice here, and no tales told if we was rescued.'

'If we were never rescued,' said Agatha, 'we should still have our religious duty.'

'Aw, forget it!' said George with good-natured contempt.

'You ought to be ashamed to say such a thing,' exclaimed Hilda indignantly.

'Well, he ain't, so there!' barked Tom suddenly. He glared beyond her to where Cecilia and Magdalene, excited and scandalized, were whispering in the background.

There was a minute of silence. The two men stared at the nuns, and Agatha felt that immediately this trance was broken something frightful and decisive would happen. She wondered where Dick and Joe were, and

Mr Smith, and whether they would hear if she called for help. 'I mustn't be afraid,' she told herself. 'If we are not afraid it will be impossible for them to use violence.' Neither Ursula nor Hilda seemed to be afraid. Hilda glared at the men with absolute confidence in her mental, moral, and social superiority. The idea that she was in any danger from these two hooligans had not occurred to her.

Marinella pushed her way forward.

'I don't see why we shouldn't have a game,' she said. 'I'ld like a game.'

Tom made a furious exclamation, spat on the floor, and stalked out of the bungalow. George grinned sheepishly, said: 'Thanks for a very pleasant afternoon,' and followed him.

Back in their hut Tom said: 'A bloody lot of use that was.' He was seething with impotent anger. He had always had his way with the type of women he had wanted. He had gone over to the bungalow determined to have his way with the nuns, with Cecilia or Magdalene. No civilized considerations were to stand in his way. He knew that Mr Smith was playing dice with Dick and Joe in their hut on the far side of the garden, out of ear-shot in the noise of the rain. As he crossed to the bungalow his imagination was inflamed and his whole being was full of purposeful lust. But this red animal power had suddenly come up against the cold, negative power of Victorian gentility. There was nothing in those women, atrophied by religion and good breeding, to meet his lust. Contact with them was like contact with a cold wind, and his animal will was defeated in a way that had never happened before. The last straw had been the intervention of the child, making the whole situation ridiculous. He turned on George, blaming him for suggesting the visit, and wanting to release his lust in a fight, which it took all George's wheedling to avoid.

The next morning the rain stopped. When the silence was ended the nuns, chattering like children, streamed out into the garden which, although bruised and disordered, appeared more beautiful than ever. The broken plants were hung with a myriad rain-drops, which glistened like diamonds in the morning sun.

Mr Smith, looking rather grave, came up to Agatha. 'The boat has been smashed to pieces in the gale,' he said. 'It's lying up on the beach like a match box that has been crushed in one's hand.'

'That seems to make our chance of escape more remote,' said Agatha, 'though personally I should not care to set out in the boat again.'

'Dick and Joe thought of making an exploration round the island in her. They thought there might be a settlement of some kind on the other side. I think it highly improbable. I have an idea that there is a taboo on this island, which is why there are no natives. Probably Macpherson knew that.'

'I wonder what has happened to Macpherson,' said Agatha. 'It is dreadful really how little thought we give to him. We behave as if the place belonged to us.'

'All you can do for Macpherson,' said Mr Smith, 'is to pray for his soul'

Agatha looked thoughtful. 'I suppose so,' she said. 'D'you know,' she went on after a pause, 'I feel as if there *was* a taboo, or some kind of curse on this place. I feel as if there was an evil spirit living here.'

'Surely you *religieuses* are able to draw on more powerful spiritual forces of good,' said Mr Smith.

'Do you believe that we can?' she asked him.

'I believe that you can if you believed that you could,' he replied.

She told him about the visit of Tom and George the day before.

'Then you did use a spiritual force against them,' he said.

'They went when Marinella suggested they should play with her.'

'A child's innocence is always an effective weapon against the beast,' said Mr Smith, 'though once in Paris an Alsatian walked into a garden and ate a baby in a perambulator.'

Agatha gave a horrified exclamation, but Mr Smith seemed only mildly amused.

'It is certainly difficult to reconcile these things with the goodness of God. The Alsatian was only obeying its instinct, though of course its instinct may have been corrupted by contact with man. By the way,' he added, 'the thwarts and floor-boards of the life-boat will be useful in furnishing the chapel.'

After the rain the whole community, except Tom and George, who now avoided meeting the women, occupied itself in tidying up the garden.

Dick and Joe and Harry collected the fallen branches and took them down to the beach to build a new beacon, as the old one had been blown away in the gale. They piled them on their heads and looked like trees walking as they made their way down the stream. Although they were a little depressed at the loss of the boat, they were cheered by the return of the fine weather, and Joe whistled an air from *The Maid of the Mountains*.

The women applied themselves to the lighter tasks, cutting away the bruised plants and flowers, and later the men came to help them. Towards noon Winifred was rather away from the others, removing litter from a clear space by the banks of the stream, where the nuns were accustomed to sit sometimes in the afternoon.

Dick saw her white coif behind a trellis of vines. He came closer and watched her through the leaves. His heart was heavy with a queer mixture of sadness and pleasure. As she bent, gathering up the twigs, and adding them to a little heap, every movement she made seemed to him significant and perfect, and he longed to touch her, but thought he would never dare.

The rich earth, soaked in the tropical rain and now drenched by the hot sun, was forcing fresh and even more urgent life into the garden. One could almost see the petals unfold and the leaves draw up the sap. Dick felt himself penetrated by this life and growth until he was a part of it. The blood rose in his veins like the sap in the thick green stems of the plants.

He moved slowly forward out of the shadow of the vine, and the sunlight was suddenly dazzling on his hair. Winifred turned with a start. They looked without speaking into each other's eyes. The light in his blue eyes was so intent and powerful that it seemed to strike deep into the centre of her own life. His eyes lowered to her mouth and before she knew how it had happened, with or without her consent, she was in his arms.

Cecilia and Magdalene were passing at that moment. They stood and watched them through the leaves, exchanged a glance with each other, and passed on whispering together, but they did not mention what they had seen to any one else.

The sun which drew the sap so strongly into the leaves and branches, withered them as quickly when they were cut off from the moist earth, their source of nourishment. The debris of the garden which Joe and Dick had carried down to the shore was soon built up into a new beacon, ready to be kindled if a ship should come in sight, and near it was a fresh piece of red linen nailed on to a post.

One day when Ursula was on watch Mr Smith came along the beach and sat beside her. It was early afternoon and the rest of the community were asleep.

'Well,' said Mr Smith, seating himself on the sands

beside Ursula, 'we are settling down quite nicely I think, don't you?'

Ursula muttered some non-committal reply. She disliked Mr Smith, chiefly because she thought he must despise her as stupid and ugly. As he appeared to be an English gentleman she thought he must be snobbish and despise her more because she was an Australian, although as a Scot she felt she ought to despise him because he was an Englishman. This was all very confusing and made her angry with him. Also she felt that he was an intellectual prig as he so often made recondite allusions. On top of all this she was painfully jealous of him as Marinella so obviously preferred his society to her own.

'Is Marinella asleep?' he asked.

Ursula grunted an affirmative.

'She is a delightful child. You will miss her when we are rescued and she has to return to her relatives.'

Ursula looked as if he had struck her.

'She may not have to go to them. They may not want her,' she said.

'They may not want her, but they'll probably take her out of a sheer, disobliging sense of duty. Most relatives are like that, I find.'

'It may be some time before we are rescued.'

'Let us hope so,' said Mr Smith.

Ursula took a little while to digest this remark.

'Don't you want to be rescued?' she asked.

'Do you?'

'Naturally.'

'Why?'

'Don't be absurd,' said Ursula.

'Why is it absurd to face realities? Compare your life here with your life at home. Which do you prefer?'

'That's my business.'

Mr Smith shrugged his shoulders.

'It's rather interesting, all the same,' he said, 'to consider which really is the more enjoyable. We assume that here we are suffering dreadful hardship, but are we? You are practically free from the irksome discipline of the convent. As I believe George said to you the other day, there are no sick and no poor to claim your attention with their miseries. In fact here you need do nothing unless you want to, as all the other sisters are afraid of you, you know.'

'Hm!' said Ursula, but there was a hint of secret pleasure in her eyes.

'Here,' Mr Smith went on, 'there is no financial insecurity, no threat of poverty, no slums, no smoke, no disease, no policemen, no politicians, no war, no taxes, no time even, unless you wish to observe it. I have lived in many places, but none that pleased me better, though I did have a delightful apartment on the quai des Grands Augustins, and another in Cheyne Walk. So I am in no hurry for rescue. I can't see why you should be anxious for it either.'

'We think it right to work,' said Ursula, identifying herself with the sisterhood when she spoke to an outsider.

'But did you join the sisterhood to do what is right, or to have a fuller sense of life?' asked Mr Smith. 'I mean, to make human contacts which you could not achieve in the outside world.'

Ursula did not reply. She looked a little afraid.

'I see I have hit the nail on the head. Well, you have a fuller sense of life here than you have ever had before. You have a new freedom if you like to take it, and this place teems with rich life, which may become richer as we stay here longer and become more reconciled to it and to each other. And you have Marinella. It is as if you were given a daughter which secretly you have always longed for. These things will be taken away from you if we are rescued. Look!'

He pointed to the far horizon where, beyond the glittering expanse of sea, a faint wisp of smoke was visible.

Ursula stood up.

'I suppose you saw that before you spoke to me,' she said. 'If you hadn't spoken to me I would have been filled with joy to see a ship coming, but you have taken away in advance my pleasure in the thing I have longed for ever since we landed here. You are evil.'

There were three boxes of matches on the island. They had been in the men's pockets. They had used a match to light a fire in the stove which they always kept smouldering, but after that the matches were kept for an emergency such as this, and were handed over as a kind of symbol of office, by one watcher to the sister who relieved her. Ursula took a box of matches from the pocket of her stained and shabby habit, and went over to the bonfire.

'You say I am evil,' said Mr Smith, 'because I have shown you what you really want, and it is painful to you to give up the idea of what you think you want.'

Ursula took a match from the box and struck it.

'Don't!' commanded Mr Smith. 'Don't light the bonfire yet. The ship is too far away to see it, and it may be burnt out before she comes close enough. I wouldn't light it for another quarter of an hour.'

Ursula turned to him, sheltering the match in her hand. The flame turned from a yellow flare to a blue quivering line along the stick, became invisible and went out.

'I have wasted a match,' she said.

'That won't matter now. But, tell me, you are not glad to see the ship come?'

She did not answer. She sat down again near the beacon and watched the wisp of smoke grow longer and more definite. Her square homely face with its hint of fair beard on the chin, had taken on a momentary nobility when she had turned and rebuked him, but now it was unhappy and abject, like that of a dog which knows it is to be left or sent away.

For about five minutes there was silence. Ursula's appearance of wretchedness increased. Mr Smith snapped suddenly: 'Why light the beacon?'

Again she did not reply, but her face became like that of a Caliban in torment. Mr Smith watched her, his eyes intent and smiling.

'You don't want the ship to come,' he said. 'You will lose Marinella. You will lose your freedom, your power. You joined the sisterhood because you wanted life more abundantly, and to satisfy your pride. Those were the only reasons. Here you will have more life than you have ever known before. Here you will satisfy your pride of life. But you are going to throw it all away, and you don't know why. Only because you have a muddled mind. You think it is your conscience speaking, but your conscience is only another form of pride. Control it. Do what you really want to do. Stay here. Don't light the beacon.'

It was terribly hot, but the sweat on Ursula's forehead was due to more than the heat, and her normally red-brown face was grey. She fumbled with the matches.

'I can't. I must light it,' she stammered, and cleared her throat. It was an effort for her to speak coherently.

'Why?' snapped Mr Smith.

'They might come down and find I hadn't lighted it.'

'They won't. They won't wake till sunset. I gave them all some drugged tea.'

She was too disturbed for this to surprise her.

'The ship will put a boat ashore.'

'She may not. You must risk that. You have to risk something. If they do I'll get you out of it. I'll do the talking. Come on.'

He leapt at the beacon and began to pull down the dry branches and scatter them over the beach. Ursula watched him for a moment and then she joined in. They worked like two furies, the lumbering panting woman and the lean frenzied man. He seemed to be possessed by a spirit of destruction which communicated itself to her. Now and then he gave a breathless laugh, but while she tore down the carefully built pile she felt she was tearing down all the things that had hedged in and oppressed her life. She was tearing down the barriers that had denied her love and freedom. She was destroying the law.

When the branches were scattered along the beach, in a line as much as possible, to make them appear from the ship like a line of seaweed, Mr Smith seized the pole to which was nailed the red flag. He tugged and pulled at it, and at last lifted it from its bed of stones. Ursula was amazed at his strength. She had thought of him as a middle-aged, intellectual weakling. Together they pulled the pole into the undergrowth, and then rested there, hiding among the leaves, to watch the steamer.

By the time they had scattered the beacon and removed the flag-pole the ship's hull was visible. She approached the island at an angle from the south-west, and came to within about two miles of the shore, though she looked much closer.

Ursula and Mr Smith, crouching in the undergrowth, acquired a primitive, animal quality. They were like two creatures of the forest—Mr Smith like a fawn, or possibly a fox—Ursula like something more savage, more earthy and hostile to the human race. Mr Smith watched the ship with an air of malicious amusement, but Ursula with a stare of dreadful intensity. When it was at its closest to the shore, it gave three long blasts on the siren. They echoed through the forest and against the mountain. Ursula uttered a faint whimper, an animal sound. She did not see how the siren could fail to bring the whole community dashing down to the shore, but no one came. The steamer went at its lowest speed, slowly along the coast. It gave three more blasts of the siren, and then in the distance another three. It was close to the island for half an hour or so, and then steamed away to the south-east. To Ursula the half-hour had seemed like a day. When the ship had gone and she came out of the undergrowth she could hardly stand. Mr Smith stretched his arms and laughed.

'It's lucky for us,' he said, 'that the captain was not more conscientious.'

He dragged the pole down the sands and fixed it again in the pile of stones. Together they began to collect the branches and to rebuild the beacon. Ursula's hands were trembling so that she could hardly pick up the dried palm fronds.

Towards sunset they had it finished and had cleared up the mess of leaves and twigs where they had scattered them. Hilda came down, four hours late, to relieve Ursula.

'I can't say what came over me,' she said. 'I was just overtaken by somnolia and didn't wake up. That's all there is to it, and nobody else did either. Why didn't you come and call me?'

She was so concerned about her lateness, and so anxious to blame somebody else, that she did not notice Ursula's curious manner.

Ursula handed her the matches, and walked away along the beach, without saying a word.

4

The chapel was finished on the Feast of the Transfiguration. Foreseeing this, Mr Smith, after a consulation with Sister Agatha, had suggested that it should be called the Chapel of the Transfiguration, and he had painted an altar-piece of this subject. To obtain his colours he had pounded up coral and shells and stones which he found on the beach, and his picture, even if it had been less skilfully painted, would have had beauty from the colour alone, a soft blending of brown and blue-grey and dull rose. Hilda said: 'It looks as if it had been painted a hundred years ago.' She did not care for it at all. The central figure had the sinister, almost malignant expression of the slit-eyed Siennese madonnas. This was unpleasant, but at least had precedent. What upset her more, as it appeared to her to be verging on blasphemy, was that the attendant figures were full-length portraits of Joe and Dick, naked.

'I had to have models,' explained Mr Smith, 'and they were the best available.'

'But they should be old men with beards,' objected Hilda, 'and they should be wearing robes.'

'People in glory are always young,' said Mr Smith, 'and they are as God made them, not ashamed of the beauty He created.'

Hilda went to Agatha.

'I shall never be able to go into the chapel,' she protested. 'Every time I lift my eyes to the altar I shall be outraged. Even if they were dressed, to have two sailors in a holy picture is simply casting pearls before swine.'

'Mr Smith says that in the Middle Ages it was quite usual for the donors to have their own portraits included in pictures of the saints. I must say I find the picture a little startling, though the colour is lovely. Still, there are thousands of nude figures in the churches of Italy. In the Sistine Chapel——'

'I've never been to Italy,' said Hilda, 'and neither have you.'

The argument went on irrelevantly for a few minutes, and ended by Agatha's saying:

'Anyhow, we can't refuse the picture now that he has been so kind as to paint it. After all, it's practically his chapel. He has designed it, and it's amazing what he has done with so few materials, and the picture, as Mr Smith says, is the eye of the chapel.'

Certainly the finished building exceeded every one's expectation.

Mr Smith had given the closest attention to every detail. The picture of the Transfiguration was a meta-cube, geometrically related to the size of the building. The windows, the altar, even the spacing of the benches all followed some subtle rule of proportion. Mr Smith, dancing excitedly about the building, explained it to Agatha on the day the last touches were given. She could not follow him very clearly, but she felt that the chapel was unusually restful and satisfying.

Hilda had another shock when Mr Smith refused to have the factory-made brass candlesticks and crucifix on his altar. He had carved a pair of wooden candlesticks from the timber of the life-boat, and had painted them with powdered pink shell. He had also carved and painted a crucifix to match, of which the figure had the same archaic and sinister expression as the central figure of the picture. Hilda thought he must be out of his senses to use this 'home-made rubbish,' when he could have had real brass ornaments from a civilized factory.

Agatha had used the beautiful silk of Belle Macpherson's dresses to make an altar frontal. She had also made a cope, and an alb from a linen sheet. Mr Smith hammered some tins into a censer, and prepared incense from the gums of the forest. They already had tapers of wild pigs' fat.

About a week before the chapel was finished Agatha said wistfully: 'If only we had a priest to dedicate it.'

Mr Smith said: 'Any one who has been baptised and confirmed has as it were the germ of priesthood in him. I don't see why one of the men who is a full member of church should not deputize for a priest, in the same way that a sub-deacon or lay reader performs certain offices.'

'Would you do it?' asked Agatha doubtfully.

Mr Smith smiled. 'I have a certain amount of theological knowledge,' he said, 'but my bent is hardly sacerdotal. Besides, if we are to choose, *faute de mieux*, someone to deputize for a priest, I feel that we should choose the most innocent, whose faith is likely to be the most simple and strong.'

'It would be rather difficult to choose the most innocent.'

'Not at all. It's obvious.'

'Who then?' Agatha could not help feeling a little supercilious as this confidence.

'Harry, the islander.'

Agatha started.

'You don't mean to say,' she said, 'that with five European men on the island we should have to ask a native to perform a religious service. Why, we set out from Melbourne to instruct the natives.'

'You might learn a little too. If you want virtue brought into your chapel, Harry is the only one whose virtue is still whole and untroubled by doubt. He still is able to see God in clouds and hear him in the wind. If you want God brought into your chapel, he alone can do it.'

So on the morning of the Feast of the Transfiguration a procession set out from the bungalow to the new chapel. Hilda walked in front swinging the censer, from which clouds of scented smoke rose and hung in fading spirals among the stronger scents of the frangipani and the kapok trees. Behind her came Magdalene and Cecilia with tapers of wild pigs' fat. Then came Harry in his white alb and cope of red linen with orphreys of gold-coloured silk. He grinned with pleasure at his grandeur and importance. Ursula and Agatha came next, and behind them Winifred and Marinella. A little way behind walked Joe and Dick and Mr Smith. Last of all came George, ambling sheepishly, and looking self-consciously about him. Tom had refused to come, but George was unable to resist any form of entertainment.

The nuns sang as they walked:

Jerusalem, my happy home, when shall I come to thee?

They sang all the fantastic verses of this ancient hymn, including those which described the gardens of Paradise.

> There cinnamon and sugar grows,
>   There nard and balm abound.
> What tongue can tell or heart conceive
>   The joys that there are found?

As they walked their stained and faded habits brushed against flowers more brilliant, they passed beneath trees more richly laden with fruit and more sweetly scented than any the seventeenth-century poet could have imagined in his nostalgic heaven, but they were so accustomed to them that they hardly noticed them, and when they came to the lines:

> Would God I were in thee,
> Would God my woes were at an end.

Hilda's voice rose in urgent longing above that of the

other women. But it occurred to Agatha, as a spray of scarlet hibiscus brushed against her shoulder, that they had already the material conditions of paradise.

When the service of dedication, conducted in broken English by Harry, was over, the nuns entertained all the castaways excepting Tom at a sort of tea-party on the veranda of the bungalow, but the food had not much resemblance to the scones and plum cake they would have provided for a similar occasion at home.

Mr Smith had tied an iron bar to a beam projecting from the chapel roof, and this served the nuns for a bell. Hilda clanged it sharply for the six daily services, and it was rung more solemnly for the Angelus at dawn, noon, and sunset. This perpetual ringing got rather on the nerves of the men on the island. Joe said: 'I feel as if I was back at school.' Tom would shake with anger when it rang, and threaten to George to throw the bloody gong into the sea, but he never went beyond these private threats.

For a day or two after the chapel was completed everybody went about rather pleased. Now and then Dick and Joe would go and look at the building. If they met one of the nuns they would say they had just come to see that it was all right and that there was nothing left to finish off, but really they went to admire their handiwork.

'It's a damn nice little building,' said Joe.

'Pity it's not a pub,' said Dick.

But in two or three days a new spirit of restlessness fell on the community. Now that their effort was no longer concentrated on finishing the chapel, they were confronted again with the prospect of waiting for months, possibly years, until they might be rescued. Ursula suddenly refused to attend the chapel services, saying that she had to look after Marinella. This was a dreadful shock to the sisters and Hilda went round talking about apostasy. They had a worse shock when Winifred announced that she was engaged to Dick.

She naturally told Agatha first. She had to screw up her courage to tell her, but she was surprised how calmly Agatha took the news. She was a little depressed by it, but after all Winifred had taken no vows. The conditions on the island were so extraordinary that it was only natural they should effect a change of attitude. If they were rescued she might change her mind again and return to religion. If they were not rescued it might be as well for Winifred to have the protection of a decent boy like Dick.

'Well, an engagement made here is not very committal,' said Agatha. 'You can't be married till you're rescued.'

'No,' said Winifred, but she did not seem to agree.

'How can you be married?' asked Agatha, sensing her doubt.

'Can't a layman deputize for a priest when none is obtainable? I mean Harry dedicated the chapel.'

'My dear Winifred, can you really see yourself—you a novice—being married to a sailor by a black man, on this savage island, among all these heathen flowers and fruits?'

As she spoke she knew that Winifred could visualize it perfectly well, and that her indignation was flat, that the standards on which it was based were like the green leaves on the branches of a tree, of which the roots were already dead.

'It was Mr Smith's idea,' she went on resignedly, 'having Harry to dedicate the chapel. I thought that when the chapel was built it would be a centre for our religious life, that it would consolidate it. The opposite has happened. Harry is a heathen. When Harry came into the chapel, robed and wreathed in incense, I felt he was bringing some other god into the place. His face was so full of animal life, so smiling and irreverent. I believe he has dedicated the chapel to his own god, the spirit that pours its urgent life into this garden.' She spoke half angrily, half ironically.

'But surely God makes this garden grow, sister?' said Winifred. 'Just the same as any other garden.'

'I don't feel it's the same as any other garden,' said Agatha. 'But perhaps I'm going off my head.' She smiled at Winifred. 'You mustn't wear your habit any longer,' she said thoughtfully. 'I'll make you a dress of that white linen. This is an odd place to return to the world in.'

Hilda was much more horrified at Winifred's becoming engaged than at Ursula's refusing to pray, chiefly because to her sterilized mind an enjoyable sin was far more wicked than one which merely brought the sinner deprivation and suffering. It would have been a deprivation to herself to keep away from the chapel, while to be engaged suggested enjoyments so great that they could not even be thought of without a loss of virtue.

She had a conversation with Mr Smith about it, as she gathered that he was theologically minded, also, although he rather shocked her at times, she found him intellectually stimulating. They had chatted together a good deal while they were building the chapel. Sometimes she thought he was 'getting at' her, and she called him a tease. Now that the chapel was finished Mr Smith had nothing to do but talk, and he hung about the shore and the garden, waiting to pounce on any potential audience for his curious ideas, and whoever he caught went away with a feeling of vague uneasiness.

Hilda complained to him that Winifred would not have dared to become engaged if she had not been wrecked on the island. She was taking advantage of the opportunity to give up religion.

'She wouldn't have met him unless the *Princess of Teck* had been wrecked,' said Mr Smith.

'She must have seen him on the ship,' said Hilda. 'She didn't take any notice of him then. I suppose its propinquitude, but that doesn't excuse it.'

'You can't expect people to behave in the same way under entirely different conditions.'

'I do.'

'Then you are ignoring nature.'

'I should hope so, indeed,' said Hilda.

'I can imagine circumstances in which you would behave in a fashion that would astonish you.'

'Then I should be grateful if you would fetlock your imagination. We are discussing Winifred, not myself. What'll she do when we are rescued? She'll look silly then.'

'We may not be rescued. But tell me, do you think it worse to be wicked or to look silly?'

'To be wicked, of course.'

'You would rather have a whole street full of people laughing at you because, say, your petticoat slipped down as you were crossing the road, then have an evil thought of which no one knew but yourself?'

Hilda said crossly: 'I wish you wouldn't talk such impolite nonsense.'

'You seem to enjoy talking to me.'

'I don't know why I listen to you.'

'Most people listen to me.'

'You're very conceited if I may say so.'

'It's because I'm so often right.'

'You think you are right about Dick and Winifred.'

'It is all experience for them. Perhaps if we stay here for long you may follow their example. Conditions may be too strong for you. You might marry George.'

'Oh, you're horrible!' cried Hilda. 'I couldn't bear him to touch me.' She hurried back along the path, between the lines of huge shells, beneath the great clusters of bananas, the sprays of flaunting, scented flowers, beneath the high, hard enamelled sky. She was like a dim Gothic fragment lost in a riot of baroque. Her heart was beating violently.

Mr Smith amusedly watched her go. Then he noticed that Sister Agatha and Dick were talking together by guava tree. Agatha looked earnest and Dick embarrassed. He picked the guavas and rather rudely spat out the stones while he listened.

'I only want you to realize fully what you are doing before you take this step,' said Agatha.

Dick murmured something unintelligible.

'She *is* a novice you know.'

'Well?' Dick looked up with a hostile glint in his eye.

'A novice isn't a nun, of course.'

'I don't approve of nuns,' said Dick.

'I'm sorry we've earned your disapproval.'

'I don't mean I disapprove of you. I mean I don't approve of the idea of nuns. It's against nature.'

Here Mr Smith joined them.

'People talk a great deal of nonsense about nature,' he said. 'By cutting pieces off a newt in a laboratory you can produce an abnormality, a thing that has sprouted out in unusual places. But nature makes it sprout, so can you say that the abnormality is against nature? Nuns by cutting off one side of their nature achieve spiritual qualities which have a part in evolution. They may, of course, more often achieve spiritual malformations, though even these have experimental value. But there's always a frightful amount of waste in nature.'

'I don't want Winifred to be part of nature's wastage,' said Dick sharply.

'Young men are so smug,' said Mr Smith. 'They think a girl's only salvation is to be found in bed with them.'

'Shut up!' Dick went scarlet.

'You started talking about nature,' Mr Smith observed mildly.

'Well,' said Agatha nervously, 'I don't think we need become quite so biological. I was just trying to explain to Dick that though Winifred is under no vows, it is a very serious step for her to turn away from her vocation.'

'We all have to go in a given direction,' said Mr Smith, 'though there are many agreeable byways. Some people rush ahead too rapidly and take the wrong turning. Others stray into the by-ways to pick flowers and sleep together, but they have to take the main road in the end. You and Winifred are about to stroll into a by-way. You will have a delightful time for a month or two.'

'It won't be for a month or two,' said Dick. 'It will be for ever.' As he said 'for ever' a note of uncertainty crept into his voice. He stood a moment sad and silent, and then turned angrily on Mr Smith.

'What's it got to do with you, anyhow?' he demanded. 'You think you have the right to poke your nose in everywhere.'

Mr Smith smiled with melancholy detachment.

'It isn't my right,' he said. 'It's my fate, my mission in life, my horrible duty to interfere, to trip you up, to injure you, to defile you, to destroy you, so that something that is in you here, which you will not release of your own free will, may finally spread its wings and ascend to God.'

He touched Dick on the breast. Dick went pale and backed against the guava tree.

'Don't!' he cried. 'Don't do that!'

Mr Smith turned away down the path, between the rows of huge shells. Dick put his hands to his face.

'God! That man's horrible,' he said. 'Why did he touch me? I feel awful. What the hell's he doing here anyhow? Does he think he owns the bloody island? If any one's in charge here, I am. I'm an officer in the Royal Naval Reserve. Blast him!' He turned apologetically to Agatha. 'I'm sorry, sister. I don't know what I'm saying. That fellow upsets me. I reckon there's something queer about him.'

'Don't worry about him,' said Agatha kindly. 'He can't possibly do you any harm, and he's really much nicer than he sounds. He has an amazing knowledge of church history and liturgies. If you are good in yourself no one can harm you,' she added thoughtfully.

'I don't feel good after he's touched me. I feel awful. I reckon I'll go down to the beach. Sometimes this garden gets on my nerves.'

'It has that effect on me, too,' said Agatha, but he didn't take in what she said, and giving a brief nod he walked away towards the exit from the garden.

Agatha went in search of Winifred, and when she found her, said: 'Dick has gone down to the beach. Why don't you join him?'

Actually, in spite of his sympathetic manner, and his knowledge of liturgies, she did sometimes feel uneasy about Mr Smith. Whenever any one showed signs of strain, or behaved in an eccentric or evil manner, it turned out that they had spent the previous hours in his company. Although she did not believe for a moment that he would countenance such a thing, still he had spent the day with Tom and George before they burst into the bungalow. He put new ideas before people, and put things back to front to amuse himself, but he really should be more careful in choosing his audience. None of these people were sufficiently educated for him. That was the trouble.

When Dick came out of the green tunnel that led from the garden to the stream, he sat down on the bank and stared moodily at the running water. He was ashamed of himself for bursting out in that emotional fashion. He had not done such a thing since he was a child. He supposed that it came of being in love. Being in love stirred up your whole internal economy. It made all things new, and the new things had to become adjusted to each other. While this was happening you had to take care not to make a fool of yourself. Sister Agatha would think him a silly boy just when he was most anxious to prove himself a man.

When Winifred came out of the tunnel and saw Dick sitting dejectedly on the bank of the stream, she crept up quietly behind him and put her arms round his neck.

'I knew you were there,' he said.

'You should have pretended to be surprised.'

'I never pretend anything.'

'You ought to sometimes. If you always say what you think you will hurt people's feelings.'

'Not saying what you think isn't pretending.'

'Yes, it is.'

'Oh, be quiet.'

'Dick.'

He turned wretchedly towards her. 'Please. I'm sorry. I don't know what's up with me. I expect it's because I'm in love.'

'But if you're in love with me and I'm here you ought to be happy.'

'I know.'

'Well, are you in love with me?' Her voice became a little shy.

He took her hands and put them against his forehead.

'There's good in your hands,' he said. 'You could heal people with them. Smith's hands have a curse in them.'

'What an extraordinary thing to say, Dick. How could you know?'

'He touched me.'

'That couldn't hurt you. He must have touched thousands of people when he shook hands with them.'

'I felt awful when he touched me.'

'That's because you don't like him.'

'I didn't know I didn't like him till he touched me.'

'You must forget about him. Be an escapist from Mr Smith.'

Dick let her hands go.

'It's no good,' he said. 'You can't escape from things. You can't escape from yourself, ever. You can stop to pick flowers and sleep together, but you have to take the road in the end.'

'What are you talking about, Dick?'

'I don't know. I'm crackers. You see, I've never been in love before.' He flung his head down in her lap.

'Neither have I,' said Winifred quietly. She played with his hair and ears, and they sat there idling until the sudden tropical night descended.

'I'm going to bathe in the lagoon,' said Dick. 'Will you come?'

'What—to bathe?'

'Yes.'

She did not reply for a moment. 'I don't think I ought to,' she said.

'Why not?' There was a hard note in his voice.

'I don't think Sister Agatha would like me to.'

'You're not a nun now.'

'That doesn't mean I should do things that are wrong.'

'What is wrong? We don't know. We never did know, but we can't escape from our ignorance. Although we're so far away from the people who talk about right and wrong, we're no more natural than if we were in Oxford Street. We can't even bathe together without your thinking it's wrong. You can't see that what is natural is beautiful. The nuns have put a curse on you. You'll never escape it.'

'Dick, don't! Please, please! I love you,' she said, almost crying.

'If you love me, why won't you do what I want?'

'It's because I'm afraid.'

'If you love me, you can't be afraid with me. You must stop being afraid.'

'I will—if you give me a little time. But I can't all of a sudden.'

He lay before her and again put his head in her lap. After a while he said very softly: 'You seem to me like everything that's beautiful, like all nature, the flowers and the trees and the sea and the birds and the animals and the fishes, all somehow collected into one person. You are like the fur of young foxes, and beech leaves when they first come out, and apples when they are turning red on the trees. It sounds crackers. I can't describe what I mean.'

'You are like that to me, too,' she said.

'Not as much as you are to me. I couldn't be.'

'You can.'

'If I did you'ld want to bathe with me. You'ld want to bathe in me—to be me. You'ld never want to leave me, not for a moment.'

She moved his head from her lap and stood up.

'What are you doing?' he demanded.

'I must go back. It's quite dark. They'll wonder where I am.'

'Does that matter?' He rested on his hands and looked up at her. He could just see her face, dimly white against the thick darkness of the trees.

'Of course.'

He leapt to his feet.

'Can't you understand that you have nothing to do with them now—that you belong to me? You must come and live in my hut. Joe will build another.'

'We're not married.'

'What is marriage? I'll marry you now. That'll settle it.' He took her roughly in his arms.

'Don't!' she cried. 'Don't be a beast!' She pushed him away.

'So you think I'm a beast,' he said quietly. 'Perhaps I am a beast. Perhaps everything I feel about you—that you are the flowers and the sea and the secret wild animals is all beastly. Perhaps you'ld better be a nun, and I'd better be a beast, if that is my nature.'

'I don't understand you,' said Winifred miserably.

He turned up the path towards the garden. She followed a few yards behind him. At the gate he waited for her.

'You see,' he said more gently, 'I don't expect our life here is so natural after all. We've brought with us everything we did and thought before we came here.'

'Yes, I think we have,' said Winifred. 'Good night!' She touched his hand and walked on across the garden to the bungalow. The scent of the frangipani was overpowering, dominating the thousand other scents of the garden. She felt calmer, but not very happy. She felt that she understood something more about life, and that the more one understood, the more one's happiness died.

Suddenly, by the stream Harry loomed out of the darkness and she gave a jump of fright. He was hardly distinguishable in the close night, but his teeth and eyeballs shone. He wished her good-night in his soft islander's voice.

'Good night, Harry,' she said kindly. He seemed like some strange dark god, walking in the tropical garden in the cool of the evening—the only one of them who really belonged there—the only one whose body, carved in wild bronze, as well as his soul, was in harmony with those superb fruits and brilliant flowers. Yet of them all he seemed the most lonely.

Dick went to his hut, where he found Joe sharpening a spear by the light of a wick stuck in wild pig's fat. Two more spears lay beside him on the ground.

They had planned when the chapel was finished to

make a tour of exploration round the island, walking along the shore, now that they had no boat. But Dick had put it off as he did not want to leave Winifred. When he came in and saw Joe sharpening the spears he knew that he intended to set out alone.

He stood leaning against the door-post, silently watching him sharpen the spear.

'I'm coming with you,' he said after a while.

'I may be away for weeks,' said Joe.

'O.K. by me.'

'What about Winifred?'

'We need a rest from each other.'

Joe examined the point of his spear. A curious aloof stillness descended on him.

'I don't think you ought to come,' he said at last.

'Why?'

Again Joe hesitated before replying.

'Someone responsible ought to stay here.'

'There's Smith.'

'D'you think he's responsible?'

'No, I don't, as a matter of fact.'

Joe gathered up his spears and leant them against the wall.

'Come for a swim,' he said. He blew out the wick and they went out into the dark, scented garden. Above them the sky was glimmering with stars, and faint chinks of light came from the bungalow, and from the hut of the other two sailors. From the bungalow too came the women's thin voices quavering their Compline psalms.

'I hate that sound,' said Dick. 'It makes me feel queer in the stomach.' As he spoke a burst of song came from the men's hut, the first verses of a long and mildly obscene ballad.

'D'you like that any better?' asked Joe.

'I don't see why you should have to choose between extremes.'

133

Joe said, 'You haven't,' and led the way down to the sea.

In the lagoon phosphorescent fish darted about leaving trails of light. The smell of the sea mingled with the scents of the forest, and the high palm fronds moved gently against the expanse of stars. The soft breeze from the sea caressed their bodies as they ran down the sands and plunged into the warm lagoon. They raced out to the coral reef where they began to fool about, pushing each other into the water.

After about an hour they swam back to the beach and lay down on the sands.

'I don't understand girls,' said Dick. 'They upset me.'

Joe laughed. 'They upset a good many people,' he said.

'I feel as if I was torn in two,' said Dick. 'I want to get away for a bit to think—or rather to stop thinking.'

'You can't escape from your thoughts by going somewhere else. You take them with you.'

'It's funny you say that. I've just said that to Winifred. At least I said that we'd brought with us here all the thoughts we ever had before.'

'It seems to me,' said Joe, 'that we begin life with a whole lot of thoughts we've brought from somewhere else, but God knows where they come from.'

Dick did not reply. He lay staring up at the stars until he fell asleep.

Joe sat with his elbows on his knees, looking out to sea. He had been there about an hour in a kind of waking dream, when he noticed Mr Smith sitting beside him.

'What the hell!' he exclaimed.

'I hope I'm not intruding,' said Mr Smith. 'It's such a beautiful night, and so much pleasanter by the sea. You are happy here?'

'I was till you came along, if you must know.'

'But you didn't realize it till I came along. You were only unconsciously happy, like a child or an animal.'

'That's the best sort of happiness.'

'It's the most innocent sort, but it can't last. From that pure state of being you have to pass to the state of knowing. Then you have to learn to know the source of your happiness to make it endure.'

'How can I learn to know the source of my happiness?' asked Joe, interested in spite of himself.

'It lies beside you.'

'You've got the nerve of the devil.'

'That's true,' admitted Mr Smith.

'Well, supposing I do know its source, what can I do about it?' said Joe sullenly.

'You can take it, once you know where it lies. When at last, after thousands of years, you have discovered this, it seems foolish not to take it.'

'What d'you mean—after thousands of years.'

'You have lived before.'

'I thought you were a scientific sort of bloke. I didn't think you believed in that rot.'

'Wouldn't you like to know your past?'

Joe laughed lazily.

'You can tell me what you think it was, if you like.'

'You were a dish-washer in Thebes in about 4000 B.C., if I remember rightly. Most people who claim to remember previous incarnations say that they were kings or queens, or tragic princesses. Unfortunately there were not so many royalties, and a great many lady novelists and fashionable clairvoyants were at one time domestic servants. When you were a slave you used occasionally to catch glimpses of a young prince whose beauty and manner of life made him seem like a god to you. Your dreams, in which you escaped from the blows and squalor of your life, were that you should become like this god. At length you began to dream that you were him, and that your spirit and his were one, and in your sleep you had those rare moments of bliss, before you were strangled to death at the age of eighteen for refusing the advances of the under-butler's wife.

'You next were a Boeotian peasant. You still had the longing for complete union with something outside yourself, but it only resulted in your marriage to a girl with broad cheek-bones and Epstein eyes, by whom you had seventeen children. The last was an idiot which you exposed. You also had a number of children by different peasant girls. Also one by a priestess. It happened accidentally during the mysteries. Almost every one in modern Greece has a drop of your blood in their veins.

'However, this peasant life which you had chosen as a contrast to the beauty and terror of your first existence, so disgusted you that you were determined to take any risk rather than face a repetition of it, and you were next born as Canthus, the son of Abas, and you accompanied Jason in search of the Golden Fleece. On this expedition you were inspired to the most selfless heroism by your love for one of the Argonauts, Atalanta, the daughter of Schoenus, who had disguised herself as a man. When you fought by Atalanta's side you were lifted into a kind of ecstasy. You felt that the only good life was one of heroic adventure by the side of a beloved companion whose nature was the same as your own. In danger and in battle your spirits were one, and when at night you slept innocently side by side, they were one in peace and understanding. When your ship was wrecked on the coast of Africa, you saved Atalanta's life, and then you discovered that she was a woman. This for some reason instead of delighting you, as now your union could be complete, filled you with bitterness and grief, as it seemed to you that the mutual trust and understanding had not existed except in your own mind. You returned to Thessaly and died in solitude.

'Next you were a favourite pupil of Socrates, and were present when he drank the hemlock. After that you were

136

a Roman soldier, and though your life was coarse in texture, you were fairly happy in the comradeship of one Lucius. But at the siege of Jerusalem you fell backwards from the wall, and your hurtling weight killed Lucius who ran to catch you. Twice more you caused the death of what you loved—once in the time of Pepin and again in the reign of Henri Quatre. Each time it was because you demanded an unhampered love, one of the free spirit, and the spirit of course is only free in death.'

'Well, it's a good story,' said Joe uneasily. 'You make me out a nice character, bumping off all my friends. Anyhow, I can't say I remember any of 'em.'

'Even if I have put it in the form of fiction, the substance of what I have told you is true,' said Mr Smith.

Joe kicked his heels into the sand.

'What the hell ought I to do about it, then?' he asked, half seriously.

'Recognize your own nature.'

'If your nature seems to be all wrong.'

'People are apt to say things are wrong which oblige them to change their ideas. No knowledge is wrong, though it can be applied unwisely. Look at the stars. They are supposed to sing in their courses in some stupendous harmony. Their tensions keep the universe together. All the universe obeys one law, and your own nature has to function in harmony with the planets. When you have learnt the note you must strike in this infinite choir, then you will be more than happy.'

'D'you reckon he ought to come with me tomorrow?' Joe nodded towards Dick who was still sleeping soundly.

'Yes, certainly.'

'His note isn't the same as mine.'

'It harmonizes with yours. He has to learn his own nature.'

'What about his girl?'

'No individual belongs to another. He belongs to himself alone. If his note as you say were the same as yours he would belong to you, if he belonged to any one. He would belong to you by the law of the spirit. He is only hers by the law of the flesh.'

'You talk like a parson,' said Joe.

Mr Smith ignored this. 'You have the prevalent Western idea that the chief end of man is to get married, and that then they both live happily ever after. Let us play this fairly tale with Dick and Winifred. You give up your own claim on him for fear it should interfere with this sacred business of marriage. Assume we are rescued. If we are not rescued their future will probably be too fantastic for the rules of the civilized game to apply to it. Every day we remain here those rules weaken and give way to a more enduring law. Well, Dick and Winifred go back to Melbourne, or to his home in Devonshire, and are legally married. They are likely to have several children and not much money. Back in the world she may regret leaving the sisterhood. A slight odium will attach to her as the woman who was almost a nun. In fact, gossip will exaggerate as it always does, and say that she was a nun who ran away in dubious circumstances. Can you imagine how Dick's mother, a respectable Devonshire farmer's wife, will receive an Australian ex-nun as a daughter-in-law?'

'What's wrong with being an Australian?' asked Joe sulkily.

'They are not popular in England, except in wartime. However, Winifred, either in a Melbourne suburban street or in a Devonshire farmhouse, will be left alone for long periods while Dick is at sea. She will be tormented by jealousy. She will hardly believe that it is possible that he is faithful to her, and that he is not taking some other girl in a foreign country as lightly as he took her on this island.'

'You make all life sound like hell,' said Joe angrily. 'Is there nothing good, and can nothing good last? Why d'you want to contaminate us young chaps with your stale cynicism?'

'I don't want to make you cynical. I want to help you to live your life against the background of reality—not of illusion.'

Joe ran his hands through his hair. 'I'm worried,' he said.

'You are worried because you find it an effort to face reality.'

Joe turned suddenly to Mr Smith. 'Show me reality,' he said, 'and I'll face it.'

'I've shown you the reality of your own nature.'

'And what am I to do about it?'

'Act according to it. You're under no obligation to take only the few crumbs that Winifred leaves you. You have your own right. Look at Dick. What will happen to him if he marries so young? People should make love when they are young, but they shouldn't marry until they have suffered. He will miss all the free adventure he might share with you. He will become pompous and too comfortable—a silly tin god in his own villa, fatuously proud because he has reproduced himself, a thing any bull or ape can do, and of which anyhow Winifred will have the labour. Can you bear to see that happen to him? And when she has a child, she will love the child more. That is only natural—and he will be puzzled and exhausted by her demands. Unconsciously obeying her instinct she will consume his effort and his freedom, until he will cry out for his youth again. Then he will remember you, but you will have failed him. A woman is caught as a tool in the hand of Nature, but in a man the spirit is free, and ultimately it is the spirit that counts.'

'I can't make out whether you're very evil or very good,' said Joe.

'Extremes meet,' said Mr Smith.

'I'm sure there's some answer to everything you say.'

'What is it?'

'I'm not clever enough to tell you, but there are chaps who could. It's easy for a clever chap like you to win an argument against me. But I expect there are chaps as clever as you who think differently and who would win an argument against you.'

'I didn't know that we were arguing,' said Mr Smith. 'What are we arguing about?'

'Well—one thing was whether he,' he nodded at Dick, 'should come with me to-morrow.'

'Of course he should go.'

'Supposing he was killed in some way. You say I always cause the death of my chums. Then I should have to kill myself.'

'He won't be killed. I promise you.'

'How can you promise me? You're not God.'

For a moment Mr Smith looked extremely angry. Then he said calmly:

'It's not in his stars.'

'That's bunk.'

'He will not be killed,' said Mr Smith indifferently.

'Why do I believe you? Are you a hypnotist?'

'No.'

'There's something queer about you. I've never talked to any one else like I've talked to you to-night.'

'People confide in me,' said Mr Smith, 'because I don't judge them. Also because I never misinterpret what they say.'

He rose from the sands and stretched himself.

'I'm very old,' he said. 'I become stiff very easily.'

'You don't seem old,' said Joe. 'When I'm talking to you, I forget that you're any older than me. What are you—forty?'

'I'm a great deal older than that. I must go and snatch

a little sleep.' He bowed, and strolled away along the sands towards the entrance to the creek.

Joe watched him till he was out of sight. Then he lay on his back and stared up at the stars. He did not feel sleepy, and to amuse himself he tried to remember a past incarnation, but he could visualize nothing.

'It's all bunk,' he said to himself. 'Anyhow, if I can't remember it, it wasn't really me.'

Then he thought that he could not remember much that he said or did when he was six. And yet he could not say that he was not really himself at six, and that it was no use having lived then. After all, memory had not much to do with continuity. The argument became too abstruse for him, and he fell asleep.

He was awakened by Dick tugging at his arm, to make him get up and come for a swim. The sun had risen, white and blinding across the sea.

After their bathe they caught some fish. They soon had enough for their own breakfast, but Dick went on fishing as he said that he wanted to take some to the nuns.

He cleaned them in the water while Joe made a fire of sticks on the sands. When they had grilled the fish and eaten them Dick threaded the others on a small branch, and they walked back to 'Balmoral.'

Dick had been very lively so far, but as they walked up the stream he became more thoughtful.

'When do we start?' he asked.

'You're coming?'

'I told you so.'

'It's your own responsibility.'

'Of course it is. You're not my nurse, are you?'

Joe flushed. 'Sorry! I forgot you were my superior officer,' he said.

'I'm not,' said Dick. 'Don't be a fool.'

'When did you stop being my officer?'

'I dunno. When I became an artist's model for old Smith, I expect.'

'That's what we all are.'

'What?'

'Artist's models for old Smith.'

'What d'you mean?'

'Nothing. I'm just talking rot.'

Joe went to their hut, but Dick crossed the garden to the bungalow. He found Agatha on the veranda, and gave her the fish.

'Could I see Winifred?' he asked a little awkwardly.

Agatha looked surprised, but went to fetch her. When Winifred appeared Dick asked her to come down into the garden with him. She hesitated a moment as she was not yet used to the idea of a young man calling for her, but she followed him down the steps, and to that shady bank of the stream where he had first kissed her.

'I'm sorry about last night,' he said. 'You can't think straight at night.'

'I know. I was silly too.'

'I didn't say I was silly, did I?' asked Dick, a little ruffled.

They laughed together.

'I'm going away,' he said, but uncertainly, as if he were playing a rather dishonest trump card.

'Where to? There's nowhere for you to go.'

'I'm going to explore the island with Joe.'

'Will it be safe?'

'Oh yes. We might find some inhabitants or something on the other side. Some means of getting away. Then we can be married. It's getting on my nerves being stuck here and not able to be married.'

Winifred was silent.

'Don't you understand?' he demanded.

'Darling, if you tell me it is, I believe you. But you can't expect me to understand everything you feel because you feel so differently from me. I shall hate it while you're away.'

'I shan't like being away from you, of course,' said Dick. 'But you see I must get away for a bit to think. This place gets me down.'

'We'ld all like to get away from it,' said Winifred.

'I want to get away from that brute Smith,' Dick burst out suddenly.

'Mr Smith! But he's been very helpful, hasn't he?'

'I hate him. He's bad. You never know what's right or wrong when you're talking to him.'

'But you're going to leave us in his care!'

'I've thought about that. It worried me a bit at first, but you see it's only his talk that can hurt you, and you're always with Sister Agatha and the nuns. He can't get at you like he gets at us. I expect he'll keep the men in order all right, and Harry's a good boy. He'll do anything for me, and I'll pass him the word.' He paused. 'Joe and I might find a port of something on the other side of the island. But if we don't, when I come back I'm going to marry you. See?'

'But how can you?'

'D'you mean to tell me that with all these nuns and all this singing and that gong going all day, you can't fix up some sort of a wedding? In Scotland you can get married by just saying together: "We're married." Well, we'll be married like that if there's no other way. D'you mean to say that if we had to spend the rest of our lives here we could never be married—simply because there isn't a parson or a registry office here? If that's morality I'm immoral.'

Winifred put a hand on his breast.

'Dick,' she said, 'if you don't go on this expedition we'll be married like that now if you like, to-day.'

There was a leap of light in his eyes, but almost immediately he looked distracted and miserable.

143

'We'll pick some fruit and flowers,' she said, 'and have a party, and Mr Smith can marry us.'

'No,' said Dick, 'I won't have that old sod marry us. He'ld put a blight on us. I'ld rather have Harry like you had for the chapel.'

He took her hand from his breast, and played with her fingers.

'Smith touched me there,' he said, 'just as you did. It was horrible.' He puckered his forehead in a worried fashion. 'Look, darling,' he said, 'I must go with Joe. I've told him I would. I can't back out. And we might find a village or some means of getting away, then you'll be glad I went.'

'I hate your going,' said Winifred, 'and I shan't rest till you return. You may meet savages, or bathe where there are sharks, or fall down a cliff, or be bitten by snakes or some poisonous spider.'

'Well, if you cross a street in a town you may be run over by a bus. It's extraordinary what some chaps get away with while others are killed going to their offices in the city. Anyhow, I don't suppose we'll be gone more than a month.'

'A month!' She went pale. 'I can't imagine how you can leave me for a month in this place. I couldn't leave you.'

'I don't want to leave you,' he said.

'Then why go?'

'Listen! When you went to be a nun I don't suppose your father liked it, did he?'

'No. He didn't.'

'You loved your father, didn't you?'

'Yes.'

'But you went to be a nun all the same. Well, I feel about going with Joe like you felt about going to be a nun. It's something I've just got to do. I can't help myself. I wouldn't respect myself if I didn't go. See?'

'Yes, I do see,' said Winifred.

He looked at her thoughtfully.

'I'll tell you what,' he said. 'We could be married to-day like you said, and Joe and I needn't start till to-morrow.'

'No,' Winifred answered slowly, looking down at his feet.

'Why not?'

'You know why not,' said Winifred. 'If you feel about going with Joe like I felt about being a nun, you couldn't be married first, hurriedly, for a day, grabbing a little of everything. It wouldn't be fair to any one.'

'There's something between us,' he cried angrily.

'I didn't put it there.'

'I know. I'm not blaming you. It's me. It's Joe. It's this place. I don't know what it is.' He turned away from her and found himself facing the smooth trunk of a loquat tree.

'See this tree,' he said. 'Cut a nick in it for every day I'm away, and if I'm away more than twenty-eight days you can ask me to do anything you like, and I promise to do it. If I'm two days over you can ask me to do two things, and if I'm six days over you can ask me to do six things, but that's an easy promise as I shan't be any days over.'

'D'you know the first thing I shall ask you?'

'No.'

'To become Catholic.'

'Why do maggots eat us?' he exclaimed. 'Why do I get this maggot of going with Joe? Why do you get the maggot of being Catholic? Why can't we just live?'

He held her closely, roughly, and kissed her. He released her as suddenly and strode away across the garden.

5

Joe and Dick left the settlement about half an hour later, so as to cover some distance before the worst heat of the day. The nuns were excited when they heard that the two young men were going exploring and they all came down to the beach to see them off—except Winifred, who had said good-bye to Dick and did not want to have to do so again publicly.

Agatha drew Dick aside.

'We shall be anxious about you,' she said. What shall we do if you don't return within a week or so? Shall we send the men after you?'

'No. I doubt if they'd go,' said Dick. 'We must take our chance. But we'll be quite all right. There's no need to worry. You'll keep Winifred cheerful, won't you?'

'I'll do my best,' said Agatha, but she was a little irritated by his assumption that a woman's moods could be so easily regulated.

Hilda fussed about with exaggerated optimism.

'I'm sure they'll find a village or something,' she said. 'I shouldn't be at all surprised if they came upon a real township on the other side of the island with steamers calling regularly. If you ask me, I think they should have gone to look for it sooner.'

Joe and Dick set out along the shore in a south-easterly direction. They were carrying only their spears, fishing-tackle, and, slung on their backs, shoes made of wild pigskin in case they should come to rocks or rough ground. At present they went barefoot on the sands, and being so lightly clad and laden they walked with a free, swinging stride.

The nuns stood in a group waving to them. Their habits, stained and faded to a greeny black, some of them patched with squares of red linen, fluttered in the wind. Joe turned and gave a farewell wave of his hand.

'Find us a nice comfortable steamer,' called Hilda.

'That woman's optimism makes me certain we won't find anything,' he said.

'She doesn't count. She's a bit cracked,' said Dick.

'If anything makes me mad it's someone else counting my chickens before they're hatched.'

They walked for some miles along the hard, sandy beach, and the farther behind they left 'Balmoral,' the higher their spirits rose.

At about midday they went for a swim, after which they made a meal of bread fruit, sitting in the shade of some rocks.

'If ever you've wanted to be free, you're free now,' said Joe. 'We have no human restriction at all. We haven't got to work, only to pull the fruit off the trees and catch the fish. This is paradise.'

'Your memory is a sort of restriction,' said Dick.

'Mine isn't. It just provides a pleasant contrast. I knew a bloke—something like Smith he was—an educated sort of chap. He said we wouldn't be really civilized until we'd reached what he called "enlightened anarchy," when every one could do what he liked, but when what he liked didn't hurt any one else. I reckon we're really civilized because we're enlightened anarchists.'

'I thought an anarchist was a bloke who threw bombs,' said Dick.

'No. He's only a bloke who doesn't want to be bossed.'

Later in the afternoon they had to climb over a small promontory of rocks, to reach the sands on the other side. Joe was ahead of Dick, who, happening to look up, saw a long tentacle whip up over the rock, trying to reach Joe's leg. He gave a yell and Joe turned, saw the octopus, and leapt away up the rock. They climbed to a vantage point from where they could look down safely on the creature. It was lying, partly concealed by a ledge of rock, in a round pool which would be covered by the sea at high tide.

'God, what a brute! I'm all of a sweat,' said Joe. 'If it had got me you couldn't have done anything. You would have just had to sit here and watch it chew me up.'

Dick looked as if he were going to be sick. 'We ought to kill it,' he said. 'We could spear it.'

'That wouldn't kill it. You have to turn 'em inside out, which would need a bloody Hercules.'

'It would die in time.'

'It's not decent to kill things slowly.'

'It would have killed you slowly—and me, too, if it had got the chance—the sod!' Dick's eyes blazed with hatred and anger.

'You don't want to lose your temper with a fish,' said Joe. 'It's just a bit of nature.'

They tramped on till late in the evening. Dick at intervals exclaimed about the repulsiveness of the octopus, and repeated that they should have tried to kill it somehow, and suggested various ways in which it might have been done.

This was the only danger they experienced for some days, although at times they risked thirst, but a number of small streams, like that by the settlement, ran down from the high mountain to the sea.

The island proved to be much larger than they had imagined and even after three or four days walking the outline of the central mountain changed very little. They lost count of time, and once or twice Dick was vaguely worried thinking that he might be longer than the twenty-eight days, and that he would not know when they ought to return. He cut a small stick on which he put a nick every day at sunset, but he only began to do this after they had been walking for a few days, and he was not certain whether he had begun with the right number.

Joe, who had talked a good deal on the first day, had become more and more silent, until now they seldom spoke. But they seemed to agree instinctively when to rest, when to bathe, and when to go into the forest in search of food. Once they were lost in the forest for a whole afternoon. Dick became rather frightened, but Joe seemed to have acquired an inner tranquillity which nothing could disturb. His eyes had the clear serenity of a wild animal's eyes. Sometimes Dick caught an expression of intense happiness on his face. It was more than happiness. It was as if his whole body had been touched by some flame of poetry, as if his body and spirit had become perfectly poised and attuned to the natural world. All his movements were graceful and sure. When Dick felt this serenity in Joe he became very happy himself, but it was only a reflected happiness. He did not feel in the same way that it had its source in his own perfect adjustment.

When they had been travelling for seven days they came to the broad mouth of a river, about a hundred yards wide. There was what appeared to be a rock or a log lying out in the middle of the stream. In the west the brilliant colours of sunset were just beginning to stain the sky.

Joe plunged into the river a little lower down than the log and swam across. Dick sat down to tie his slight equipment together to fix it on his back. The string had broken, and he dawdled on the bank of the river mending it, stopping at intervals to look back at the amazing sunset. Joe reached the other side, brushed the spray from his body, and turned to watch Dick swim across, but Dick was still looking at the sky, and had not yet started. The log in the middle of the stream suddenly moved, swirled, and disappeared below the surface, and Joe realized that it was an alligator.

He shouted across to Dick, who thought he was hurrying him, and he strolled down to the water's edge to swim across. Joe shouted again, but Dick seemed unaware that he was being warned and walked on into the creek. Joe waved his arms and signalled to him to go back, but it was rapidly becoming dusk, and Dick, bemused by gazing at the brilliant sky, could not see what he meant. Joe realized that the only way he could stop Dick was by swimming back himself. When he saw him returning he would probably wait for him. He ran back into the river and began to swim rapidly across. He lifted his head and saw Dick, standing on the opposite bank, watching him. Half-way across the giant jaws seized him and dragged him below the water. He felt a prolonged piercing agony of his body, and an awful suffocation. Everything he saw was scarlet. Then the scarlet changed to golden light, and the piercing agony of his body to a piercing joy of soul. In the golden light he saw Mr Smith, who somehow had become the personification of evil. Beside him was the personification of good, and then the two blended into one being, transfigured by light.

Joe's pain and his joy became one thing. He saw all the good and evil he had known as one thing, and then he realized that he himself was one, and there was no more doubt nor conflict in him. His body and mind seemed to dissolve into the light, and he was no longer an individual, but only a vibration, a note of music, a beam of light.

*

Dick sat on the bank of the creek all through the night. Occasionally he dozed, but he soon awakened to try to grapple with the realization of what had happened. He stared at the place in the river where Joe had given a cry and disappeared. He knew that Joe had deliberately swum back through the alligator-infested creek to save him. He felt that this demanded some terrific response from himself of which he was incapable. Now and then he groaned, not with grief at the loss of his friend, but at his own intellectual inability to adjust himself to the circumstance. At one stage this sense of inadequacy became so painful to him that in resentment he blamed Joe, and exclaimed aloud:

'The silly damned fool.'

He then felt even more ashamed of himself. He felt that he should have done something to save Joe, although he knew that this was impossible, and that it would have been suicide to have plunged into the stream to go to the rescue. Joe would not have wanted him to do this as it would have made his own sacrifice useless. He felt further entangled in shame at using this argument, and his tension became so great that he shouted a stream of curses. They echoed and died away eerily up the dark river, and he was horrified that the only words he had said over his friend's grave were filthy oaths.

He remembered when he was a boy reading about two young men who were bathing in Sydney harbour. One was seized by a twelve-foot shark. The other dived in, attacked the shark, and dragged his friend away, at the cost of a leg. He had been uncomfortable at reading about it, as he felt that he could never bring himself to do the same thing. It seemed that the things that struck you forcibly when you were young, were things which would somehow apply to you when you were older, although you had no idea of it at the time.

At last the sudden dawn flared across the sea. Dick crawled into the shade of some trees and went to sleep.

He awoke at noon from a dream that he was on a

holiday on Dartmoor, and that he had crossed a bog and could not get back, and was likely to be marooned there for the night. When he awoke to see the dazzling tropical sunlight on the river, and on the lacquered green trees, he had a sense of relief that he was not really lost on the grey and dangerous moor, but the awareness of his true situation following immediately on his relief, made him feel as if a black, almost physical weight were being pressed down upon him.

He went down to wash in a pool, and as he bent over it he started at his reflection. In his mental distress he had forgotten his appearance. He knew that he had a beard, and that his skin was brown, but he had somehow expected his face to be familiar. But his face was a darker brown than the bleached gold of his hair and beard, which framed it like a startling aureole, a kind of sun-burst—and his blue eyes were arresting, staring tragically from the dark face. His body, naked, shining, superbly developed, was like that of a native. He plunged into the pool to destroy the image. It was too bizarre. It destroyed his identity as Dick Corkery, a Devonshire farmer's son, and identified him with some kind of ancient European savage, a Tartar or a Scythian.

He remained by the river for two days, in an agony of indecision. He was ashamed to return to the settlement, to have to announce that Joe had been killed while trying to save him. What would Winifred think of him? He was sure she would despise him. In the small hours of the morning he felt that he could never return to face them all, the nuns and that swine Smith. What would Smith say? Now he could not bear even the thought of Smith.

If he did not return what would happen to him? He would stay here going crazy in solitude. Perhaps in twenty years' time some ship would call and find him, wild, dirty, and gibbering. He would become horrible.

He had this vision in the middle of the night, but in a panic he rose and set out at once, back along the coast the way they had come. He walked for two or three days, and then began to feel an impulse to return to the river. He did not know how long he had been away, as after Joe's death he had forgotten to cut the nicks in the stick. He found that he was still carrying it, and he threw the useless bit of wood away.

At last he came to the rock where they had seen the octopus, and he knew that the settlement was now only a day's journey. He climbed on to the rock above the pool, and saw the octopus still lying there under its ledge. All his detestation of the obscene creature returned. He half blamed it for his present plight. All his hatred, his repudiation, every destructive impulse he had was focused on the octopus. He made a vow to himself that he would not return to the settlement until he had killed it. When he had made that vow he had a sense of peace.

It was evening when he arrived at the rock, and he decided to wait until the morning to begin the attack. He went a little way into the forest to cut new spears, and he spent some hours sharpening them before he went to sleep.

In the morning he approached the rock and stood looking down on the octopus, soon to be his victim. It gave such an impression of evil power that it was some time before he could muster the courage to launch the first spear. He was afraid of discovering that his weapons were ineffective. At last he took aim at one of the creature's eyes and hurled the wooden spear. He was so nervous that he missed his aim by some inches, and the spear, weighted with no metal point, did not penetrate deeply enough to inflict more than a slight wound, but the effect was terrific. At once the pool became dark with the ink shot out by the octopus, and the huge tentacles waved and lashed about in the black water, and whipped up the rock towards Dick, who jumped back and ran some yards along the sands, where he waited, pale with fright. Normally he had plenty of courage and he had more than once been apparently close to death without showing fear. It was not now so much any danger from the octopus that he feared. His reason told him that if he kept well out of reach of its tentacles it could not harm him. What he feared was the sight of those white limbs writhing in the black water. They had for him an obscenity which made the whole of life and nature seem evil. He thought perhaps that Joe was right, and that the only thing to do was to avoid the evil thing and let it be. He had a moment of temptation to do this, but he knew that if he did so he would never again trust his own courage. He forced himself to return to the rock. The octopus had calmed down. Its tentacles showed here and there like the roots of a tree above ground, but he could not see its head in the black clouded water. One of the tentacles made a slight movement, and again Dick jumped away, and then despised himself for his lack of nerve.

There was nothing he could do while the head of the octopus was hidden. At noon it would be high tide, which would cover the rocks and wash away the black fluid from the pool. Dick went up into the shade of the forest to wait until the afternoon before making another attack. As he flung himself down under a palm he saw that his legs were splashed with black drops, and he ran down to the sea to wash them before he could rest. He leant against the trunk of a palm tree, and watched the breaking waves slowly encroach farther on the sands, until their racing fringes touched the line of dry seaweed which marked the last high tide. He romanticized himself. He remembered a picture he had seen of a young knight watching before the altar in preparation for some ordeal. He felt it a symbol of his own situation, not that he ever prayed. He disliked the idea that his independence of mind and action could be influenced by an unseen being. It produced in him an unpleasant sensation, not very different from the revulsion he felt from the obscenity of the octopus. The idea that the octopus with its thick white twisting limbs should touch and entangle his own free body was more dreadful to him than the thought of the actual death which would follow. As he wanted his body to be free, moving in the sunlight, so he wanted his mind to be free to decide in its own light of reason. He hated darkness. He hated what was unseen.

The wind which waved the fronds of the palm trees against the hot high sky ruffled his bleached hair. His pupils as he stared out at the brilliant sea were narrowed to pin points, so that he had an extraordinary wild ferocity of appearance, like someone who was born to kill. And yet as the waves began to recede, so his heart sank, and he dreaded the return to the rock, and half hoped that the octopus, having been attacked in its pool, would have left it, and have gone out with the tide.

At about four o'clock in the afternoon the rocks were again quite bare. Dick took his spears and climbed up to where he could look down into the pool which was now as clear as glass. The octopus was still there. The spear had not stuck in its head, and had evidently floated away on the tide. He could see the trivial wound that it had made.

Dick began to tremble. The creature had suddenly acquired a horrible fascination for him, and he had an impulse to fling himself into the pool and end this tension. He climbed down the rock and went along the sands to pull himself together. He wondered if he were going mad from the sun or from solitude. It seemed to him now that it would be an outrageous effrontery for him to attempt to kill the octopus. He felt as if he were ranging his puny strength, his petty individuality, against some essential force of nature. He avoided contact with God in prayer, contact with the spiritual force greater than himself, and yet he had undertaken contact and conflict with this greater physical force, and one which in some horrible way was also spiritual.

'I'm mad. I'm off my head,' he said aloud, and shutting out all argument and fear he raced back to the rock, and making his body simply an instrument of his will he hurled a second spear at the creature's head. The result was the same as before. The black ink shot in thick clouds into the clear water. The writhing tentacles lashed up grey spume.

Dick, when he came to himself on the sands a few minutes later, found that he was covered with this beastly spray, and he ran into the sea to wash it off. But now even the sea which bred and sheltered such creatures seemed evil to him, and he hurried away from it, up under the palm trees where he fell into an exhausted sleep.

He awoke to find himself looking up through the eternal waving palm fronds at the morning sky. At first he looked around for Joe, and then, as the realization of all that had happened in the past week came to him, he felt a kind of deadening of his mind. He rose slowly, stretched himself, and walked down the beach. In the east the sun was rising behind a headland, which loomed dark and cool against a vast splendour of rose and green. The beach itself and the forest were still in shadow, but out at sea the waves were dancing and glistening in the morning light. The breeze was still cool on his skin. He stared wondering about him, at the distant line of light on the sea, at the astonishing blaze of dawn behind the headland, and the waving feathery silhouette of the palm fronds against it.

He thought of cold grey dawns on Dartmoor, but without much nostalgia. It seemed to him no longer his natural home, but part of another life, another world which he had left far behind, and which would now prove insipid. With all its danger and insecurity he felt that he belonged to this life on the island, and that he would suffocate elsewhere. Here his body and soul had made sharp contacts which tested and formed them. As his body had become as nature designed it, his beard grown and bleached, his skin naked and brown, his every muscle proportionately developed in free movement, so he felt his spirit was growing untrammelled towards its natural pattern, its instinctive vibration, like a piece of dried seaweed which placed in water unfolds into some beautiful frond or star. Even the fear he felt, his horror at the death of Joe, his dread of the octopus, when it was past, released some tendril of his spirit so that he became more wise and free.

As he stood on the cool-shadowed beach, with the resplendent dawn behind him, the dazzling sea ahead, standing as it were in the centre of a vast reflective shadow with the brilliant urgency of life as a distant promise, the knowledge of this worked in him to make him accept his coming conflict with the octopus. He knew that it was his lot, and that if he killed the octopus his spirit would unfold a further stage, and that if he was killed, that too in some way would be inevitable. But he knew that he would not be killed unless he allowed fear to dominate him. And yet Joe had been killed in the very moment of contempt for fear. This thought deepened his reflection. To accept death in contempt of fear was perhaps the final freedom.

He went back up the beach to where he had left his spears, his small red linen haversack, and his sandals. As he picked up the spears he noticed that Joe's spears, which he had been carrying, were straighter, of harder wood, and better balanced than his own. He had not used them before, having a sentimental reluctance to part with them, but now he decided to use one against the octopus.

He climbed the rock, and looked down into the pool which was once more cleared by the tide of the black liquid. The octopus still lay under its ledge, and he felt its eyes watching him. A huge tentacle squirmed up the rock towards him, but he felt a sense of power and of indifference to danger. He launched Joe's spear, and with a leap of his heart which forced an involuntary cry from his throat he saw the spear go straight and deep into the creature's eye. It shot out its black fluid, its tentacles gave a few convulsive lashes, and it was dead.

In his excitement he ran back to the sands. He longed to tell somebody what he had done. He shouted: 'O God! O God!' and burst out laughing. He lay on the sands and laughed and hugged his knees. He was enormously proud of himself, more than he had been at any other time of his life. Now he could return to the settlement. He picked up his few things, strapped his red sack on his back, and set out westwards along the beach. Before he left he took a last glance at the octopus, lying in its black pool, with Joe's spear sticking up from its pierced eye, but somehow now the sight gave him no pleasure, and he frowned and turned quickly away. Then later, as he walked homewards, he thought of his skill and he sang aloud.

In the middle of the day he had a swim, ate a breadfruit, and went to sleep in the shade. When he awoke he felt a strange depression, and when he remembered what he had done he could not understand why he did not still feel exultant. He wished he could tell Joe that he had killed the octopus. But Joe had said they should leave it alone to live its own life.

Was the octopus better as it had been before he came, alive in the clear water or was it better as he had left it, dead in its black juice? Soon it would begin to stink frightfully. The brute had tried to get Joe. The alligator had got Joe. The only way he could get even with them was by killing the octopus. He had visited the sins of the alligator on the octopus. It was only when you tried to injure the octopus that it squirted out black juice. But the brute would destroy you if you got too close to it.

He was going crackers. What was he arguing about? The bloody brute was dead. That was the main thing. And he had killed it, and that was the least he could do to avenge Joe. But did Joe want to be avenged?

'Oh, shut up arguing!' he shouted to himself.

Anyhow, he couldn't face them at the settlement unless he had killed something, and if old Smith was going to sneer at him let him go and kill a bloody octopus himself.

At sunset he was only a few miles from the settlement. He sat down partly to rest, to compose himself before appearing among men again, partly from habit to watch the familiar gorgeous spectacle. He marvelled at its splendour, at the changing crimson and green, the gold and the purple. The prodigal splendour of life in this place intoxicated him. It stirred him in a curious way, half-sensual and half-religious, as if he were to see the naked body of an infinitely beautiful woman, one too lovely for him to dare to love her. And as he felt his being stirred by this worship he became suddenly aware of the infinite beauty of living forms, and even as he became aware, he thought of the octopus lying dead in the black pool, where soon it would begin to stink, and the depression returned to him.

He wanted to put his head between Winifred's breasts and to weep there—not to make love to her, but to be comforted—not to make love to her because he had killed the octopus, the living thing, and he felt that he would bring death with his love.

6

Although before he had set out with Joe, the settlement had seemed the remote and savage refuge of castaways, now as he picked out familiar land-marks, just visible in the rapidly fading light, the line of the coral reef, the headland that hid the creek entrance, he had the same sense of peace and security, mingled with excitement at the prospect of a reunion, that he had known as a boy returning from school, when he had left the bus at the corner of the Dartmoor lane, and dumping his playbox and heavy luggage by the roadside to be collected later, he had raced down between the steep banks of foxgloves, simmering, bursting with love for his mother and his dog, which when it got wind of him, would tear to meet him in a mad intoxication of welcome, jumping to lick his face, and then, overwhelmed and whimpering with the ecstasy of the moment, would writhe, retreat, and hesitate in an agony of delight.

He rested for an hour or more after sunset, and then set out on the last stage of his journey. As he approached the headland he noted with surprise that there was still a red glow in the sky beyond it. He thought it must be some kind of prolonged after-glow of the sunset, though it was too late for that, but the light did play queer tricks in the tropics. As he drew closer he thought his head was throbbing, until with a start he realized that he was listening to the insistent monotonous beat of a drum. When he reached the headland he saw that the glow in the sky came from the beacon, which had been lighted, and he stared out to sea, thinking there must be a ship passing, which the castaways were trying to attract.

Now, in addition to the beating of the drum he heard singing and occasional wild shouts. There were people dancing round the bonfire—at this distance little black silhouettes. Not quite knowing who or what they might be, he approached more cautiously, keeping in the shadow of the fringe of palms. The rhythm of the drum stirred a queer kind of excitement in his own blood. The singing was dominated by a male voice of extraordinary vitality, and followed the rhythm of the drum.

There was a body suspended over the fire—roasting, turning on a spit. He could see that the people dancing round the fire were naked, and with a surge of horror he thought that cannibals must have landed in canoes or come from the interior of the island, and had killed and were eating his companions.

Fear succeeded his horror, and he stood there, resisting the impulse to run for his life. After the first shock of fear he remembered Winifred, and his fear evaporated. He moved swiftly into the fringe of trees, and crept along towards the creek entrance and the bonfire.

When he came close enough to identify the naked dancers he experienced a different kind of horror. They were his fellow castaways, and the roasting body was only that of a wild pig.

Harry the islander seemed to be the leading spirit of the orgy. He shouted and chanted his wild songs, all the time dancing rhythmically round the bonfire, but it was Mr Smith who set the rhythm, beating on a huge pigskin drum. Harry seemed to be completely himself for the first time since Dick had known him, completely the animal, but magnificent, wild and free, possessed by the spirit of all animals, but the animal become conscious of itself, of its power, its lust, its liberty.

The others were intoxicated by him. Hilda's shrill laugh had become a wild cackle. Magdalene leered and swayed as she danced, her movements flowing with a kind of evil poetry. Mr Smith sat at the drum, his face smiling and glistening with the effort of his incessant beating, but he was the only one who appeared to be still himself, still a self-possessed human and not an animal caught in howling lust.

Dick stood at the entrance to the creek and watched them. He felt his blood beating faster in his veins with the beating of the drum. He half moved forward as if drawn against his will towards the orgy, but again the thought of Winifred came to him, and he had an illusion that he heard her singing a bar of that plain-song music which normally he disliked, but which now was like a fountain of limpid water, cooling his blood.

He brushed his hand across his eyes and turned up the creek, feeling his way into its overhung gloom, though for a short distance it was faintly lighted by the glow from the bonfire. He had just passed beyond this light when a scream from the bank made him jump. It came from Marinella, who, as he approached her, backed away still screaming.

'What's the matter?' he asked, and took her arm. At first she seemed terrified of him, but soon her screaming subsided to fitful sobs, and he managed to extract from her that she had escaped from Agatha and Winifred, and had followed the other women to the feast, but when she got there she was frightened by the drum and by Harry's singing, and had run away.

'Where is Sister Agatha?' he asked.

'In the bungalow.'

'And Winifred?'

'She's there too.'

'Why didn't you go to them?'

'I was frightened of the path,' said Marinella. 'It was dark.'

He took her hand and led her up the creek, and into the tunnel through the forest. He had to feel his way slowly.

The sound of the drum penetrated even here, and Marinella began to cry again.

At last they came into the garden. The scent from the exotic trees was sweet and heavy on the night air. The glow from the bonfire on the shore was in some curious way reflected from above, down into the garden, so that the flowers and trees were bathed in a rosy dusk. He could see the huge blooms of the zinnias, the mauve shining more palely, the red and yellow almost black. The melons and marrows, hanging among their enormous leaves and giant tendrils, loomed like a drunken gardener's dream. To Dick this riot of life and richness of fragrance was a kind of affront, because he felt that half of himself was dead.

The bungalow and the other huts were in darkness, but a faint light came from the chapel door, and he led Marinella over there, knowing that there he would find Agatha and Winifred. As they approached they heard the quiet murmur of voices, coming out with the rectangle of pale light into the garden. It was as if the quiet voices and the pale light were a solitary thing, one feeble protest of the disciplined spirit against the riot of life in the garden, the distant shouting of the flesh on the shore, the throbbing of the drum, and beyond it all the steady thunder of the breakers, a reminder of the natural force which might at any moment, ignoring flesh and spirit, assert its own eternal senseless power.

Dick and Marinella were barefoot so that they came silently up to the door of the chapel and stood there unnoticed, watching the two women recite their office. The light from the two tapers of wild pig's fat illuminated the picture over the altar, the 'Transfiguration,' with its portraits of Dick and Joe, and its sinister Siennese Christ. Mr Smith had used powdered mother-of-pearl in the paint for Joe's body, and now some curious effect of the light gave it a faint glow, and the whites of the Christ's eyes also had a luminous quality. Dick had never been in the chapel at night before, and this effect startled him.

Agatha and Winifred were facing the altar, with its frontal made from the silk of Belle Macpherson's dress, on which Hilda had embroidered the symbols of the Passion. There were no flowers, perhaps because Agatha felt that their life here should be a continual Lent, or possibly because the flowers of the garden were no longer for her the creation of the Christian's God.

'By the waters of Babylon,' murmured Agatha, 'we sat down and wept, we remembered thee, O Sion.'

These words, which Dick had heard so often with indifference or boredom in the church at home, heard in this setting remote from all the rather stuffy associations of the rector and the village choir, seemed to him infinitely beautiful and sad, and yet it was a sadness which did not touch him deeply, because he felt that it was a nostalgia for something so remote that it had no relation to their present circumstances. He stood watching, calmed by tranquil sadness, as on a hot day one may enjoy for a moment a breeze which passes, but which cools one for no longer than it lasts.

The curious peace of the moment was broken by Marinella. As Winifred ended the psalm, saying: 'Happy shall he be that taketh thy children: and dasheth them against the stones,' Marinella ran forward, and weeping loudly flung her arms round Agatha, who hushed her impatiently and ended the service with a collect and a perfunctory reference to the faithful departed. Then she turned to Marinella and said:

'Where is Sister Ursula? What are you doing here?'

'She's on the beach,' sobbed Marinella. 'She's horrible. They're all horrible.'

Agatha turned instinctively, to listen to the incessant throbbing of the drum, as if that could tell her something. Winifred noticed her look of sudden amazement, and she too turned and saw Dick standing in the dark, open square of the doorway. His body was that of a native. His hair and beard were longer and more wild than when he had left, and their aureole made a more startling contrast with his brown face. With all his arresting physical beauty his face was tragic, his blue eyes wide and sad, and at her first glance Winifred gave an involuntary cry, which was not one of pleasure nor of surprise, but almost of grief, as if in some way he had passed beyond her. His beauty made him seem too dear for her possessing, and his tragic face, young and yet seeming to know so much, gave him a quality which she had not sensed before in any human being, and made him appear to belong to another age and civilization, where the soul and the body were evolved to a tension of beauty beyond man's present achievement, to contemplate which tore the heart. She stood still, unable to move forward to greet him.

Agatha too felt that he had acquired some strange new personality. Even Marinella, now when for the first time she saw him in the light, forgot her sobbing, and like the two women was still with surprise.

Dick said: 'Winifred!' and the spell was broken. She moved down the chapel to him, and he took her hand. At her touch he felt a terrible weight lifted from his heart and mind, and he longed to go to sleep. Agatha saw the expression of his face change. The illusion of superhuman beauty left him, and he appeared an ordinary tired young man. Marinella recovered from her momentary surprise and began to whimper again.

Agatha led her over to the bungalow, and tucked her up in bed. Almost immediately she fell asleep, and Agatha returned to the chapel.

Left alone Dick and Winifred sat, holding each other's hands, on one of the benches which had been a thwart in the life-boat from the *Princess of Teck*.

'This is the twenty-eighth day,' she said after a while. 'I longed for you to come. It has been awful.'

He did not know how long he had been away. It had seemed a very long time, but now that he was back it did not seem so long since he had left.

'Then you can't ask me to do anything,' he said and smiled.

'There may be too much for you to do without my asking,' she said. 'I feel as if something awful was going to happen.' She looked at his face and ran her hand across his eyes. 'You looked so different when you came in. You were like yourself, but as if you had acquired a different soul. It startled me.'

'What d'you mean?'

'I don't know. It was just something I felt when I saw you. But it's all right now. You're the same, but your hair is longer.'

'I don't feel quite the same. I'm so tired.'

'You didn't find anything—any village or people?'

'No.'

Agatha came back into the chapel.

'Where is Joe?' she asked.

Dick stood up. Again that look of tension, of aloofness, of tragic beauty came upon him. He let fall Winifred's hands and she stared at him, afraid.

'He's dead,' he said. 'He was killed.'

Agatha said wearily: 'We seem to be nearly down to zero,' but Winifred felt a sudden relief, and was confusedly ashamed of herself.

'Oh, how horrible life is!' she cried bitterly.

Dick thought she was distressed for Joe, and a warmth of gratitude was added to his love. He sat down again beside her and put his arm round her shoulder.

'It will be all right,' he said tenderly. 'We can't have come through so much for it not to come right in the end.'

166

Agatha turned away, and looked at the portrait of Joe in the altar-piece. She crossed herself.

'What did you find?' she asked Dick after awhile.

He looked up from Winifred.

'Nothing,' he said.

'I was afraid you wouldn't. It didn't seem possible. And Joe—what happened?'

Dick told them of the journey, of their first encounter with the octopus, and of the river infested with alligators, and of how Joe had plunged into it again to save him, and of how, on the way back, to avenge Joe he had killed the octopus.

'It was a pretty tough job,' he added, hoping they would sense behind this laconic remark that he too had shown a fair amount of courage.

When he had finished speaking Agatha said thought-fully:

'I don't think Joe would have wanted to be avenged. I think that he had accepted every condition of life and so he was ready to leave it. You say he was very happy on the journey?'

'Yes,' said Dick, but grudgingly, feeling that Agatha was minimizing his own effort. He would not have minded so much if he had not himself thought that perhaps it was useless. It was damned silly really. How could the life of an octopus compensate for Joe's life? But that was not why he had killed it. He had done it to prove his courage to himself. He should not have told them about it. It had only to do with his inner self, and by revealing it he had somehow weakened again his inner self which he thought he had strengthened by the deed.

'What has happened here?' he asked brusquely, to get away from the subject.

'What hasn't happened?' exclaimed Agatha. 'As soon as you had left Mr Smith went round telling every one that they should enjoy themselves, and lead a fulfilled life, as he calls it. He said it all in that cultivated, detached manner which makes one unsuspicious of what mischief he's up to. He told the men it was foolish to subscribe to the artificial conventions of a society from which they had fortunately escaped. He flattered Hilda so that all her silly suppressed vanity came to the surface, and now she is always exclaiming: 'Oh, Mr Smith!' and bursting into hysterical laughter. He corrupted Cecilia and Magdalene with some beastly decadent poetry, which he recited to them in the scented corners of this dreadful garden. I think his insinuations to Ursula were more gross. And then he made that drum and taught Harry to dance and sing to it. Harry was only too apt a pupil. Mr Smith said that he had learned the rhythm and the songs in Haiti. Heaven knows where he hasn't been. But all the time his conversations with me were intelligent and sympathetic, and I couldn't feel that he was a humbug. He seems to reflect what one wants oneself to be. He's like a mirror—its extraordinary. It's only when he's not with me that I see how vile he is. And yet while he has been giving me quite good advice how to cope with these bad and crazy people, all the time he has been inciting them to further badness and craziness. This morning he said we ought to have a feast. He said that it would be a good thing and give the men a chance to release their spirits, and that after it they would settle down better. I said that nuns could not possibly attend a festivity of that kind. He only smiled and bowed and went away. Then late this afternoon he began to beat his drum on the beach. After an hour or so it seemed to get into every one's blood. Ursula went first, then the others. I couldn't stop them. To be frank it was all I could do to stop myself. Winifred and I came over here and said our offices to keep out the sound of the drum. It was the only way we could save ourselves.'

'Did you want to go too?' Dick asked Winifred.

'Only when I didn't think of you,' she said. 'But I thought of you all the time, and I looked at your picture there.'

'He's a complete swine,' cried Dick angrily. 'He ought to be shot.'

'Possibly,' said Agatha, 'but at times I feel we all ought to be shot. If we were not like we are Mr Smith wouldn't be like he is.'

'I don't follow that,' said Dick.

'The function of a religious community in the world is to tap the forces of Good and use them for the whole of mankind. When we arrived on this island the religious community was a half of the whole, so the forces of Good should have had an unusual opportunity, which they don't seem to have used,' she added drily.

'Perhaps the forces of evil were strong here before we arrived,' said Winifred. 'Mr Smith said that the natives think there is a curse on this island, which is why it has no population.'

'Perhaps we brought the forces of evil with us,' said Agatha, 'and we shall only escape when we have shed them. Joe shed them and he escaped.'

'I don't call that escaping,' said Dick.

'Because you don't believe in God.'

'I don't believe in getting killed to see God,' he exclaimed hotly. 'It's damned silly. A proper life is doing good work, and keeping healthy and loving someone, and having kids and living as long as you can without being a bother to people. That's all any one wants who's got any sense in their heads.'

'I am sorry, you are right,' said Agatha. 'At least what you say is right for you—absolutely right. But every one's lot isn't the same. That wouldn't have satisfied Joe. He wanted something more, and he found it. The nun, too, is seeking for something more, but we were not true nuns. We had only become nuns because we were disappointed, or wanted to be romantic, or grand, or to escape every responsibility except that to God, who we thought would let us down lightly. Even Winifred here was not a true nun, as you have shown her. I'm glad you have, as that was the best way for her to find out.'

Winifred took Agatha's hand and kissed it.

Dick said curiously: 'Are you a true nun then?'

'I don't know. At least I do know that I'm not one yet, but I still want to be one. What should I do if I gave up now? I should be destroyed, as those wretched women on the beach are destroying themselves. Or perhaps not like that, but I should sit here in intellectual sterility, useless to God and man.'

'Then you're only going on with being a nun to keep your self-respect?' said Dick.

Agatha looked at him sharply. She laughed uneasily, but at once became serious again.

'Perhaps I am,' she said, 'but in a place like this I don't know that that is altogether a bad motive. I may become a bit of a prig, but I daresay that in Sodom Lot was thought a prig.'

They laughed. Agatha stood up and said: 'Well, you two must want to be alone, and I must go back to Marinella.'

'No, don't go,' said Dick. 'I'm jolly interested in all this.'

Winifred looked surprised and hurt. Agatha saw her expression and said: 'No. I'd better go.' At the door she turned and looked at Dick.

'The important thing,' she said, 'is to know your own motives, what you really want. If this island can teach you that, you may thank your stars you were wrecked here.'

'I know what I want,' said Dick. 'I want Winifred and to get home again.'

'Then why do you ask me to stay here and discuss religion with you?'

She did not wait for an answer, but went out into the garden. Evidently the bonfire had died down, as the garden was no longer illuminated by its rosy reflected glow, and the rhythm of the drum at last had ceased. Instead there was a complete silence, which struck Agatha as eerie and a little frightening. Then she noticed that the wind had dropped completely, almost for the first time since they had been here. The palm fronds no longer rustled high above the garden, but hung still against the huge moon just risen in the east, and two days gone on the wane so that it had an odd, misshapen appearance. Not only had the palm fronds ceased to rustle, but she could no longer hear the steady thunder of the surf, beating on the coral reef.

In the chapel Dick turned to Winifred.

'What a lot they do argue here,' he said, 'but I don't argue with you, do I?'

Winifred did not answer. She played thoughtfully with the ends of his fingers. She was oppressed by his apparently irrational changes of mood. A minute ago he was asking Sister Agatha to stay and continue the discussion. Now as soon as she had gone, he spoke as if only she were responsible for it. Winifred could not point this out to Dick, as it would sound like fault finding. Also she had been too hurt at his wanting Agatha to stay to be able to mention it.

He lifted up her face and looked questioningly into her eyes. He smiled playfully at her as if she were a child.

'Do you really love me?' she asked.

'Of course I do, silly.'

'Did you think of me all the time you were away—every day, as I thought of you?'

The expression of his eyes changed.

'I thought of you a lot,' he said, 'but I couldn't all

the time, because sometimes when it was dangerous I, had to think of the danger—when I killed the octopus, he blurted out in spite of himself, seizing on the ready excuse.

'But when it wasn't dangerous, did you think of me a lot then? Did you wish I was with you?'

'Sometimes I did.'

'How often?'

'It wouldn't have been suitable, darling, for you to be with us very often.'

'You tell me the truth,' said Winifred. 'That is something.'

'Aren't you happy now I'm here?' asked Dick a little resentfully.

'Yes, I am. I must be. But I feel as if you had left part of yourself behind, away somewhere along that wild beach. Perhaps you left your love at the river where Joe was killed, and perhaps you left your fear at the pool where you killed the octopus, and you have come back to me without love and fear.'

As she spoke she watched him, and he seemed to grow more aloof from her, and the strange wild tension of beauty returned to him. She went on talking as if she were hypnotized, feeling that she was risking her dearest possession as she spoke, but feeling desperately that she must know if it was really hers.

'Perhaps your love only came to you from Joe, and without him you cannot really love, and now when you think of him love returns to you, but it isn't love for me. I can see from your face that your soul has left me.'

'Why do you say that?' asked Dick. He did not meet her eyes, but looked at the picture above the altar, where Joe's body, painted with pearl dust, glimmered between the two tapers of wild pig's fat.

'Because you were happy with him, more than you were with me. I was only someone on whom you could come and release the happiness you found with Joe.'

'That isn't true. You don't know what you're saying. How could you possibly know?'

'Tell me what you did—when you were not in danger.'

'We just walked steadily eastwards along the beach. We talked a bit, but not much after the first day. We bathed, we ate breadfruit, we slept on the sands. That's all.'

'Then I might have been with you. I could have done those things.'

'Yes. You could have done those things.'

'Did you sleep beside Joe?'

'Yes.'

'And soon you will sleep beside me.'

At that he met her eyes again, and the tragic aloof expression left his own. He looked at her long and searchingly, with increasing tenderness. He drew her towards him, and at the touch of her breast against his own a stinging sweetness passed through his body and he cried aloud:

'Oh, damn Joe!'

This shocked them both so much that they fell apart.

'I'm so terribly tired,' said Dick. 'I don't know what I'm saying.'

'We've talked too much,' said Winifred, 'but we ought to be so happy.'

'We shall be to-morrow, when it is light.'

'Good night.' She lifted her face to be kissed.

'You're like a child,' he said. 'I don't know what makes you think of the things you say.'

She went to the altar and took a carved wooden extinguisher which Mr Smith had made, and ceremoniously put out the tapers. He watched her, half-touched, half-irritated by this glimpse of what must hitherto have occupied so much of her attention. She bowed and they went out from the dark chapel into the moonlight. They walked hand in hand along the path to the bungalow.

173

At the steps on to the veranda Winifred turned to him.

'Isn't it still?' she said quietly.

'Yes. The wind's dropped.'

'It's rather frightening.'

He put his arms round her shoulders and kissed her again.

'To-morrow,' he said.

'Yes, to-morrow.'

She turned at the top of the steps, smiled, and went into the bungalow. Dick walked slowly across the garden to his hut. He picked some grapes and ate them as he walked, spitting the pips into the flower-beds beside the path.

He pushed open the door of the hut, lay down on the floor, and went to sleep. When he awoke again it was still dark. He had expected to sleep for twenty-four hours, but he could only have slept for two or three. He had not slept under a roof of any kind for a month, and the silence of the sea and the trees was strange. He went out into the garden, and instinctively, without thinking of his direction, he turned his steps towards the sea.

When he came out of the creek on to the shore he remembered the orgy, which in talking to Winifred had passed from his mind. The few hours' sleep back in his hut had dimmed his recent memories, but now they returned in vivid successive waves, until his brain was alive with images—of Joe shouting to him across the dark river; of the octopus writhing in its black spume; of the distant bonfire with the roasting pig, and the naked dancing bodies silhouetted against it; of the faces of the two women in the chapel as they turned and stared at him standing in the doorway.

He was moved by curiosity to see what had happened, and he walked along the beach towards the site of the bonfire, above which hung the misshapen moon. A few wisps of sweet-scented smoke rose from the still smouldering fire, and bones from the broken carcass of the pig lay round it. There were also tin mugs from the bungalow. Dick picked one up in an idle adolescent fashion, and smelt it. It contained the dregs of rum, and then he saw two of Macpherson's barrels lying a little way off from the bonfire. Smith, who originally had hidden them, must have unearthed them again.

He strolled a little beyond the fire and saw in the moonlight something black and white lying on the sands. It was Cecilia lying across the dark body of Harry the islander, both asleep. He stared at them, and was seized by a gust of sheer sexual desire, so that he trembled. Everything but this desire faded from his mind. It possessed him body and mind, and the inability to release it was torment to him. Further away he saw other couples, but he did not move towards them to see who they were, as he did not want his wave of lust to be identified with individuals. Harry, the native, and the white girl were a sufficient symbol. He stared at them, hypnotized, and then their black and white enlaced limbs became the black and white of the octopus in the pool, and the revulsion he had felt at the octopus returned to him and slowly strangled his desire, so that he felt as if he were in hell, while lust and revulsion were in conflict in him.

He turned back along the beach, crossed the entrance to the creek, and sat down on the eastern side. He put his head in his hands and said: 'O God, is there no escape?'

He did not know from what he wanted to escape. He only knew that he wanted his life to be simplified, with his love turned unconfusedly in one direction. Hell, it ought to be simple on this island, if anywhere. What had made him complex? What had made him torment himself about nothing? Was it Joe—or Mr Smith—or

Winifred? But Winifred was simple, simpler than he was. The thought of Winifred made him ashamed of the mood that had seized him at the bonfire. He could not connect those feelings with her. It was vile, impossible to think of her while they possessed him. But they had nothing to do with Joe or Mr Smith. They were in himself.

A voice said: 'So you found no way of escape?'

Mr Smith was standing beside him, sober, unruffled, wearing his usual shirt and flannel trousers.

'No,' said Dick shortly, and he continued to look out to sea. It was colossal impudence of Smith, who was responsible for all that had happened last night, to come and talk to him with such assurance.

Mr Smith ignored the disapproval expressed by Dick's back, and in his usual manner, which was a mixture of banter and kindness, touched occasionally with patronage when he thought his listener was being stupid, he said:

'The adventure was too great for you.'

Dick felt his naturally slow anger rising in him, ready to boil over into physical violence against Mr Smith. He felt the blood beating at his temples, and a new sort of lust rose in him, that would take an infinite pleasure in an orgasm of murder. He wanted this moment to come when his anger would boil over and he would be possessed. But it has been said that it takes two to make a murder, and Mr Smith sitting beside him, completely indifferent to his mood, prevented the final bubbling over, and his inhibited fury sank again, leaving him impotent and immeasurably depressed.

He had intended when he met Smith to scare the wits out of him. He had imagined himself standing over a contemptible creature, sozzled and bleary after the night's debauchery. But Smith appeared as fresh, as urbane, as self-possessed as ever, and it was himself who had the feeling of being called to account. The whole situation was back-to-front and barmy, and yet he felt that it was inevitable and that he must accept it. His reason told him it was all wrong, but something deeper than his reason, an instinctive sense of truth, told him it was right. On this island reason and truth did not seem to be the same thing, and that in itself was barmy.

'You wouldn't have done any better,' he said.

'I suppose not,' said Mr Smith, 'but I am an old man. It's a young man's business to succeed in dangerous adventures. An old man's function is different.'

'To make everybody tight, I suppose,' said Dick, 'and work them up to that,' he jerked his head towards the bonfire, 'and to put decent women and a young girl in danger. That's an old man's business, I suppose.'

'If and when you all leave this island you will want to feel that the experience has been valuable to you in some way. The most valuable experience you can have is one that gives you a little further knowledge of yourself. I was merely helping them to know themselves. Sister Agatha and Winifred were in no danger because those particular characteristics were not crying for release in them. Marinella, on the other hand, had a wholesome check. The sequence of life is folly, learning, sorrow, and wisdom. If you never commit folly you will never have wisdom.'

'Now you've made 'em commit the folly are you going to teach 'em wisdom?' asked Dick, still trying to keep the moral ascendency.

'I've done my bit. The wisdom will begin to develop quite soon now. But I am more interested in you at the moment.'

'I don't want your interest,' said Dick with weakening resistance.

'You can't escape it. And really you do want it. You were very anxious to justify yourself to me on your return, and you were very offended that our little community was not wild with excitement at your arrival, although relieved that you did not have to explain Joe's death to us all at once.'

'Who told you about Joe?' demanded Dick.

'I heard of it. Did you enjoy your excursion?'

'Hell!' exclaimed Dick indignantly.

'It was only hell after you failed.'

'Well, I couldn't go on, could I? What was the use of crossing the river and getting eaten too? And even if I had got across I couldn't have gone on alone.'

'You have learnt something then.'

'What d'you mean.'

'You've learnt that you can't go on alone.'

'Who can, anyhow?'

'Joe could. He went on alone, but he had to come back for you.'

'That wasn't my fault.'

'Not entirely. It was your nature that you weren't ready to cross the river as soon as you arrived at it. Actually Joe did not come back for you. You thought he loved you, didn't you?'

Dick looked extremely uncomfortable, and made an unintelligible reply.

'You needn't be a humbug about it,' said Mr Smith. 'Anyhow, you're wrong. Joe thought he loved you too, but even before he plunged back into the river to save you his love had begun to die. Joe loved an image of a perfect man which he had conceived in his heart. He loved the idea of the noble mind and the generous heart in the beautiful body. Because you have great physical beauty and many attractive qualities his imagination clothed you with this little bit extra, this human divinity which he had always been seeking. But when he shouted to you not to cross, and you stood deaf and dithering on the opposite bank, already his love began to die a little. By the time he was half-way across, and you still stood there stupid and hesitating, his love for you died completely, and at that moment the alligator took him. He still loved you in a way, but as he would have loved his dog, not his god. You were no longer the beautiful incarnation of the spirit he was seeking. If you had been you would have swum to meet him, but the adventure was too great for you. He then realized that it was the spirit he was seeking, and that though the spirit may blow through you intermittently, you are not that spirit, nor could you hold it long enough to hold his exclusive love. Oddly enough his last human thoughts were of me.'

'Do you want to take everything from me?' cried Dick desperately.

'Only what does not truly belong to you so that you can be happy following the true pattern of your life. You still have Winifred. I haven't taken her from you.'

'You'd better not try.'

'I couldn't if I tried.'

'I'm glad there's something you admit you can't do.'

'There are a great many things outside my *métier*.'

Dick did not know what *métier* meant. He became engrossed in removing the sand from his toes.

'Anyhow, I killed the octopus,' he said sullenly, after a while.

'I should like to take away your satisfaction in that,' said Mr Smith.

'You want to take away my self-respect, don't you?'

'You don't respect yourself for the right things. Why did you kill the octopus? Because you could not achieve the goal you aimed at, so you turned back to destroy something which might have impeded the early stage of your journey—a silly and useless victory. You can only pride yourself on something negative and sterile. You should make up your mind which world you want and make the best of that world.'

Dick laughed bitterly. 'How many worlds have I to choose from on this bloody island?' he demanded.

Mr Smith looked up at the sky. 'It appears,' he said, 'that soon we may not have even one world to choose.'

Since they had been on the island they had seen many strange and gorgeous atmospheric mutations, but nothing to equal the aspect of this moment. The sea stretched like a mirror to the horizon, and on its glassy surface were reflected the thousand colours of the morning sky, which radiated from the blinding vermilion womb of its splendour, the point where the sun was just rising. The palm fronds hung absolutely still, enamelled against the sky. The whole world was so still and silent, the colours so incredible, that it was like being in the carved interior of some mammoth jewel. The heat already was terrific.

'Something is going to happen,' said Mr Smith, and as he spoke the stillness was broken, and the sands beneath them gave a faint tremor, and there was a rumble as of thunder towards the centre of the island.

'Look,' he said, and turned towards the volcano. A brown column of smoke rose in slow, softly unfolding curls from the crater, and spread like a mushroom out across the sky. On this side of the island the tremendous expanse of brown cotton wool crept steadily towards the sunrise, obliterating first the high expanse of blue, and then the fringe of the brilliant colours. It poured in an inexhaustible column from the crater, a pillar of brown wool that rose for two or three thousand feet, and then spread itself in a soft blanket over the world. The edge of this blanket reached the point in the sky above the shore where Dick and Mr Smith were watching, and moved steadily on towards the horizon.

'It is shutting out God,' said Mr Smith.

Dick gave him a scared glance and looked back at the sky. After awhile there was only a narrow band of light between the edge of the blanket and the sea, but this band still held all the brilliant colours of the dawn. Its rays glowed along the underside of the layer of smoke so that it was like the colour of a fading red rose whose petals were turning brown. In this curious rosy twilight the faces of Dick and Mr Smith were yellow, like the faces of people in a room lighted only by red lamps.

The sun for a minute or two blazed in the centre of the band of light, and then had passed above it, or the blanket had moved on to hide it. The rosy glow left the underside of the smoke and the folds loomed dark, oppressive, seeming almost to threaten suffocation. The twilight was grey-brown. The soft folds of the blanket became wispy and ragged, and descended lower towards the earth and sea.

Mr Smith wiped his face and left a brown smudge. A fine ash was falling about them, like brown snow. Dick went down to the sea to wash it off, but the usually crystal clear water was itself discoloured, and when he came out the ash stuck more unpleasantly to his skin, and in his wet hair and beard.

'We had better go indoors,' said Mr Smith.

They went up the creek where the overhanging boughs sheltered the water, and before they turned into the forest path Dick was able to wash himself more satisfactorily. In the tunnel it was as dark as a moonless night, but no ash penetrated the thick foliage overhead, though the place smelt faintly like a railway tunnel.

When they came to the garden Dick gave an exclamation of dismay. All the gorgeous flowers, the brilliant leaves, the superb golden melons were covered with the brown snow. The place looked like some extraordinary drawing in sepia, with the sky, the flowers, and the earth all brown, and even the light was a paler brown that took the colour from the lower leaves of plants which the ash had not yet touched.

Dick hesitated before leaving the shelter of the tunnel.

'I'd better go to the bungalow,' he said, 'and see how Winifred is.'

'If you put my handkerchief over your head,' said Mr Smith, offering him a large square of red linen, 'you won't get your hair full of ash again.'

'What about you?'

'My hair is thin and dry. The ash won't stick. Yours is thick and wet.'

Dick thanked him, put the hankerchief over his head, and dashed across the garden to the bungalow. The red handkerchief was an odd spot of colour in the sepia landscape.

Mr Smith followed more leisurely and when he reached the shelter of the veranda lightly shook the ash from his clothes, while Dick rubbed himself down with one hand and knocked on the door with the other.

Marinella put a peaky tear-stained face round the door, and called out: 'It's Dick.' She then withdrew her head and shut the door in his face.

Agatha opened it again and came out, followed by Marinella who stood close beside her as if for protection. When Agatha saw Mr Smith her face became cold and set. She turned to Dick.

'What is happening *now*?' she asked.

'Seems to be Ash Wednesday,' said Dick, and grinned apologetically, uncertain whether Ash Wednesday was too sacred a subject for a joke.

'The volcano is in action,' said Mr Smith.

'Is there any danger?' asked Agatha. 'Not that it matters if there is,' she added.

'There is the possibility of burning lava engulfing us from the mountain, and also the possibility of a tidal wave engulfing us from the sea. This delicate brown ash which enfolds us so tenderly like a soft Angora blanket gives a false sense of security. We are in fact between the devil and the deep sea.' He laughed.

'Can you suggest anything?' asked Agatha sharply.

'Nothing, except to take a vivid interest in life while it lasts, and to get as much pleasure as we can from watching these strange phenomena.'

Agatha turned her back on him. Winifred came out on to the veranda. Her eyes met Dick's inquiringly, and he gave her a glance of mingled tenderness and half-amused resignation. They drifted automatically together and stood side by side.

'Ooh, how dirty the ash is!' cried Marinella. 'I hate it! I hate it!' She flung herself weeping against Winifred, feeling that she and not Winifred should be the object of any love that was going. Winifred absently put a hand on her shoulder, but Agatha said with good-natured irritation: 'Oh, do be quiet, child, you'll get so ugly if you cry any more.'

Dick said: 'I haven't had any breakfast.'

Agatha gave him a piece of old stuff to keep off the ash, and he went down into the garden and brought back a supply of grapes and melons. Winifred went through into the kitchen and fried some rashers of bacon and made some coffee. Meanwhile Dick took a couple of pails down to the stream, and filled them with fresh water, while it was still possible to obtain it. He made this journey two or three times, until they had filled every vessel in the bungalow.

At last Dick and Mr Smith sat down to an appetizing, almost European breakfast on the veranda. Agatha and Winifred watched them eat while Marinella picked at their grapes.

'If you eat any more fruit I can't think what will happen to your inside,' said Agatha.

'Do you think this ash will kill the garden?' asked Winifred, a little anxiously.

'Not if we are fortunate enough to be visited by another

storm,' said Mr Smith, 'to wash it away, which I think is probable.'

'Unless of course it is washed away by a tidal wave or finally buried under molten lava,' said Agatha.

'Naturally,' said Mr Smith, dipping his grapes in a cup of water to remove the ash.

A silence which seemed to clothe a sardonic mutual understanding settled on them. It was broken by Marinella going off into wild fits of laughter. To the adults the sight which caused this was more sordid than comic. Hilda was returning from the revels.

She was wearing her habit, but she had lost her wimple, and her hair, now grown fairly long, hung in wisps round her eyes and ears. It was covered in ash, and in trying to brush it off she had merely rubbed it in, and her forehead was covered with brown smudges. Her skirt trailed in the ash which was now nearly a foot deep. She left deep footprints in the ash as in snow.

When she climbed stiffly on to the veranda she looked so woebegone that Marinella rolled on the floor with laughter, and cried: 'Oh, you do look funny.'

This had the slight advantage of distracting the general attention to Marinella, and easing for a moment the awkwardness of the meeting.

'Oh, my head!' exclaimed Hilda, and sank on to a form. 'I do feel awful.'

'That is called a hang-over,' said Mr Smith amiably.

'You!' Hilda darted him a malevolent glance from her neuralgic eyes. 'You serpent!'

Agatha could not say anything. The situation was too grotesque. She felt the corners of her mouth twitching, and was horrified at her indifferent, half-amused reaction. That a religious should come back after a night of debauchery, and be chaffed about a 'hang-over' was so remote from anything she had ever contemplated that she had no idea how to cope with it. She felt that she should be full of outraged grief. At one time she would have affected outraged grief, and believed that she really felt it, but the island had freed her from the obligation to pretend moral indignation, perhaps because there was so much occasion for the genuine thing. But surely Hilda's condition was an occasion for the genuine thing? No, because Hilda had never really been a virgin at heart. She had only been a fussy, over-conscientious, bossy little woman, and she could not betray the self she had never been. There was no more occasion for outraged grief than over one of the slatterns of Little Bourke Street. Of course every fallen woman was an occasion for outraged grief, but Agatha had seen so many that she could not pump it up every time.

Hilda, poor creature, looked woebegone. She was waiting for the rebuke which did not come. Mr Smith went on eating his grapes, while Marinella, having recovered a degree of composure, stood beside him and picked at the bunch, spitting the skins over the veranda edge, and grinning mischievously at Hilda. Dick and Winifred had moved away to the far end of the veranda, and stood hand in hand, watching the ash falling. Agatha sat aloof and faintly smiling.

'Well, aren't you going to say anything?' demanded Hilda at last. 'I suppose you think I'm too wicked to speak to.'

'Do you think you are?' asked Agatha.

'That's right. Be cold and sarcastic. You're too grand to do your duty, I suppose.'

Agatha flushed.

'You're not as stupid as you appear to be,' she said. 'You have the power to get under one's skin, though it seems to be unconscious. If you can get under your own skin you won't need me to say anything.'

'I don't know what you're talking about,' said Hilda. 'Oh, my head! If only we had some aspirin.'

'You had better go and lie down,' said Agatha.

'How can I lie down in these clothes. I'll make my bed all black.'

'You could take your clothes off.'

Hilda began to frame an automatic shocked protest at the idea of a nun going to bed with nothing on, and then she remembered the past night. Her face twisted, and she stammered. Her conventional self appeared to be so affronted by the glimpse of her natural self that her single body was scarcely able to contain them both, and her gestures were tormented and pitiful.

'It is more painful,' said Mr Smith, 'to face the truth about oneself than to undergo an operation without an anaesthetic.'

Agatha looked at him angrily, but he went on unconcernedly dipping his grapes in the cup of water.

'I was only trying to help her,' he said. 'If you understand the cause of your pain it isn't so bad.'

Agatha went over to Hilda, and took her by the hand and led her into the bungalow.

'Do you still acknowledge my authority as your religious superior?' she asked her kindly.

Hilda nodded wretchedly. She could not speak.

'Then you must take off your stained and torn habit and go to bed. You must acknowledge your body to yourself. Then you may bring it to God for His forgiveness.'

With trembling fingers Hilda undid the fastening at her neck. Agatha left her and went back to the veranda.

As she came out Ursula, also covered with ash, was mounting the steps. She looked like some great she-bear, or underground creature, covered with the earth of its cave. Marinella turned from picking at the fruit on the table to stare at her with an expression of utter repudiation, and with the contempt that only a child can achieve. Ursula gave her a furtive glance, and when she saw her cold contempt a queer look of infinite pain showed in her small, animal eyes. She lumbered heavily across into the bungalow, shedding ash as she went, and no one spoke until she had closed the door behind her.

Mr Smith said to Marinella: 'Some day you will regret this moment.' Marinella answered with pert incredulity: 'Me?' and went on picking at the grapes.

Dick and Winifred remained at the far end of the veranda. They seemed to be absorbed in each other, and they took no notice of the others, to whom their backs were turned.

It was not long before Magdalene and Cecilia arrived. This proved the most embarrassing of all the encounters. Magdalene was emotionally repentant. Cecilia emotionally unrepentant. When they had gone indoors Agatha said to Mr Smith:

'I suppose you think they're improved.'

They were startled by the sound of Harry's voice, somewhere down in the garden, muffled behind the curtain of falling ash, raised in a monotonous dirge. This lamentation continued throughout the morning, while the carpet of ash became thicker on the ground, and now and then a loud crack announced that a branch had broken under its weight.

Mr Smith invented a game with orange pips, which he played with Marinella. Dick and Winifred sat holding hands as if in a trance. At what she thought was noon Agatha put a piece of sacking over her head and went across to the chapel where she recited her office alone. When she had finished, despair like a physical weight descended on her. She could almost feel it pressing her head towards the ground. Everything she had hoped for in life now seemed finally to be taken from her. This morning the last two things that had sustained her had gone—her confidence in her own commonsense ability and fairness and her hope of salvation, and Winifred's love. All the morning on the veranda, while Mr Smith had played his game with Marinella, and Dick and Winifred had sat apart mutually absorbed, she had felt an intolerable isolation of spirit. She knew that Winifred must turn from her to Dick—that it was right—and yet she could not easily accept the loss. But now she had accepted it, and at last she had reached the zero of the spirit. The ash that fell from the brown sky had blotted out the colour of the earth, and even possibly their means of subsistence. So it seemed that these waves of denial which she felt descending on her, bowing her head to the earth, blotted out the last vestige of colour in her soul, and even her hope of survival.

For a time she made an effort of will to fight against these dreadful waves of depression, but they were too strong for her, and at last she remained, still and bowed, as one who waits defenceless for an inevitable blow, and in her heart she accepted the destruction of her desire and of her will.

With this completeness of abnegation came a sense of peace, in which she remained quiescent while she was unconscious of the passage of time. Again Winifred and Dick came into her mind, and with the thought of them came a new stirring of love which was curiously impersonal and undesirous, and rooted elsewhere than in her human will.

She had a pencil in the pocket of her ragged habit, which she had taken from Macpherson's desk. She found that a verse was forming in her head, and slowly, stopping frequently to think, she wrote it on the back of the bench in front of her.

> O God let me not seek for love,
>   But let love dwell in me.
> For if I seek he lies without
> And I in darkness walk about
>   And search but cannot see.

Then let me grow in my own heart
What I have asked my friend,
That I may give the thing I sought,
And though in turn I'm given nought,
I have no lonely end.

When she had written this she found that the weight
of her depression was lifted, but the tears streamed down
her face.

She did not know how long she had been in the chapel,
when at last she sat back on the hard wooden bench, and
looked about her, as after a long night one might look
idly out of a window at the new day. The chapel seemed
lighter, and she went to the door to find that the ash had
ceased falling, and that there were rifts in the brown
blanket which spread across the sky.

The close heat was terrific, and Agatha became aware
that her habit was wringing wet.

With amazing rapidity the gaps in the brown sky
widened, leaving hard lakes of blue, in one of which
suddenly burst the blazing sun. The brown garden was
now flooded with metallic light, and appeared like a vast
extension of the burnished gold efflorescence round a
baroque altar.

Agatha walked slowly through the thick ash back to
the bungalow. She felt that something extraordinary
was about to happen; but it did not disturb her serenity
because she now felt in herself the power to endure most
things.

Dick and Winifred, Mr Smith and Marinella were
standing at the edge of the bungalow watching the sky.

'I think that now we're for it,' said Mr Smith.

As he spoke there was a long whine across the sky,
high above their heads. In a few moments the ash laden
palm fronds began to move, and at first it seemed as if
the fronds were sprouting, as the ash blew from them
in fantastic spirals.

'Inside! Quick!' shouted Mr Smith, and pushed Marinella before him into the bungalow. Agatha entered last, and he slammed the door behind her. As he did so they were surrounded again by thick darkness. The gale whipped the huge volume of ash a thousand feet into the air, so that no light could pierce it. Agatha groped her way to the desk and lighted a taper that was standing on it. Through the small square panes of the windows showed only an opaque density like that of a London fog, but unlike in a fog, instead of a muffled silence they were surrounded by the howling and screaming of the gale. The fine ash crept and eddied through the chinks of the loosely built bungalow, and the smell of railway tunnel was stifling. The four nuns who had spent the night on the beach were huddled under their thin coverings at the far end of the room. They awoke one by one at the noise of the wind, and Magdalene cried: 'It's the judgment of God.'

Suddenly a fresh sound froze every one into an intensity of listening. Almost before they were aware what the terrific crashing in the forest meant, the tidal wave struck the bungalow. The walls slanted in, and then the whole building gave a lurch upwards, and swayed off on the crest of the wave, while water spurted in like the jets of a fountain through the cracks where lately the fine ash had blown. The people and the furniture in the bungalow were shot into one corner, and Hilda's naked body, like a figure in some medieval picture of the last judgment, flew headlong down the room. The bungalow did not travel far. With another shock it hit something solid, and its occupants clung desperately to each other while the receding wave rushed past, wrecking the outside world but leaving the bungalow high though not dry, as it was feet deep in water which continued to pour out after the tidal wave had gone.

It was some minutes before any one dared to move. At last Mr Smith pulled himself up the slanting floor to the door which he tried to open, but it was jammed, and Dick, who had bruised his knee, limped to help him. Hilda, made innocent by fright, examined Cecilia's cut forehead before she remembered her own nakedness, and then she looked about without fuss or hurry for a covering. Marinella had at last become inoculated to terror, and she had ceased to scream. Her expression was waiting, alert, afraid, and yet at the same time resigned to what might happen next. She clung to Ursula, whose eyes had become straight and calm.

By splintering a strip off the door Mr Smith and Dick managed to get it open. They found that the bungalow was jammed between two trees at the edge of what had been the garden. The wreck of the veranda still overlooked the enclosure which was now like the mud flats at the estuary of a river. Every shrub and flower and most of the smaller trees had been uprooted and washed away, and there remained only an expanse of grey, glistening mud, from which rose here and there the trunk of a ravished tree.

The forest beyond this expanse, between it and the sea, was like a colossal heap of rubbish where someone had been weeding a giant's garden. It stretched as far as they could see, and the vast entanglement of broken vegetation was covered with grey slime.

Agatha came out and balanced herself carefully on a loose plank of the veranda, and contemplated the desolation. Was God determined to give them as much as they could bear? A little while ago, it seemed in another life, she had made the complete abnegation of her will and her own desire. She had thought it impossible to sink any farther in loss and despair, and having reached the nadir she had found her inner security. And now she saw that there were greater depths and her new strength was already being tested. She had disliked the garden and thought it evil, but it had given her shelter and food, and beauty if she had cared to see it with innocent eyes. She had brought her own guilty mind to impair its beauty, and now she had to accept a further judgment. Her face was heavy, her acceptance of loss so profound, that it appeared almost expressionless.

Mr Smith laughed and pointed upwards.

High on the top of a palm tree was perched their little chapel, looking like a child's toy.

7

From out the broken jungle, across the undulations of grey slime, crawled some creature that might have been bred of the mud on which it clambered. It was not until it was within a few yards of the veranda that they were able to recognize Tom. He crawled on to the veranda, and lay there gasping for breath. The blood trickled from wounds and scratches all over his body, and made curious soft red blotches on the film of grey mud that covered him.

'Bring some water,' said Agatha, but where recently there had been so much clear water, now there was none.

Dick took a bucket and went across to the stream which, swollen with the last of the receding wave and stained to the universal grey, raced across the former garden. They washed Tom as well as they could with this, and powdered him with boracic, and bound his wounds with bandages from the bungalow medicine chest. Agatha was afraid he might be in danger of tetanus, but Mr Smith said one only caught this from over-cultivated soil.

They spent the rest of the day straightening up the bungalow, and mending the veranda, which was as wavy as the brim of an ancient straw hat. Dick and Mr Smith chopped some logs to give it a more secure foundation, but they were unable to make the floor level or the uprights vertical, and it was hard to recognize their former embowered and vine-garlanded dwelling in this crooked shack, hanging on the edge of the mud.

When Tom was able to speak they asked him what had happened to the other men, but he had seen nothing of them after the tidal wave had swirled down on their hut. Dick and Mr Smith slithered across the enclosure to the broken jungle to see if they could find any trace of them, but they only found Harry's body caught in a tangle of creeper, like a fly in a web. His hands were gripped round two thick tendrils, and apparently he had died from drowning. They released him and brought him to the edge of the jungle, leaving him there to be buried the following day.

There was still enough red linen in the bungalow to make a partition, and the women slept on one side, and Dick and Tom on the other. Mr Smith preferred to sleep on the undulating veranda.

They were now faced with the problem of providing food and drink. Even when Dick went higher up the stream the water he brought back was still discoloured with ash. They had to leave it to settle, and though it was then possible to drink it, it remained a brown colour and had a strong taste of cinders.

The sweeping away of the garden robbed them of their main source of food, and for two or three days they suffered from hunger. On the day after the tidal wave Dick and Mr Smith, when they had buried Harry, began the laborious job of cutting a new passage through the jungle to the stream. When they had done this they were able to walk up the stream to a point higher than the wave had reached and to gather bread-fruit. They thought they would be able to catch fish as usual, but when they went down to the shore they found that the ash had killed thousands of fish, which were washed up on to the beach where they were going bad, so that the smell was appalling.

Now that the enclosure was robbed of all shade, the heat there was almost unbearable. The air was steamy and still smelling of ash in spite of the wave. The women cut a passage into the jungle on the side away from the sea, and hollowed out a kind of bower, where they could sit in comparative comfort. They offered to help Tom to move into it during the day, but he would not budge from the bungalow. It seemed to give him some queer satisfaction to be there, as it might a peasant after a revolution to sleep in the state apartments of a ransacked palace. They all became weak from the diet of bread-fruit and water, and the smell from the dead fish on the beach penetrated inland as far as their bower in the forest. The wild pigs had fled up the mountain, and neither Dick nor Mr Smith were able to trap one.

In two or three days after the wave the expanse of mud began to break into green. Seeds burst and bits of root sprouted, and it seemed that, if growth continued at this rate, in a few months the garden might be restored to its former rich fertility. But Agatha wondered if they would survive to see it. She was afraid they might be wiped out by some plague or fever, started by the steaming mud or the decaying fish, and they were all too weak, she thought, to have much resistance to germs.

The small community in the bungalow were now one intimate family, battered by circumstance into complete equality, with the exception of Mr Smith, who still remained a little aloof, and to whom they turned for advice as to a father. But none felt superior to another. Agatha no longer felt herself wiser than Hilda, nor more virtuous than Magdalene. They were different but they were equal. In those dreadful weeks they came to know each other, and after momentary outbursts of irritation, to forgive each other with an absolute intimacy. Mr Smith was quiet and thoughtful, and in their worst moments he would say something which strengthened their endurance.

When Dick and Winifred were together with them, in the bower in the forest or in the bungalow, they were happiest. From these two there seemed to emanate a sense of peace and life which made their days more tolerable. Dick or Winifred alone did not have this effect, but only when they were together. Only Tom did not accept their lot and his share of affliction with the same inevitability. At first he was too weak to say much, but as he became stronger he was inclined to speak with an air of self-importance, and he appeared to be insensible to the wisdom of Mr Smith or the virtue which spread from Dick and Winifred.

Every now and then he would say: 'What you want to do here,' or 'If this were my place——' The others let him talk, but they listened to him as one might listen in tolerant absent-mindedness to a boasting child.

As soon as the enclosure began to sprout they put what energy they had into caring for this new growth, weeding round the food-producing plants, and arranging a trellis for the young shoots of a vine. Tom lay on the veranda and directed them, but each one of them as he bent to his work seemed only conscious of himself and the plant he was tending, and the voice from the veranda had no more significance than that of a dog which barks aimlessly at a distant sound or at a flight of birds.

One afternoon there was a heavy downpour of rain which lasted for some hours. It cleared at sunset, and after the clouds had passed there was a delicious scent of wet woods and fresh earth, and the awful stench of the fish and the lingering railway tunnel smell of ash had completely gone.

The setting sun caught the myriad raindrops which hung on the forest leaves, so that all the east wall of the enclosure glittered with rosy diamonds.

'Now there's a pretty sight for you,' said Tom. 'I remember once being caught in a storm in the botanical gardens in Melbourne, and afterwards the sun came out, and the trees was just like that. A fair sight it was.'

But nobody answered him, because in each of them was so much happiness that his voice was something irrelevant, like a passing car below the window of a room where two people are in love.

He looked at them in a puzzled way, half-hurt, half-aggressive, and repeated: 'A fair sight it was.'

After a while Agatha said: 'I never thought I should be happy again, and yet I think I'm happier than I have ever been.'

'You're easily satisfied,' said Tom, but she did not hear him.

Mr Smith said: 'I should think no one was satisfied with more difficulty. She could not be truly satisfied until she had lost everything. No one can be, because until we have lost everything, nothing has its true value.'

'That's all my eye,' said Tom.

'When we have lost everything,' Mr Smith went on, 'we are left alone with our real selves. Then we can begin to make our outer things accord with those which are within. And that is the heaven we are all seeking, if we only knew it.'

'You mean a little of what you fancy does you good,' said Tom.

'Not quite,' said Mr Smith.

'I know what I want,' said Tom. 'I want to catch my old man, and make him fork out what he stole from me, and then I'm going to buy a pub, and marry a widow with a bit of money too, just to be a bit more secure-like, and then I'll settle down comfortable.'

'And then you'll be happy?'

'I'll say I will.'

'In spite of your unpleasant experience,' said Mr Smith, 'you seem to be the only one who has learnt nothing from this island. But I have no doubt you will learn your lesson. Everyone else has, so you are not likely to escape. I should say that every one here, except you,

has been granted his most earnest wish—the desire that
has haunted him all his life.'

'They must have bloody queer desires,' said Tom
scornfully.

'Possibly. But you will probably get your wish too,
before you leave—if you leave, of course.'

'If I had my wish,' said Tom. 'I'ld like to see my old
man, the bastard, come up those steps. I'ld wring his
bloody neck.'

Mr Smith smiled. The others were absorbed in their
own thoughts, and though they heard this conversation
which in other days would have shocked them, it now
made no impression on their minds.

'Talking of leaving,' said Mr Smith. 'It seems foolish
not to keep a signal on the beach. It is always possible
that a ship may come past. There are still a few yards of
that scarlet linen left. I think I shall take it down and
fix up a flag.'

He went indoors, and after a few moments, in which
they heard him opening a cupboard, he came out, and
carrying a roll of scarlet linen under his arm, he made
his way across the enclosure, along the new narrow
paths, between the fresh young plants, whose growth
was so unblemished, so vivid, so confident that it made
the heart leap with joy.

Before he reached the other side there was a crash.
The Noah's ark chapel, sodden with rain, had fallen
from its perch on the tree-top. For some reason Agatha
was very happy to see it go, disappearing finally from
sight into the thick undergrowth.

*

One afternoon, three weeks later than this, they were
seated on the veranda. They had been working in the
garden all the morning, and they had just come out
from the bower in the forest where they had been resting

during the hottest part of the day. Ursula was inside brewing the tisane which did for tea, to wake them up properly before they began their work. Their clothes were now dreadful rags, though kept clean, but their bodies were strong and graceful from the healthy work. From Dick and Winifred there shone a kind of beauty which was reflected in the others. Cecilia and Magdalene had begun to bloom, and were happy in their close but not jealous companionship. Tom alone did not appear to belong to the company. This was not only due to his more gross physical appearance and coarser habits, nor had it anything to do with his being originally from a less educated social level. He was like an animal among them, which they treated kindly, but which was necessarily excluded from their conversation. What he said did not meet with any response. They turned when he spoke, and tried to listen to him, but his words were like a noise about their feet. His self-opinionated importance was meaningless. Mr Smith alone spoke to him occasionally, but with a kind of banter which ruffled rather than satisfied him.

As Ursula brought the tray of mugs, invisibly steaming in the heat, out on to the veranda, Marinella, who was following her with the kettle, cried: 'Look, there's a man!'

They turned in the direction in which she was pointing, and saw a bent old man, limping with the aid of two sticks across the garden. As he came closer it appeared that he only had one foot. They were too amazed to do anything but watch his laborious approach. He was about sixty years old, with reddish hair and beard. He wore an improvised hat made of plantain leaves, and his clothes were as ragged as those of the people on the veranda, but they were also filthy.

When he came close to them he seemed to be convulsed by a paroxysm of rage. His reddish-brown eyes glared. He waved one of his sticks and shouted:

199

'Get out! Get out of my house! Get off my veranda!'

Mr Smith murmured: 'The Lord of the vine-yard, apparently.'

The little old man continued to shout until he was almost foaming at the mouth, when his eye met Tom's, who was staring at him with goggling eyes and a gaping mouth. The old man's jaw dropped. His face turned from an angry mahogany red to khaki colour. At last he managed to whine with sickly affection:

'My boy!'

Tom said very quietly: 'So I've found you, you old bastard!'

He rose from the bench where he was sitting, and hooked the old man by the scruff of his neck up on to the veranda, and dumped him on the floor.

'Where's my money?' he demanded.

'Here,' cried the old man. 'I bought all this stuff with it. Now you're here we can share it and live comfortable like. I was getting a bit lonely. I've had a terrible time, Tom, my boy,' he began to whine again. 'I went out fishing and my boat got blown round the island, and I got out on a coral reef and put me foot in one of they big clams, and it ate my foot off and I lost me boat, and I had to crawl all the way back. A year I must have been. And now you're here to look after me. It's just what I wanted. God sent you, my boy.' He began no snivel.

'Did he hell?' said Tom. 'I sent meself. I've been going round these here South Sea Islands for ten years lookin' for you, you lousy old thief, and now I've found you. I'll show you if God sent me.'

'You can't treat your father rough. It's not right,' said the old man. He looked ghastly, not only with fright, but from the ravages of his recent experiences which showed more clearly as the blood drained from his face. Agatha had seen the same expression in people who were about to die.

'It's right to spend your son's money, I suppose. Where's the rest of it?'

'There ain't no more.'

'You spent the lot on this damned shed!'

'I had to get a boat to take me here. And I had to buy all the gear and stuff, and me new teeth cost £50.'

'You spent my £50 on your teeth?'

'And I had to buy all the seeds and plants.'

'You're a bloody old liar. You've got a bag of gold hidden somewhere. Where is it? Is it in this shack?' He jerked his head backwards.

The others stood about watching them, feeling that the quarrel was too personal for them to interfere. Dick did make a move forward, but Mr Smith put a hand on his arm to stop him.

'There's no gold, I tell you,' whined the old man. 'Aren't you glad to see your old dad?'

'There's no gold!' It took some time for the implication of this to sink into Tom. He stood holding the old man by the neck, his forehead twisted with the effort of thought.

'There's no gold,' he shouted. 'Only this damned shed. Then it's mine!' He yelled. 'It's mine. It's been mine all the time, and I've let you bloody women live in it. I'm the king of this place, I tell you. It's mine! Mine! I own it!' He put his hand on the wooden wall of the bungalow. 'This plank belongs to me, every nail in it. Those mugs are mine. I can do what I like with them.' He gave a kick and sent the tray full of enamelled mugs over the rail of the veranda, and the tisane spilt in dark splodges on the boards and dripped through the cracks. 'All that rum was mine. Every plant in that garden is mine, every grain of earth. I'm the king of this place, d'you hear? I own it. I rule it. It's bought with my money, and you're going to do what I tell you, you superior bitches. And you too, you old sod,' he yelled at Mr Smith. 'And you too, you pretty young pimp. You've got to work, work like hell, to pay me the rent you owe for all the time you've lived here free, eating your heads off on my property. It's mine, d'you hear? I'm the king!'

During this tirade the old man had been recovering his spirit. Tom had let him go while he thumped the walls and kicked over the tray.

'I made this garden,' he shouted back. 'I built this bungalow. It's mine! What have you done, but eat what I grew?'

Tom had burst into the bungalow in his rage, and when he came out he held in each hand a set of the gold false teeth which he waved in his father's face.

'And these are mine, too, you old swine!' he shouted. 'You think you're going to eat with my money, do you?'

This roused the old man to his original fury.

'You give me them teeth,' he said. He stood up unsteadily and made a grab at one of Tom's hands.

Tom laughed and held the teeth in the air above the reach of the old man, who was seized by a fresh paroxysm of rage. He put his hand to his hip, and drew out a long knife which he plunged into his son's heart. Tom's surprise when he saw the knife delayed him for a fatal moment. He crashed his fist down on his father's head, but only simultaneously with the thrust of the knife into his own heart. The old man collapsed without a sound. Tom thudded to the floor, raised himself a moment on his e bow, gave an astonished gurgle, and died.

The women looked at the two corpses with wondering pity, as one might look at tragedy on a film. Marinella asked almost indifferently: 'Are they dead?'

No one answered her. They turned to each other with wild surmise, their faces suddenly illuminated with hope. From out at sea, beyond the garden and the belt of jungle came the insistent, staccato hoot of a steamer's siren.

Marinella cried: 'A ship!' and tore across the garden. Cecilia and Magdalene followed her, and the others trailed after them, Ursula waddling in the rear. They ran through the jungle path and splashed down the stream, Marinella leading with her excited cries, and the women half-laughing, half-fearful that even yet it might not be true that they were to escape.

When they came on to the shore they saw a steamer of about two thousand tons, lying out beyond the coral reef, and a boat rowing through the entrance to the lagoon, and they ran down to the water to meet it. But at the mouth of the stream Winifred halted and caught Dick's arm, and turned him towards her.

'We're going to leave the island,' she said.

'Yes. Aren't you glad?'

'Are you?'

'I'm happy anywhere if I'm with you.'

'But you've never been with me except in this place. D'you think you will still love me in another place?'

'I love you, not places.'

'I love you, but I love this place too, although it has done such dreadful things to us, because it has given you to me. Without it I feel that I could never have loved you so much—that our love has been through death and has survived it—that it has passed the absolute test.'

'Then nothing can separate us now—not the world or anything.'

'But while we are here our love is fixed in the place of its security. Now that we can go, I don't want to. That's silly, I suppose.'

'It is a bit.'

'D'you know what I feel—this is silly, too, I suppose. I feel as if we were leaving God.'

'We're leaving the devil, too,' said Dick.

'They've both been fairly useful to us.'

'I don't know what you mean.'

'I don't know myself, really,' said Winifred.

He put his hands in her hair and drew her face up to his own and kissed her. He gave a husky laugh.

'Smith tried to tell me that we wouldn't always be happy,' he said.

'I wonder if we shall be.'

'You don't believe him, do you?'

'Not exactly. But I don't think we can expect any worldly happiness to last for ever, however good it is. We don't complain of the beauty of a daffodil because it will be dead in a few days, nor of a sunrise because it changes as we watch it. The important thing about beauty and happiness is its quality, not its permanence. In that way we have to live from hand to mouth. You can't plan happiness ahead. It comes at you suddenly out of the skies and then is gone. Our only permanent happiness is in our own souls.'

'You're not regretting that?' asked Dick suspiciously.

'What?'

'Being a nun.'

'No. How could I?' She passed her hands over his face and laughed, and the tears came into her eyes.

'You don't think I've ruined your soul?' asked Dick.

'Marriage doesn't ruin your soul. Why Monica was the mother of St Augustine.'

'I don't reckon I'm likely to be the father of a saint,' said Dick doubtfully. He took her hand and went down to meet the boat, which was waiting a few yards out from the shore.

*

If Agatha had been asked which of the passengers of the *Princess of Teck* was least likely to cause grief at her loss, she would probably have named, in spite of her kindness with the brandy bottle, Mrs Bright. But Mrs Bright's twin brother in Sydney was actually as rich as she had boasted, and could not bear the thought of his flesh and blood sitting naked and non-alcoholic on some coral reef, so he had sent a steamer to look for her. He had done the thing well, and the ship was provided with everything necessary to bring comfort and relief to people who had been cut off from civilization for some months. There were cosmetics, cases of wine and spirits, cigarettes, and clothes enough to stock a small *modiste's*, though thinking mostly of Mrs Bright he had ordered nearly all the dresses to be made in an outsize.

When the castaways had climbed up on to the deck of the steamer the captain said:

'Which of you ladies is Mrs Bright?'

They looked at each other awkwardly, suddenly ashamed of being the only ones to be rescued from a ship-load of two hundred people.

'I'm afraid Mrs Bright was drowned in the *Princess of Teck*,' said Agatha.

'Hm! That's bad luck on the old boy,' said the captain. 'He's sunk £10,000 in this expedition.'

'You don't think us worth so much,' suggested Mr Smith.

The captain was ruffled.

'No, no! I didn't say that. But naturally he hoped to rescue his sister. How long have you been here?'

'Since the *Princess of Teck* sank,' said Agatha.

'But I came here before. There was no sign of life. It was just a stroke of luck I decided to have another look.'

'We were some days in the life-boat, reaching the island,' said Ursula.

'Well,' said the captain, feeling that the occasion demanded more geniality. 'I'm sure this little girl is worth at least £10,000.' He ran his hand through Marinella's curls.

'Could you tell me,' asked Agatha politely, 'the name of this island?'

The captain looked serious.

'It's got some long native name,' he said, 'but it's generally called Hell Island. It belongs to a chief who won't sell it, and who won't let any niggers go near it. It's supposed to be full of dead souls or some nonsense, and they say that if you land on it you either die or else the dead souls do something to you which makes you unable to mix with ordinary men again. But I must say you don't look like ghosts. You ladies seem to be blooming with health if I may say so—blowing with health.' He seemed pleased with this phrase, and smacked his lips over it. 'But you may have noticed,' he went on, 'that my men who took you off didn't land on the island. They waited a few yards out for you to wade to them. Sailors are very superstitious, you know.'

'There are two dead men on the island now,' said Marinella with pleased importance. 'They killed each other half an hour ago.'

The captain took his hand out of her curls as if they had been Medusa's vipers.

'What!' he exclaimed.

'Yes,' said Marinella brightly. 'One had a knife and the other bashed him on the head. They were horrible.'

'It doesn't seem to worry you much,' said the captain sternly.

'Well, they were such horrid men.' explained Marinella with airy indifference.

'Perhaps you could send some sailors to bury them,' suggested Agatha.

The captain looked from one to another of the party of castaways. He appeared to be nervous, and cross because he was nervous.

'I don't know that I can do that,' he said. 'I wasn't sent out here as an undertaker.'

'One has duties beyond one's occupation,' said Agatha.

Again the captain scrutinized the group.

'You're a queer crowd, aren't you?' he demanded. 'You're not dead souls by any chance?' He burst into uneasy laughter.

'We are nuns,' said Agatha, 'and there is, I suppose, a sense in which nuns are dead souls.'

'D'you mean to tell me that out of a whole ship full of people the only ones saved are half a dozen nuns? That's queer, that is. I've known some funny things happen at sea, but that's about the queerest. Makes you think there's something in religion. Not that I ever said there wasn't, mark you—that's funny, that is. But what about this little girl here and you two gentlemen, why didn't the ghosts get you?'

'As you say,' said Mr Smith, 'the ghosts could not get at the nuns because even the most imperfect of them was partly inoculated against death. This young man was redeemed from death by the love and death of a friend. As for this little girl, her soul has not developed yet, so love and death are as remote from her as mountain snows from the fish in a tropical lagoon.'

'You seem to be an odd customer yourself, if you don't mind my saying so,' said the captain. 'How did you escape? Are you a priest?'

'As a matter of fact,' said Mr Smith, 'I do mind your saying so,' and he offered no further explanation.

'H'm!' grunted the captain. 'Well, the sooner we get away from this place the better I'll be pleased, and I don't suppose you'll be sorry yourselves to see the last of it.'

He was turning to give an order when Dick stepped forward, holding Winifred by the hand. When Mr Smith had spoken about love and death, that strange, aloof expression had returned to Dick's face which Winifred had noticed when he came into the chapel on the evening after he had killed the octopus.

'Please, could you marry us?' he said.

'Marry you! We'll see about that to-morrow.'

'But we would like to be married now—before you weigh anchor.'

'Would you, indeed? You seem to be in a great hurry, young man.' The captain's manner was facetious to cover his increasing uneasiness. 'I don't suppose you want to be married while you're dressed no better than a naked savage?'

'Yes, I do,' said Dick calmly.

'Well, you can't be, see? I'm busy.'

'I want to be married now,' repeated Dick insistently, 'before you weigh anchor.'

'Who gives orders here?' barked the captain. 'Let me tell you you're damned lucky to be on this ship, and for two pins I'd put you back on the island. I was sent to find Mrs Bright—not a crowd of nuns and half-wits.'

It seemed to Dick of desperate importance to be married before they left the bay. He felt that the island had given him Winifred, and that if he did not secure her while they were still under its influence, the civilized world might take her away from him.

Mr Smith said: 'It seemed a harmless request.'

The captain turned to glare at him, but when he met his eyes his own wavered and he grunted: 'All right, but hurry up. Hi! Fetch me prayer-book,' he shouted to the cabin-boy, who was standing on one leg, watching the scene with an air of derisive detachment.

Having given way, the captain affected a brusque joviality. He told Dick and Winifred to stand at a certain place on the deck, and the other castaways grouped themselves behind them. Behind them again, beyond the railing of the ship and the expanse of sapphire water, rose the clear, glittering green island surmounted by its pile of ancient, Leonardo rocks, and the faintly smoking cone of the mountain. The captain, having fumbled for the place in his prayer-book, glanced up at them, and was momentarily arrested. Some streak of atavistic culture was disturbed in him by the strange beauty of the group before him, standing in careless grace against that brilliant background. They seemed to have recovered the natural freedom of the child and the animal, but in their eyes was a look of sadness or wisdom which made them appear more human than the ordinary civilized man. They were cool and dignified in their rags, while he sweated in the tight, dark uniform he had put on for the occasion. It may only have been that they awakened in him the memory of a noble painting or piece of statuary he had seen when he had strolled into a gallery in some Mediterranean port. Whatever the cause, the effect they had on him was to destroy his composure, and give him a sense of having lost something in life. Hitherto the only service he had taken at sea was the burial service, and disconcerted, staring at the group of castaways, he blurted out:

I am the Resurrection and the Life.

He stammered, corrected himself, and began the marriage service with a slightly absurd pompous reverence.

*

Agatha lay awake in her cabin. She had been in bed for at least two hours but she could not sleep. The rescue naturally had excited her, and this state was curiously sustained by her contact with the commonplace objects of life, which formerly she had taken for granted. She stretched out her hands every now and then to feel the smooth linen of the sheets. It had excited her to clean her teeth once more with ordinary soapy, peppermint-scented toothpaste. The port-hole was open and moonlight flooded the cabin, and she could see all the civilized details of its appointments. She could see her tooth-brush sticking up in the common tumbler on the washstand,

and every time it caught her eye she gave an absurd, pleased giggle. She shut her eyes and tried to forget these exciting objects, but it was useless. They danced in her brain. She tried looking out of the port-hole. It was only pleasantly rough, and the swirling lace of the sea was beautiful in the moonlight. Neptune! Who was it had once said something to her about the influence of Neptune?

Her brain simmered with thoughts and queries. At last she gave up the attempt to sleep, and taking up a purple velvet evening cloak, part of the wardrobe sent by Mrs Bright's brother, she decided to try to clear her head and calm her nerves by a walk on deck.

As she came out into the corridor she saw Mr Smith ahead of her. She had a slight shock, a feeling that this had happened before, and then she remembered that on the morning of the day that the *Princess of Teck* had gone down, she had first met Mr Smith in the small hours of the morning in a corridor like this, and of course it was he who had said something about Neptune. She had an uncomfortable feeling, almost of fear, and half thought of returning to her cabin. Then she thought that would be too weak-minded, and she followed Mr Smith up on to the deck.

He was waiting for her outside the starboard door of the lounge.

'Have you come up for an airing?' he asked.

'Yes. I couldn't sleep.' She laughed nervously.

'If you come and look over the stern, you will see all the phosphorus churned up. It's very pretty.'

Agatha laughed again. 'I'll come,' she said, 'because these tropical splendours may seem soothing and commonplace to me after the beauty of a tube of toothpaste.'

He helped her down a ladder, and led her between the ropes and hatches of the well-deck up on to the poop, where they stood leaning against the stern railing, looking down at the foam with its darting streaks of light.

'Tell me,' said Mr Smith, 'if you could have avoided your experience on the island, would you have done so? Perhaps I haven't put that question quite right. I should say, would you do so? English grammar can't cope with all aspects of time. I don't mean would you deliberately face so much suffering, but now that it is over would you rather it hadn't happpened?'

'I suppose I should say 'of course,' said Agatha.

'But you don't say "of course."'

'No.'

'Why not?'

'Because,' said Agatha slowly, 'I'm different now from what I was before the wreck, and I think I'd rather be like I am now.'

'Outwardly,' said Mr Smith, 'you seem much less changed than any of the others, if I may say so.'

'I haven't done anything so extreme.'

'In what way are you changed then?'

'When I was a younger woman I found that I had a rather attractive, direct manner. I used to say things that startled people a little by their unusual approach, and which made them laugh. That made me popular, but I was kind too, and when I had done little kindnesses and had done thoughtful things I had a pleasurable glow inside me. At first I did these things instinctively, but afterwards I did them deliberately, for the effect they produced in me, or to attract people. What I have learnt on the island, and what I hope I shall remember, is that it is as easy to be corrupted by one's virtues as by one's vices, and that it is more tragic, because then one turns a little of the good in the world into evil.'

'But your experience has not strained your faith?'

'I have never known a time when my faith was not a little strained, but if it wasn't strained it wouldn't be faith, would it?'

She suddenly became aware that he was watching her intently, and she thought that in the moonlight his face looked sly and evil.

'Why do you ask me these things?' she demanded sharply. 'I don't know why I have revealed so much to you. You talk about people's souls, about good and evil, but I don't believe you care for either of them. You only play with the idea of them. You like to arrange them in patterns, as an artist arranges colours on a palette.'

'You only half perceive my motives. You do me some injustice.'

'Then perhaps you will explain yourself. You pry into other people's motives. You presume to direct them or misdirect them. What authority have you to do this? We don't even know who you are or where you come from.'

'If my advice is wise, and if what I say is true, surely that is sufficient authority?' said Mr Smith mildly.

'Your advice was often equivocal.'

'I only wanted each of you to derive the full benefit from his experience. You would rather be as you are now than as you were a year ago. Don't you think the others would say the same?'

'I don't know,' said Agatha doubtfully. 'But you haven't answered my question. You haven't told me who or what you are.'

Mr Smith laughed, but rather sadly. 'I've been many things,' he said. 'I am a bit of a rolling stone. I was a great disappointment to my Father.'

'What did he want you to do?'

'He wanted me to go into the Church. I studied for it for quite a time. As you know, I am an authority on liturgies.'

'Why didn't you go on with it?' asked Agatha more kindly. 'You have real wisdom and sympathy, I believe, if only you would direct it into the channels of good.'

Mr Smith did not immediately reply. He bent over the railing.

'Look at all that water,' he said, 'full of darting phosphorescent light. The Spirit has been compared to fire, but I think that it has been compared to water too. The Church now seems to me like someone guarding an antiquated and crumbling aqueduct, through which a little stagnant fluid trickles, while the great bulk of water rushes wildly about the land, eroding mountains, flooding villages, altering the face of the earth. But the guardian of the aqueduct still affirms that he possesses the only existing water supply, and he won't change his opinion, even if the flood washes away his aqueduct.'

He turned and laughed in her face. She was a little frightened, and she could not think of an answer to his argument.

'What did you do after you left the Church?' she asked.

'I wrote a book, but it shocked the public by its high moral tone.'

'Oh! And then?'

'I have been many things. An architect, a painter, a flautist. In fact, I've dabbled in all the arts and some of the sciences. I love knowledge and the admission of truth. But most of all I love life. I love it wherever it breaks out into beauty or free movement. I love it from the first cry of a baby to the happy death of a good man or the tragic death of a bad one. And I love all the things in between. I love the obvious beauty of flowers, and all the exquisite sentimentalities of adolescent love. And I love to see a group of boys robbing an orchard, and a stallion leap on a mare, and to hear young men shouting. I love to see everything acting according to its nature. I love the bounding heart and the teeming brain. But the bounding heart must come first. You must become all that your natural self is capable of being before you can stop to think about it, otherwise you just shrivel up. You mustn't prune the seedling. Excuse all these analogies. They result from my ecclesiastical associations.'

Agatha felt that he was making some demand of her—a demand that was too extreme for her to accept.

'It is no use,' she said, 'to strive after things which are more than your nature can bear, even if they are good in themselves. An adult's tastes and interests are more extensive than a child's—and an adult can touch things that would injure a child. You seem to me far more grown-up than I am. I can't make that direct approach to the universe. I should be destroyed. I have to make my approach through the convention of God.'

He was smiling at her again with that evil intentness, as if he were amused at some knowledge he had of her, which was hidden from herself. Then she realized that she had referred to God as a convention, and she was distressed.

'I must go down,' she said.

He merely bowed. The churned-up phosphorescence from below them threw a curious pale glow on to his face. Agatha again had a tinge of fear.

'Good night,' she said, 'or perhaps I should say good morning.' She laughed nervously and hurried away along the deck. He did not follow to help her down the ladder, nor up on the other side.

He did not appear again on deck, nor in the saloon for the rest of the voyage. Agatha asked a steward if he was unwell. The steward only grinned and said: 'Not as I knows of, miss.'

Agatha was a little hurt that he did not come to say good-bye when they landed at Sydney, but by the time she was seated in the Melbourne express she had almost forgotten about him, as people are apt to forget the enforced acquaintance made on board ship. When she reached home she was so full of joy at being back with old friends and among familiar things that her companions on the island, excepting of course the other nuns and Dick and Winifred, passed completely from her mind. The most ordinary things like the taste of butter and the clean smell of the convent floor polish filled her with delight, while the really beautiful things which she had loved long since and lost awhile, small, simple flowers like daffodils and violets, awoke in her a kind of rapture, and she felt that she had only seen them before with a film over her eyes. It was as if she had come to a world in which all things were made new.

In June she was godmother to Winifred's twin boys.